I0822518

JOHN F. CARR

Pequod Press

PARATIME TROUBLE
A Pequod Press Adventure Novel

First Edition

Printed in the United States of America
First Printing, 2017

V 10 9 8 7 6 5 4 3 2 1

ISBN: 978-0-937912-71-3

Pequod Press
P.O. Box 80
Boalsburg, PA 16827
www.PequodPress.com

Paratime Books

Paratime
The Complete Paratime
Time Crime
Paratime Trouble

Lord Kalvan of Otherwhen
Great Kings' War
Kalvan Kingmaker
The Hos-Blethan Affair
Siege of Tarr-Hostigos
The Fireseed Wars
Gunpowder God
Down Styphon!

Terro-Human Future History novels

Fuzzy Ergo Sum
Caveat Fuzzy
The Fuzzy Conundrum
Cosmic Computer
The Merlin Gambit
Space Viking
The Last Space Viking
Space Viking's Throne

ACKNOWLEDGEMENTS

Special thanks go to Pequod Press's Editor Victoria Alexander for her hard work and efforts to make this book as professional as possible.

I'd also like to give thanks to all the members of the Copyediting and Post-Proofing Team, Dwight Decker, Dennis Frank, Larry Hopkins, Wolfgang Diehr, and David Williams.

Thanks go to Alan Gutierrez who came up with the cover design and executed it so well.

PART ONE

ONE

I

August 21, 1962 A.D.

Davran Thal, director of Stochastic Studies at the Rhogom Foundation, used a detection sensor to see if there were any tattle-tales, eavesdrop meters, sticky dots or other listening devices planted in the Foundation Tower's subbasement since their last meeting. The room was clean, except for his own tattle-tale. His hideout was a former maintenance storage room that had been walled over during one of the tower's many remodeling projects some two thousand years before. He had discovered it by accident while going through some ancient files that were about to be purged from the building's records.

There was a knock at the door. The small room had a recessed thumblock that even his visitor didn't know about. There were no electrical door openers since that might attract the attention of one of the tower's robot custodians. He used the handgrip to open the door, revealing Marthon Larl, Dean of Parapsychological Research.

"Come in, Larl," he said.

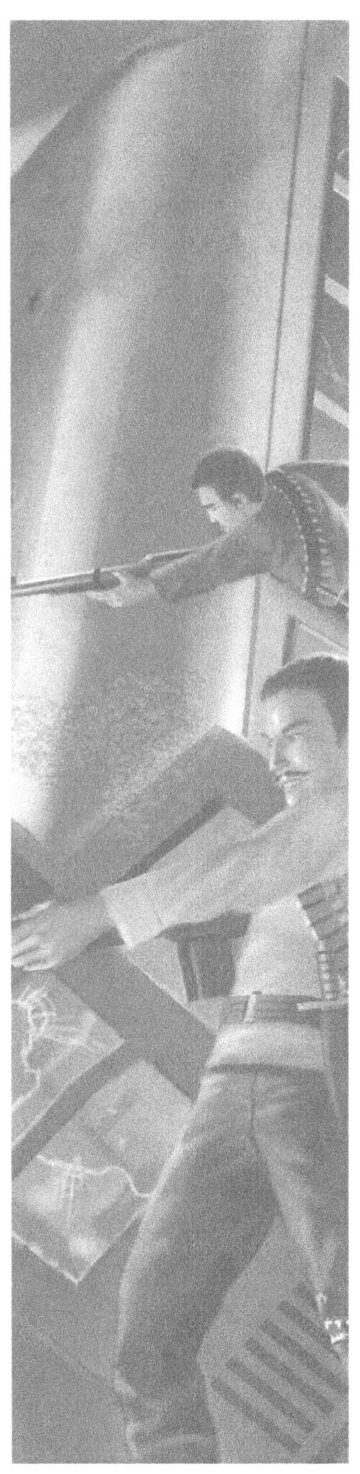

Marthon Larl was a big man with a shaggy head of gray hair that always looked as if it had just been tousled by a windstorm. Without the black and red Foundation tunic, he could have easily been mistaken for a maintenance prole. "What is it this time?"

Thal put a mental lid on his growing frustration. *Am I the only one around here who sees the danger the Paratime Police represent with all their meddling into the Foundation's affairs?*

"We need to talk."

"That's why I'm here," Marthon said with barely suppressed irritation. "What's the latest crisis?"

You'll be laughing out the other side of your mouth in a minute, he thought. "Did you know that Dalla Hadron has just been made Paratime Police Special Chief's Assistant's Special Assistant?"

"No, I didn't," Marthon exclaimed. "But isn't that a conflict of interest with her work for the Foundation?"

"Not in *her* mind or Verkan Vall's. One thing it does mean is that the Foundation's going to get a lot more attention from the boys in green. And that, my friend, is not good."

"Thal, we can't afford to have the Paratime Police looking over our shoulders. We're in a precarious situation here. We've got Dalla's crazy brother making insane demands and too much invested here to pick up and move to some outtime hideaway."

"I agree," Darvan Thal said. "We need to find some way to distract Dalla and get her outtime where she can't cause us any problems."

"Hmm," Marthron mumbled. "There's a real mess on a recent Europo-American break-away belt—much of it predicted by a local psychic, Jeane Dixon. Well, on this branch, which for identification purposes I'll call the Lavrentiy Beria Branch, the Cold War is heating up to full boil."

"Interesting," Thal interjected. "But what does this have to do with the Dalla Hadron problem?"

"From what our Special Investigator has unearthed, this Dixon woman has been right on about eighty percent of her predictions, on most Europo-American time-lines, way above any normal probability. Her latest prediction on the Beria Belt is that a nuclear war is about to begin."

Thal reared back. “You’re taking this seriously? Most of these so-called psychics turn out to be con artists, if not outright frauds. Has she made similar predictions on the other Europo-American subsector time-lines?”

“She’s made some highly accurate predictions throughout the Fourth Level, Europo-American Subsector; and you know how unusual that is. We have investigators on several hundred time-lines throughout the Europo-American Subsector investigating her abilities. However, this is the only divarication where she predicts a nuclear war. Do you see where I’m going with this?”

Thal grinned from ear to ear. “Yes, I do. We’re going to bring this case to Miss Busybody’s attention and let her run with it.”

“Exactly. Ever since the Reincarnation Fiasco on the Abkor Neb Sector, she’s become Volzar Darv’s special pet and can do no wrong.”

“I know. Dalla’s been getting all the interesting assignments. So you’re suggesting we release some of our findings as bait and wait for her to bite.”

“Exactly, my friend. Then we can cry into our beards when she’s discorporated in their little atomic war.”

“Will she be in the target area?”

“I expect so. This Jeane Dixon lives in Washington, D.C., the capital of the United States of America. The Subsector that everyone’s afraid is headed for a full-out nuclear holocaust. I’m sure Washington is number one on the Soviet Union’s hit list.”

II

Hadron Dalla stepped into Director Volzar Darv’s office, which was filled with bound books, boxes of data wafers, recording cubes, rolls of storage discs and even a few scrolls. “Come in, Dalla. Good to see you again. You’re going have to find your own seat.”

She removed a stack of recording cubes and reader screens from one of the chairs and sat down.

Volzar was a very tall, thin, bald-headed man of indeterminate age; he looked anything from two hundred to five hundred years of age. His eyes were a watery-gray and his complexion was mahogany with hands that looked like claws at the end of stringy arms. Looking up from his datapad, he said, "I haven't seen you in a while, Dalla. What have you been up to?"

"I've been busy working with the Paratime Police." Dalla quickly briefed him on the Kali Operation, where the Wizard Traders had infiltrated a rarely visited Fourth Level Gutapa Belt and started a Death Cult to steal young women, whom they sold as slaves both outtime and on Home Time Line.

Volzar shook his head as she finished her tale. "I would like to believe that as the oldest recorded human culture, we would be above such actions. Sadly, we are not. We have been told that the Bureau of Psychological Hygiene would cure our people of such atavistic and non-productive emotions, but it appears their screening methodology has some serious flaws."

Not to overstate the obvious, Dalla thought. "They're certainly not doing the bang-up job they claim to be doing."

Volzar nodded, but it was obvious that he had something else on his mind. Impugning BurPsyHygiene was like complaining about the weather, everyone did it but no one did anything about it.

"The reason I requested your presence today," he announced, somewhat stiffly. "Is that I have an important assignment and—because of your recent successes—I want you to look into this matter for the Foundation."

Dalla all but rubbed her hands together in anticipation. *This is going to be a good one.*

He shook his head. "I'm doing this against the recommendations of several colleagues who believe I'm showing favoritism." Suddenly, he stiffened up. "If that's what giving the job to the best person is being called these days, they can go hang themselves!"

Atta boy, Dalla thought. *I knew I was stepping on toes, but I hadn't realized just how bad. I'll have to be a little more circumspect, as Verkan would suggest.*

"I suspect you are familiar with the Fourth Level, Europo-American psychic, as they're called there, named Jeane Dixon;"

"Yes, her name has come up frequently in the Foundation's journals. I've never had the pleasure of meeting her, though."

"Exactly. She's attracted a bevy of admirers, each of whom believes he's an expert on Mrs. Dixon. Unfortunately for them, none of them are objective. They're all more concerned with their papers and studies than the facts. I need someone who doesn't have anything to gain or lose in this operation."

"Just what are you proposing, Director?" Dalla asked.

"You can skip the title, Dalla. Call me Darv," he said with a wink.

If I didn't know better, I'd think the old fool is flirting with me... "Sure, Darv. What's this all about, really?"

With his face suddenly pinched around his long nose, Director Volzar looked like a raptor about to strike. "We now have several reports from a new Europo-American divarication belt that Jeane Dixon is claiming to have seen a nuclear attack on the capital of the United States of America and several of the major cities on the eastern seaboard."

Dalla jerked back, not saying anything. One of the Paratime Police's biggest worries was that the economic and verbal rivalry between the US and USSR would turn into a nuclear slugfest. Not only would it endanger millions of Paratimers ensconced all over that Subsector, but possibly bring an end to one of the most vibrant and interesting cultures that had sprung up in the last ten thousand years. To say nothing of the immense cultural and physical treasures the Paratimers would lose access to if such a war broke out. Dalla had been on Second Level time-lines where such doomsday scenarios had played out with dismal results, as a result she realized the seriousness of the problem.

"What do you want me to do?" she asked in all seriousness.

The Director nodded, then smiled. "Your usual thorough job. I'm going to send you to one of the time-lines on this new Europo-American belt, called the Beria Belt."

"Beria Belt? What's the divarication?"

"It's more of a who, than a what. You're familiar with the Union of Soviet Socialist Republics that has spread across much of the Major Land Mass in the Europo-American Subsector?"

Dalla nodded. "Of course, it's a nasty statist theocracy which contains many of the worst traits of both an autocracy and a theocracy. It's been ruled for the past forty years or so by several iron-handed dictators, the most recent of whom has been Nikita Khrushchev; all in the name of communism, a utopian vision created by flawed idealists."

"Basically, correct. However, on this branch we have a different leader; Khrushchev has been executed, his place taken by Beria. Lavrentiy Pavlovich Beria was one of Stalin's right-hand men and the longest-lived of his secret police chiefs. During Hitler's War he served as Marshal of the Soviet Union and commanded the anti-Nazi partisan units in the field. He was especially hard on deserters, turncoats and cowards. After Stalin's death and the chaos that ensued, Beria was promoted to First Deputy Premier and was briefly part of the ruling *troika*.

"On most Europo-American sectors, Beria's overconfidence in his position led him to misjudge the Politburo members and he was arrested and executed. On the Beria Belt, he was more suspicious and removed most of his competitors within the military and Politburo on trumped up charges, then made himself the absolute ruler of the Soviet Union. The internal struggles have left him paranoid and worried about threats from both inside the Soviet Union and outside."

"Not a good position for someone in charge of the second largest military machine on most Europo-American sectors," Dalla noted.

"Exactly," the Director said. "Which brings me to your assignment: I want you to vet Mrs. Dixon and find out if she's really a gifted clairvoyant—as so many psychists here believe—or a fraud with a hidden motive. She doesn't take money for her gift, but it has given her unusual access to important political and industrial persons within the Washington, D.C. social register. From all the Dixons, on different time-lines, we've interviewed, I personally do not believe she is a fraud or personally mendacious. However, it is also possible that she has turned some lucky guesses or a mild clairvoyant talent into a private sideshow for her friends and social acquaintances."

"From what I've read, Director Darv, she appears to be the real thing, a true clairvoyant, as rare as that is. I've always wanted a chance to study her—"

"Well," the Director interrupted, "this is your opportunity, Dalla. I want you to determine, once and for all, if this Jeane Dixon is a clairvoyant. If so, you will return with her for further study."

"What about the nuclear war she's predicting?"

The Director shrugged. "The Beria Belt is the only belt where she is predicting one. She predicted the war would begin on 'the ides of October'."

"Ides, I know the Ides of March Shakespearean reference, but what does that have to do with this case?" Dalla asked

"According to Records, in the Roman Calendar there were festivals that occurred on the fifteenth of March, May, June and October; or on the thirteenth day of the other months of their calendar. So, you might want to consider the fourteenth of October to be the last safe day of leave taking."

Dalla nodded. No sense cutting it too close, she decided. Atomic bombs made no differential between enemies and friends, nor non-combatants.

Director Darv began, "Here's what we do know about Jeane Dixon. First, she avoids tests by parapsychologists on her time-line. She insists that her 'gift,' as she calls it, to foresee the future comes from 'God' and that she has no inclination to be anyone's guinea pig—a small animal often used for experimental purposes. Her husband is independently wealthy, runs a successful real estate company in Washington, D.C. Thus, she is not amenable to the usual outside pressures since she has no interest in proving herself as a clairvoyant and no need for additional income or fame. Indeed it appears she eschews publicity—although, that's almost impossible considering the prophecies she's made over the years.

"She has made a number of predictions in quite considerable detail and with lots of names and dates. I don't have to tell you how unusual that is, Dalla. One of Dixon's most important predictions was when she predicted the date of February 20, 1947—to use the local's dating system—as the date of the separation of India and Pakistan, many months before there was any specific evidence that such a move was in the works. As early as 1956 she predicted the 1960 election would be won by a Democrat, and that he would be assassinated in office—not necessarily in his first term. The election of John F. Kennedy throughout most of the Europo-American subsector proved her veracity.

"Obviously, Kennedy was elected, but he's still early into his first term so there's no proof that this prediction will prove out. However, we are keeping a close watch on several time-lines to see if there are any indications that her prophecy is true."

Dalla interjected, "What about this new Beria Belt? Is John F. Kennedy president?"

Darv nodded, but his face took on a wary cast. "Yes, he was elected, but he did not defeat Richard Nixon—he beat out another Democratic candidate, Hubert Humphrey. But it turns out that Adlai Stevenson was the outgoing President, not Dwight Eisenhower."

Dalla's eyes grew big. "Then this belt branched off some time ago."

Darv shrugged, looking guilty as though it were his fault. "There are so many time-lines on the Europo-American Subsector that it would take ten million men a thousand years to map even a tenth of them. It's the largest subsector in Fourth Level, and it's throwing off new divarications faster than Paratime Police Survey Department can map them."

"I understand that, but how far back in time does this Beria branch go?" she asked.

"As far as we can ascertain, it branched off shortly after Hitler's War. But the Belt's a new discovery and the early surveys pointed out the Beria ascension as the defining event of this branch. So the Belt was named after him."

"So there might be other changes I'll have to be alert for?" Dalla asked.

"Yes. We don't know how pronounced they are, but you need to keep that in consideration as you travel. From our agent's superficial survey, it appears to be a 'typical' United States; that is, there are no major changes such as breakaway regions or internal strife not typical of the country, as we know it from previous visits and surveys.

"I do suggest you be very careful. And I can't say this any stronger, but be certain that you depart before the Ides of October. I do not want to be the man who has to inform your rather formidable husband of your discorporation."

Dalla grinned. "Yes, boss."

TWO

September 5, 1962 A.D.

"What do you mean, I shouldn't transport to the Beria Belt!?" Dalla demanded.

Paratime Police Chief Tortha Karf could tell by the tightness of Hadron Dalla's jaw and the sparks in her green eyes that he'd gone too far in warning her off the Beria Belt. *When will I ever learn?* he asked himself. The problem was he was too emotionally involved with her and Vall.

Maybe I should have had some kids of my own, he mused. Then he shook it off; it wasn't like him to get so overtly emotional.

"Chief, I'm going and there's nothing you can do to stop me. If you want, I'll resign my commission in the Paratime Police. I've already got the okay for this mission from Director Volzar Darv."

"No, that's not what I want," Tortha said, shrugging apologetically. "Sorry, Dalla, I didn't mean to ruffle your feathers. But with Vall still gone on assignment, I feel I should act in his place. After all, this Beria Belt is an unknown area. Your assignment is very dangerous. What if this Jeane Dixon is

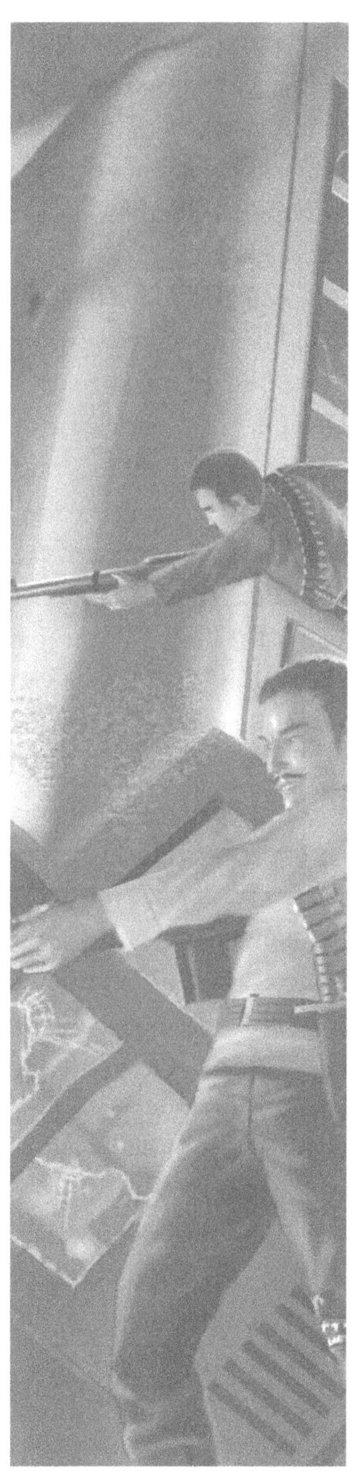

right and there is a full-blown nuclear war? Do you want to be stuck in the middle of it with no way home?"

Dalla sighed. "But that's the whole point. I want to be there to see if Dixon's prediction is correct, and get a chance to watch her in action. When it looks like the fireworks are about to begin, I'll do my best to bug out beforehand."

Tortha shuddered. "Dalla, we only have one conveyer-head on one time-line in the Beria Belt, which belongs to Tharmax imports. It's in New York. This belt is a brand new divarication; the Paratime Police Survey Division hasn't even logged it in yet. You may not be in a position where you can, as you put it—'bug out.' Furthermore, the best we can do is set up one or two temporary conveyer depots before the war heats up to boil. You could easily find yourself caught in the middle of a nuclear slugfest with no way out! And guess who Vall will blame?"

Dalla winced. "You may be right, but I believe you're both way too paternalistic. The two of you remind me of a couple of tribal patriarchs on Fourth Level Indo-Turanian. Jeane Dixon is the most important figure in the study of psychic sciences today. This is a pivotal point, too. I want to be there on the front lines and see if Dixon's prediction comes true. Sure it's dangerous, but I've survived outtime in a lot of other such situations. If nuclear war breaks out and I can't leave, I'll find a good place to weather it out. I'm not going to give up a choice assignment because you two old hens are worried about my safety!"

Tortha shook his head. He knew stubbornness, and Dalla's was legendary. "Okay, but let's set up some ground rules. First, see if you can talk this psychic into leaving Washington, D.C. If war breaks out, that place will be the first to be hit—and hit bad. Maybe even obliterated. If she won't leave, you get yourself out of there before it's too late."

Dalla nodded.

"Next, I want you to take along one of my best Field Agents, Maldar Dard. Maldar will put together a special five-man squad for support. Sardrath Darn was the one who did our initial survey of the Beria Belt; I know it wasn't exhaustive, but there wasn't time for detailed study. I'll have Sardrath brief you momentarily. As far as Maldar is concerned, I won't saddle you with him directly, but I want him in the vicinity of the Dixon domicile so that you'll have some help if you have to move out in a hurry."

"Okay," Dalla replied. "I've met Maldar before. He's a good man and one of Verkan's buddies. He's smart enough not to pull rank unless he really has to."

Tortha nodded. "I've also put some field agents to work and you'll find temporary conveyer-heads in Washington, D.C. and New York upon your arrival. Make sure you're close to one of them just in case this fracas starts early. This Cuban Missile Crisis is heating up all over Europo-American and it may well turn nasty on more time-lines than just the Beria Belt. There's some evidence that it may be sector-wide; if so there will be very little that the Department can do if you're stranded. The Opposition Party has been making noises in the Executive Council that it's time to pull out of the Europo-American sector entirely."

Dalla shook her head. "More Opposition rhetoric. We have too much invested in the Europo-American Sector for either Management or the Opposition to pull out."

"I agree, although I don't like it," Tortha said. "However, if a sector-wide nuclear war between the US and USSR does happen, we won't have any choice."

"True. Look, Tortha, I'm not interested in being discarnated on some god-forsaken time-line." She gave him a big smile. "Vall and I are in a really good place; he gives me all the breathing room I need, and I do likewise. I like my work here with the Department and what I do for the Rhogom Foundation. So I'm not going to take any stupid chances, but on the other hand I have a hot one here and I'm not going to let go of Dixon until I have to."

"Okay, Dalla," Tortha said. "Truce?"

"Truce."

"Okay. Sardrath Darn's a Second Class Field Inspector and one of the best we have. I'll have him give you his impressions of the Beria Belt."

"That's fine," she replied.

Tortha made a quick call on his squawk box and a few minutes later Sardrath Darn, dressed in his field greens, entered the Chief's office.

"Hi Chief," he said, then turned to Dalla and said, "I'm looking forward to working with you, Special Chief's Assistant's Special Assistant."

"Me, too, Inspector, but enough with the titles. What do you have to tell us about this new Belt?"

"First of all, I don't think the divarication is as recent as we first thought," he said. "The time-line I visited is a far shabbier place than most of the United States time-lines that I've visited on Europo-America. New York City's population is around five million. On most Europo-American time-lines, it's closer to eight million. The buildings are smaller, not as developed. The post-war boom that happened throughout most of Europo-America didn't occur here. Also, there are some significant political differences."

"What are they?" Dalla asked.

"On this belt General Eisenhower didn't run for election in 1952," Sardrath said, "so he was never elected president."

"Why not, Darn?" she queried. Eisenhower was one of the great Cold War warriors and had had a major role in Soviet containment.

"There was a scandal. One of the Hearst papers leaked information about Eisenhower's wartime mistress, Kay Summersby. I don't know if his wife, Mamie, knew about this British temptress, but when the papers reported she was moving to D.C. in 1950 all hell broke out. His wife didn't divorce him, but the scandal took the luster off his gold bars. Instead, the Republicans ran one of the leaders of the conservative faction, Robert A. Taft. Taft lost the presidential race to a Democrat, Adlai Stevenson, a representative of the eastern liberal wing. The Democrats have run the country ever since."

Dalla nodded. "So we'll have to be a little more careful than usual since we don't know all the particulars."

"Right. There are some other oddities, too. Rock and roll, the latest music fad throughout most of Europo-America, never happened on this Belt. Another thing, Walt Disney went bankrupt during the war and closed Disney studios, so there's no Disneyland and all its cultural detritus. I know, I know Disney characters are popular with the First Level hoi polloi but I can't stand them. Also, television is still in its infancy; most of the country still listens to radio and goes to the movies. Overall, in appearance and attitudes, this Belt is about a decade or more behind the primary Europo-American Subsector. The Jesus Brokers are more prominent here, as well. The entire country is Bible-soaked. So we'll have to be more circumspect than we're used to on this subsector."

"That's good to know, Darn. If you can get me a couple local histories to hypno-mech while I'm on the transposition conveyer, I'd appreciate it."

"Can do, boss."

"Good. I think we're done here, Chief. Anything else you want to add?"

"No," Tortha leaned back in his chair, lighting up a cigar. "Just come back in one piece, or I'll never hear the end of it!"

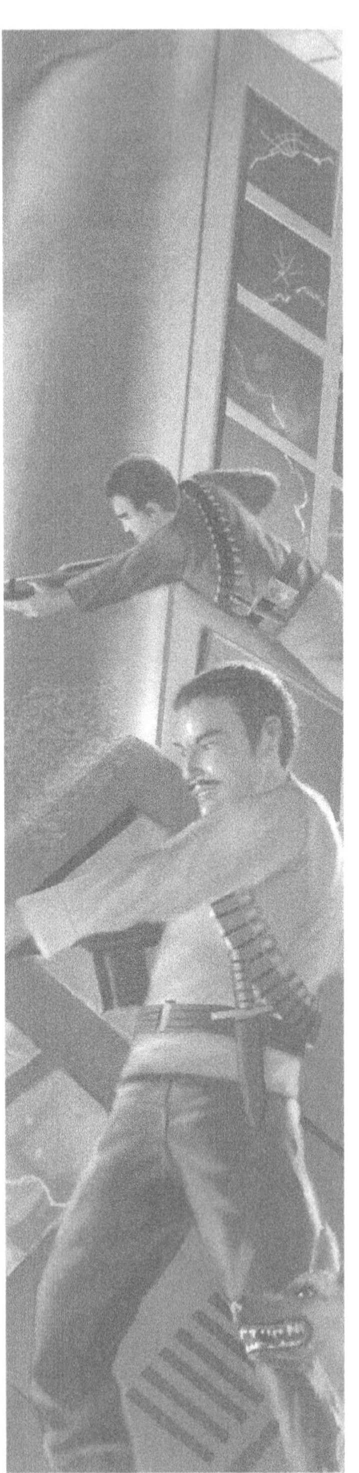

THREE

Dalla Hadron studied the two-story clapboard gray Victorian house from a distance. The house was located in upstate New York in a small town, Silchester, in a heavily wooded area. It was late fall and most of the leaves had turned and were beginning to drop off the trees. With a white picket fence, the house appeared quite normal from the outside. According to one of Jeane Dixon's long-time clients, Miriam Mosby, the famed psychic was inside. She'd left her Washington, D.C. home shortly after her vision of the coming nuclear war. This assignment reminded Dalla a lot of a recent case, where a man's extra-ego component had been "projected"—for lack of a better word—from the future and into his younger twelve year-old self.

Her husband, Verkan Vall, had convinced her to keep the entire event secret, even from the Rhogom Foundation. Verkan had correctly intuited that if they identified the man he would have been picked up and quarantined for the rest of his life while the Foundation's psychists and mentalists picked and pried his brain apart. They were both still waiting to learn how Alan Hartley's actions would play out against the recollections of his future self. Maybe one day, after his death, she would write up the entire case.

That's one advantage of living four to five centuries, Dalla decided. A lot of First Level Citizens found the years weighing heavy after the second century, but she thought that was just a failure of the imagination. She loved watching over the various sectors, subsectors, belts and time-lines, never knowing what new surprise might pop up. Of course, this unpredictability was what gave her husband headaches, but for her it was invigorating.

Dalla opened the gate, walked up the stone pathway and knocked on the door. An old lady, with bluish hair, cracked open the door. "Yes?" she asked carefully.

"I'm Doctor Hadron from Duke University, here to see Jeane Dixon."

"Oh, how did you find her?" The woman kept herself between Dalla and the door, as if she could keep out unwelcomed intruders with her wasted body alone.

"One of her clients, Marian Mosby, told me."

"Marian! Then you must be okay. My name is Sylvia Crosthwaite. Come in, Doctor? Miss…what did you say your name was?"

"Mrs. Hadron. You can call me Dalla. I've brought six of my assistants with me, but they're looking for accommodations in town."

Sylvia nodded. "They should find something. This is the slow season except for leaf peepers. And they're mostly weekend folk."

As they walked into the parlor, a busy room filled with overstuffed furniture and knickknacks. The walls were covered with wallpaper, showing a rose design, and had a dark wainscoting. Lighting was minimal.

"Please have a seat, Dalla. Oh, it isn't an unusual name. I used to have a Chinese cook, but her name was Dolla—are you Chinese?…you don't look Chinese, although you do have an exotic look...dear, I do hope I'm not being too nosy…I can be such a nosy parker."

"No, I'm not Chinese. I was born in Albuquerque, New Mexico."

"Oh," the lady replied, as if that explained everything. "Please take a seat." She pointed to a lushly flowered and overstuffed armchair. "If you want to speak to Jeane, I'll have to go fetch her. She's in the sitting room; she woke up this morning with such a terrible headache. It's the prophecy, you know." She ended with a wink.

"Please," Dalla implored, as she sat down. A small tortoise-shell cat jumped in her lap and began purring when she began petting it. A few minutes passed before Jeane Dixon entered the parlor; she was a moderately attractive brunette, full-figured with an over-sized nose and lush lips. Her eyes, like limpid pools of amber, were her most arresting characteristic.

Dalla put the kitty on the arm of her chair, then stood and introduced herself.

Instead of shaking hands, Jeane Dixon touched the tips of Dalla's fingers. Dixon drew back as if she'd received an electric shock. Her eyes widened and she said, "Please, excuse me, dear. I often read the tips of the fingers for a quick reading, but I've never had such a strong contact." She wobbled on her feet for a moment. "Very strange; it's almost as if you're from another dimension."

Dalla shrugged.

Jeane blushed. "This is a first, Mrs. Hadron. I apologize."

Dalla responded. "I have a touch of talent myself, Jeane."

"Phew, I'm glad to hear that. I've been blessed—though some of my critics might say 'cursed'—with my talent since I was a young girl."

"Me, too," Dalla said. "When did your gift first appear?"

Dixon smiled. "I was only eight years old. My father, Frank Pinckert, moved our family from Germany to the United States after the First World War. He was quite wealthy and dedicated himself to studying the local Indians and gypsies. Upon learning that a gypsy woman was encamped on Luther Burbank's estate—they were good friends—father suggested that my mother take me to see her.

"It was a magical moment. The gypsy lady lived in a covered wagon with an old stovepipe peeking out of the canvas roof. I saw chickens sneaking looks at us out of the wagon door. The gypsy woman lived mostly outdoors, but the grounds were swept clean—I remember noticing that. She was telling a woman her fortune with cards when we arrived. When it was my turn, the gypsy looked at my palms and cried out: 'This little girl is going to be very famous. She will be able to foresee world-wide changes because she is blessed with the gift of prophecy. Never have I seen such palm lines'."

Dalla could read the truth of her words in her eyes. Jeane had a good heart, but was maybe too trusting.

"Let me see your palm?" Dalla asked. She was familiar with palm-reading from a stint on Fourth Level Alexandrian-Roman where almost everyone believed in palmistry and astrology. She had passed herself off as a sorceress while studying under a local wizard, who turned out to be a complete fraud, but a good sleight of hand magician.

She studied Dixon's palm, noting the star on the Mount of Jupiter and the hump at the base of her index finger. In her right palm was a huge star that reached out in all directions. Her head line completely crossed the palm and wrapped the hand, with a half-moon on its outer cuff. Never before had Dalla run across such pronounced markings....

"I see from the look on your face that you find my lines unusual," Jeane noted. The gypsy woman told my mother that they mean I would grow mightily in wisdom and that she had never seen so much potential in a child."

Dalla nodded.

"Then the gypsy went into her covered wagon and returned with a beautiful old crystal ball. She told me, 'It is for you to keep. You will be able to meditate on this and see wonderful things in it.' I looked into the shiny ball and I saw pictures begin to form inside. It was almost as if I were watching a TV screen—even though this was decades before I ever saw one."

She went on to tell Dalla about seeing waves of blue water. "Somehow I was seeing a faraway land where the gypsy had come from. Then I cupped my hands around the crystal ball and I saw her reaching for a cooking pot of some sort. I sensed danger and told her to be careful and not scald herself. When we returned for another visit, the gypsy woman's hands were bandaged; she had burned her hands from scalding water which she had upset while cooking."

Dalla was impressed. Never in her time with the Foundation had she run across anyone with such raw psychic talent. "How did your mother respond to this?"

Jeane shrugged. "Mother didn't act as if it was at all unusual. She said that if God had given me this gift he wanted me to use it for good. She always told us children, 'You do not belong to me, but to God.' And, from that time on, she encouraged me to develop my talent or 'sixth sense' as she called it. None of my other six siblings showed any unusual abilities. Once, when my father was on a business trip to Chicago, I told mother that he would bring back a big black and white dog. I saw it in a vision. When he returned home, he had a black and white collie with him.

"But enough about me. Tell me about yourself, Mrs. Hadron. By the way, that's a most unusual name."

Dalla smiled. "I was a student at Duke University during the war. There I met Dr. Joseph D. Rhine and, when he discovered I had a small talent myself, he invited me to join the Duke Parapsychology Labs. I completed my doctorate and I've worked at the Labs ever since. When Dr. Rhine learned of your latest prophecy, he sent me to do an article on it for the *Journal of Parapsychology*."

"The great scoffer. I'm sure Dr. Rhine expects me to fail—although in this case, I very much hope my vision does not come true." Dixon's face fell and she suddenly looked a decade older.

"Tell me about your *vision*," Dalla requested.

Jeane Dixon's eyes began to roll back into her head. Dalla quickly grabbed her blouse to keep her upright, then put her arm around her shoulders and helped her over to an overstuffed couch.

"I'm sorry," Dixon gasped. "I'm usually stronger than this. I find that as the time draws nearer I'm seeing more and more blackness and death symbols. When I saw the first sign, I was in bed alone—my husband Jimmy was out of town—when suddenly I saw a huge black cloud hovering over the White House. It kept getting bigger and bigger until it covered all of the Washington. Every night it grows and keeps moving downward. Then an inner voice announces, 'The Ides of October.' This voice comes to me a lot, and I always listen to it."

She shuddered, "Now, I also see a black cloud hovering over New York City, Philadelphia, Washington, D.C., Baltimore and Boston. I don't know where it's going to end!"

PART TWO

FOUR

I

October 12, 1962 A.D.

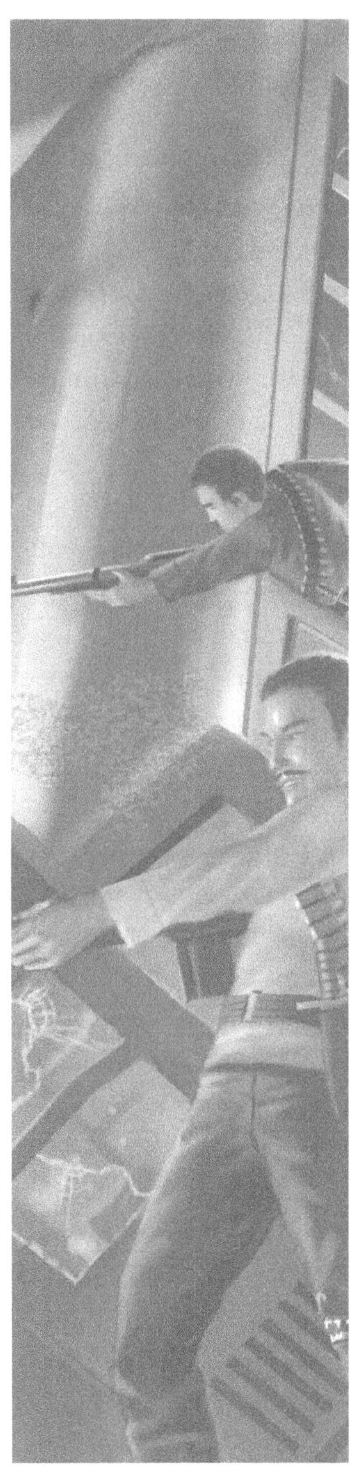

Kostran Galth bulled his way past the Chief's secretary, shouting, "Out of my way. This is a red alert!"

Chief Tortha Karf was talking to someone on his visiscreen, and raised his head when he saw who it was that had just barged into his office. He jerked his thumb, pointing to one of the chairs in front of his horseshoe desk, and quickly ended his conversation and asked, "What is it, Kostran?" Knowing Galth, he knew it was urgent.

"You won't believe what this idiot in Survey did!"

"Oh, no? You haven't worked with this outfit as long as I have, Galth. What's this all about?"

"As you know we still haven't heard a word back from Verkan, or Dalla from the Beria Belt."

"That's why I put you on the job, two days ago," he said. "What have you found out?"

"Second Survey Level Avlarn Farth was put in charge of setting up the temporary conveyer-heads in Washington, D. C, Baltimore and New York since we were unsure of Jeane Dixon's location at the time of Dalla's transposition to D.C. It took Dalla several days to locate someone in Washington who knew where the Dixons had moved; then she and her team left for Hartford, Connecticut by airplane. Meanwhile, not having heard from Dalla, Avlarn took it upon himself to close the Washington, Baltimore and New York depots since he was worried about the threat of an imminent nuclear attack."

Tortha felt his blood pressure rise. "This moron made this decision on his own without confirming it with anyone higher up on the food chain?"

"That's what happened. Now, he's most apologetic—for all the good that will do."

"Very little," Tortha snarled. "When I'm finished with this Avlarn, he'll wish he'd never been born! I'm going to send him to Fifth Level, End of the Line Survey."

Kostran whistled. "That's pretty harsh, Chief."

Tortha nodded. End of the Line Survey was the worst job in the Paratime Police Department; it meant transposing to the last known time-line on Fifth Level, then visiting each adjoining time-line in succession, planting locator beacons so that the time-line would be available via temporal transposition conveyers. Since there were no known limits to Paratime, that meant a career of going from one uninhabited time-line on Fifth Level, with only subhuman brutes and vicious animals for company, to another. It was the most hated assignment in the Department. Avlarn would spend the rest of his career there; or maybe, even better, he would quit.

"So, in a nutshell, Dalla and her party are stranded somewhere in Connecticut, while Verkan is somewhere on Fourth Level Gutapa Belt. At least we know his coordinates."

"That's right, Chief. Verkan should be returning soon anyway, but I'm going to send an agent out to Gutapa to fill him in on what's happening. I'm surprised no one has contacted him before."

Tortha sighed. "This Cuban Missile Crisis had been the Department's major focus. We have tens of thousands of police on those time-lines, not to mention millions of tourists. Everyone in the Department has been focused on setting up immediate evacuation points if it looks like war is going to break out. Dalla and Verkan got overlooked with all that's going on. Have Verkan report to me the minute he returns."

"Yes, sir," Kostran replied.

II

October 15, 1962 A.D.

In his office high atop the Paratime Building in Dhergabar City, Verkan Vall, Paratime Police Chief's Special Assistant, was talking out his final notes into the vocowriter about the Way of Kali Case when his secretary buzzed the intercom. He'd spent the last six ten-days on the Fourth Level Pandyan Imperial Sector, Gupta Empire, straightening out the mess left behind by the Wizard Traders most recent slaving operation. Or, at least, the most recent one they'd run across. He shuddered to think of how many more were out there that the Paratime Police hadn't uncovered.

Verkan pressed a switch on the intercom box, asking, "What is it, Karoth?"

"I just received a Code Red call from the chief's office. He wants to see you immediately."

"Thanks," he replied.

Verkan rose to his feet, stretching out his arms and shaking his legs one at a time. *I just got back and I'm already feeling desk fatigue. Maybe the Chief has run across something outtime that'll get me out of playing chair jockey.*

He left his office and went to the nearest antigrav kiosk, where he took the ascent shaft up to the next floor. From there he made his way to the Chief's office. Tortha's secretary, who was working with his vocowriter, just nodded and pointed to the Chief's door.

Inside his office, Paratime Police Chief Tortha Karf sat behind his horseshoe desk smoking a cigarette and reading through a red file. Chief Tortha was a big man, portly but not fat. He was well into middle-age, well over his three hundredth year. His hair was iron-gray and starting to thin out in front.

"Have a seat, Verkan. This is going to take a few minutes."

Verkan sat down and waited while Tortha finished shuffling through the folder on his desk.

Tortha held up the red file. "This just came in from Survey Division. Normally, I wouldn't have contacted you about this Red Alert, but it's personal."

Verkan sat up straighter in his chair. *What kind of trouble has Dalla gotten herself into now?*

"I know you got tied up on the Pandyan Imperial Sector cleaning up that Kali business and the mess the Wizard Traders left behind. However, Dalla came home early, four ten-days ago, and shortly transported out to Fourth Level, Europo-American Subsector to a new time-line divarication to check out on a precog that the Rhogom Foundation wanted investigated."

Verkan shook his head. "She didn't waste any time leaving."

"You know Dalla; the minute she heard about this Jeane Dixon woman a team of wild aurochs couldn't have held her back. This precog has made a number of valid predictions on other Europo-American time-lines, but on this particular one she's been dead-on accurate. Of course, Dalla, as a Foundation Fellow, thought it was her duty to check it out personally. Nor did it help that Director Volzar Darv requested her assistance personally."

"Don't they have anyone else at that Foundation who can do outtime investigations other than Dalla?" Verkan asked between gritted teeth.

Tortha laughed, shaking his head. "No, not to hear old Volzar tell it. I think he's got a bit of a crush on your wife."

He's at the bottom of a long line, Verkan thought as he looked down disgustedly. "So what kind of trouble has Dalla gotten herself into this time?"

"For once, it's not her fault," Tortha replied. "You've been away from your office so you probably haven't heard about the latest goings on throughout the Europo-American Subsector. It looks like the two major competing sovereignties are about to come to blows over what the locals are calling the Cuban Missile Crisis."

"What happened?" Verkan had visited the Fourth Level, Nile and

Tigris-Euphrates Sector, Europo-American Subsector many times on various assignments. Fourth Level was the maximum probability level and was divided into many sectors and subsectors, on most of which human civilization had first appeared in the valleys of the Nile and Tigris-Euphrates, and on the Indus and Yangtze. The Europo-American Subsector was the largest subsector on Fourth Level and the one that Home Time Line had the most invested in.

The cultures there were like rioting petri dishes, displaying almost every social and civil construct, many of them developing sophisticated technology at a frightening rate. Verkan had seen what nuclear warfare had wrought all through Second Level and it appeared that much of Europo-America was headed in the same direction. One of the problems with the Terro-human animal was that any terrible weapon it invented—it used.

The biggest source of tension on Europo-American was the growing hostility between the US and USSR. He suspected that this latest round over Cuba was just posturing by the Soviets to test the new US President's resolve, since John F. Kennedy had backed down over the Berlin Wall fracas. The young President had already lost face when the Cuban President, Fidel Castro, had gone from liberator to communist lackey in the American's eyes. Several failed operations to unseat Castro had turned the new President into a laughing stock worldwide.

Kennedy reminded him of several of the Opposition Party's leaders, all surface charm and good looks, but hollow inside.

"Right now it's a stalemate on most time-lines," Chief Tortha said. "The Soviets atomic arsenal has only a few dozen Intercontinental ballistic missiles, while the American's have over a hundred and eighty. It's pure bluff on Premier Khrushchev's part. However, if the Soviets can successfully transfer a good portion of their over seven hundred nuclear armed medium-range ballistic missiles onto Cuban soil, Khrushchev believes they will have parity with the US arsenal."

"What does this have to do with Dalla?"

Tortha paused as he took out his Zippo lighter to fire up another cigarette. Self-igniting cigarettes were easily available on Home Time Line, but many citizens, like the Chief, preferred the ritual of lighting up. Fortunately,

First Level medical advances had eons ago removed the threat of lung cancer and heart attacks. After releasing a small cloud of smoke, he continued, "Unfortunately, on the new Beria Belt—that's what the Foundation's calling it—the Soviet's intercontinental ballistic nuclear arsenal is much larger. Agent Second Class Sardrath Darn has provided credible intelligence that the Soviets on this time-line have closer to seventy ICBMS."

"Who is this Beria?" Verkan asked.

"Lavrentiy Beria was the head of Stalin's NKGB and many had expected him to become First Premier upon the dictator's death. Unfortunately for Beria, he'd made a lot of enemies, especially during the purges during the 1930s. After Stalin's death he quickly married the intelligence services to the MVD, Ministry of Internal Affairs. Beria was promoted to First Deputy Premier, where he carried out a brief campaign of liberalization. He was briefly a part of the ruling *troika* with Georgy Malenkov and Vyacheslav Molotov. Beria's overconfidence in his position after Stalin's death led him to misjudge the feelings of his associates, many of whom had suffered under his previous reign as intelligence czar.

"A *coup d'état* directed by Nikita Khrushchev, and assisted by the military forces of Marshal Georgy Zhukov, had Beria arrested on false charges of treason by Zhukov's soldiers. The full Politburo met in special session and condemned him to death. The compliance of the NKVD was ensured by Zhukov's troops, and after interrogation Beria was taken to the basement of the Lubyanka, headquarters of the KGB, and executed there along with his most trusted supporters."

Verkan nodded. "I remember we had some of our own agents spirited out of the Lubyanka before they were executed."

"Yes, Khrushchev's sudden takeover left the Fourth Level intelligence specialists in the Bureau of Outtime Intelligence flabbergasted. Never saw it coming."

"That's not the first time," Verkan chuckled.

"Nor the last," Tortha echoed. "Look at how they missed that Jewish carpenter's son."

Verkan shook his head. "That was a real disaster in every direction. But what about Dalla?"

"Well, according to Agent Sardrath Darn, things are coming to a head there. It looks like a full-blown nuclear war. They've happened many times before, all over Second Level, and you know the devastation they leave behind. Sometimes the time-lines decivilize all the way back to stone axes and fire-hardened arrows. Or worse…."

"I know, Chief. I spent some time on Second Level Trisaurian Empire Sector shortly after their all-out nuclear slugfest. It made me wish we could outlaw the damn things…."

"You know how that goes, Vall. Once the atomic genie gets out of the bottle, it's impossible to stuff it back in."

Verkan nodded. "So, how much danger is Dalla in?"

Tortha frowned and his face sagged like that of a Basset hound. "First, the good news: she's with First Class Field Agent Maldar Darv and a hand-picked squad of Paratime Police. The bad news is that this Jeane Dixon she went to investigate lives in Washington D.C.—"

"Ground Zero!" Verkan interrupted. "We've got to get her out of there."

Chief Tortha shrugged. "I'm sorry, Vall, but it's not going to be that easy. From what we can ascertain, Jeane Dixon has relocated with friends in upstate New York or Connecticut—we don't know for sure. After her prediction of an all-out nuclear war she decided to leave the nation's capital. Unfortunately, our closest conveyer-head is inside New York City itself; I ordered it reopened when I heard that Dalla was still missing. I'd have already sent in an extraction team, but the entire country is on war footing and no one is above suspicion. You can see that sending in a large group would only attract the wrong kind of attention."

Verkan nodded. "Paranoia about Communist agents runs rampant throughout that subsector—not that there isn't some truth to it. However, one or two men could do the job."

"Exactly. I thought you'd want to pick the other agent yourself."

"Yes, is Inspector Ranthar Jard available?"

"Let me see." Tortha looked down at his computer and typed in a message. "I'm contacting the Department of Personnel. They should know whether Ranthar is here or outtime."

"While we're waiting," he paused to type some more, "I've just put in a requisition with the Bureau of Outtime Disinformation for ID and personal effects for both you and Ranthar, assuming he's on Home Time Line."

"Good. I don't want to waste any time. Is there a briefing on this time-line?"

Tortha shook his head in the negative. "The divarication is too new. The Rhogom Foundation were the ones who discovered it, quite inadvertently. They've got about a hundred investigators studying Jeane Dixon on different time-lines scattered through Fourth Level, Europo-American. True precognitives are pretty rare and even those who test out are unreliable. Dixon's precognition record is far above average and the Foundation wants to know why.

"One of their investigators noted Dixon's success record on this particular time-line was higher than usual, and was smart enough to nose around and find out it was a new branching. I sent Sardrath Darn there to do a quick survey. You can talk to him if you'd like."

"I'd like. It might give me a better feel for what kind of mess I'm about to step into."

III

Verkan took the descent shaft down to his office and shuffled through the files, as if some answer were hidden there, while he waited for Ranthar Jard and Sardrath Darn to arrive. The only conclusion he came to was that his wife was in real trouble. According to the files, Jeane Dixon had a well-stocked bomb shelter, but he knew the shelters were more a cynical marketing gimmick than a survival tool, especially if the bombs landed anywhere nearby. And the Russian missiles were known to be inaccurate....

Ranthar Jard, who towered over even Verkan, was the first to arrive. Verkan raised up and they touched hands in greeting.

"What's going on, Assistant Chief?" Ranthar asked.

"Dalla's in trouble again, nothing new."

Ranthar laughed out loud, showing large well-formed white teeth.

"Here, take this file. You can read it while we're waiting for Agent Sardrath Darn to show up."

After lighting up his pipe, Ranthar settled in and started reading while Verkan waited impatiently. He'd really been looking forward to spending some time with his wife. The Path of Kali case had been horrific with thousands of young girls tricked into slavery by answering what they thought was a call from their savage goddess, Kali the Dark Mother. Typically, First Level Paratimers were beneficent parasites, careful not to harm their hosts and only taking that which would probably never be missed. But, every once in a while, some of them turned into the most voracious of leeches, like the Organization or Wizard Traders, which the Paratime Police had been trying to put out of operation now for almost eight years.

A few minutes later Sardrath Darn made his way into the office. "Assistant Chief, I got here as soon as I got the red alert. I take it this is about the Beria Belt."

Verkan nodded. "Yes, it turns out my wife is stranded there."

Darn flinched. "I'm sorry to hear that. That time-line's about to go up like a Roman candle." He shrugged his shoulders. "Sorry, I should have phrased that better."

"I don't want it candy-coated," Verkan said. "Call it like it is."

Darn went into a far more detailed background description than Tortha had, naming names and giving specific examples.

"That's good background, Darn. But, you were agent-on-hand on that time-line. What's your gut telling you?"

"That whole time-line's in peril. If you want to help Dalla, you'd better get going. Today is Doomsday if this Jeane Dixon is to be believed."

"How much time do we have?"

Darn looked at his watch, which had readouts for both Home Time Line and Europo-American time. "It's only 0920 hours there, so you've got some time to pack and get a conveyer there. I'll contact the Department of Conveyer Dispatch and Scheduling to reserve you a conveyer."

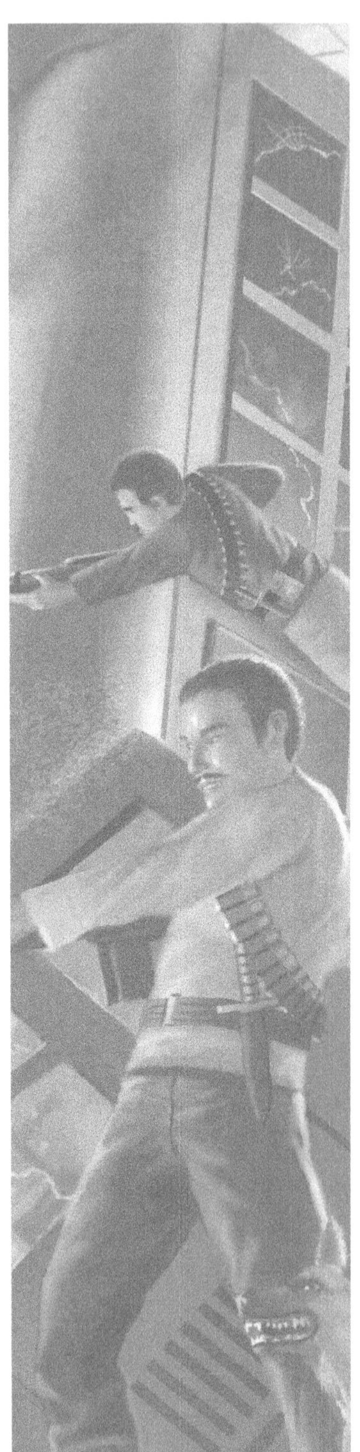

FIVE

I

As they transported in the small twenty-foot diameter transtemporal conveyer, Verkan watched as uncountable numbers of time-lines flickered by through the silver mesh dome. They were traveling too fast to see actual time-lines; what he was seeing was the passage of hundreds and thousands of parayears of time-lines condensed into fleeting images. On most levels the area was filled with first growth forests, but when they reached Fourth Level humanity began to make its presence known, buildings, street cars and crowds of people appeared and disappeared as ghostly after images.

The situation on the Beria Belt was unpredictable. If war broke out Dalla could be in real trouble, Verkan thought. He used his first level mental discipline to keep negative thoughts at bay. *At least she isn't staying in Washington D.C., although New York is another priority target.*

"How long has it been since you've visited Europo-America?" Verkan asked.

Ranthar shrugged. "A few years."

"Then you're going to need a hypno-mech update with me. Slang and technology change faster on this subsector than women's fashions." Verkan took one of the blue plastic helmets on swinging arms and placed it over his head.

Ranthar did likewise. They were attached to square metal cabinets bolted in place behind them. The cabinet was loaded with a current language tape for Europo-American as well as the latest news and customs, including fashions, popular music and sports.

The pilot adjusted their helmets and gave them their injections.

When the conveyer arrived at the New York City conveyer-head, it was completely empty. The conveyer-head was located on the first floor of a large export warehouse owned by Home Time Line interests, in this case Tharmax Imports. According to Paratime Police Survey Division, the entire time-line had been evacuated two days earlier. The room's only occupant was a large German Shepherd dog which ran over to Verkan and began to rub up against his legs.

"Looks like you just made a friend," Ranthar Jard said.

"Some fool left him here to starve," Verkan said. Then he turned to the dog, saying "Whoa!"

The dog immediately came to attention.

"Good dog, good dog," Verkan said, leaning over to scratch behind the Shepherd's ears. Turning back to Ranthar, he added, "This is a highly trained animal. I can't believe one of our people just left it behind with no food or water."

It was obvious from the way his tongue was hanging out that the dog was thirsty. Verkan looked around until he found an old hubcap. He took it into the washroom, filled it up and brought it back and set it down in front of the Shepherd. The dog looked at the water longingly, but didn't touch it.

Verkan nodded, and the dog lapped up the water as if it hadn't been watered in a week.

"What are we going to do with him?" Ranthar asked.

"Take him with us," Verkan replied. "He might be useful."

Ranthar smirked. "Sure, he can sniff out Dalla's hiding place."

"Speaking of Dalla, we'd better get out of here. I don't know how much time we'll have before the bombs drop. I don't buy this Ides of October nonsense."

"I'm glad to hear that, boss. Because, guess what? Today is the 15th of October!"

As they left the conveyer-head, Verkan made sure to use the thumblock on the door to make sure no one busted in, although it reminded him of locking the barn door after the horses had fled. The dog followed behind Verkan as they made their way down the stairwell to the first floor.

Outside the harsh wail of the alarm siren sounded through the streets, startling the few people outside in the heat of the day. It rose and fell, warbling in the Red Alert signal, bringing both men to a halt.

"Well, Verkan," Ranthar said. "Do you think we've got time to get back to Home Time Line?"

"No. Damn-it! Attack or no attack, I've got to find Dalla. I was a fool to bring you. We'll never make it back."

He stood, looking up and down the street. They were in the Bronx borough of New York City. A few blocks away was a busy shopping district. In the other direction were apartments, tall buildings with stores on their first levels. Farther away were the towers of Manhattan and the Empire State Building. Where they stood, there was little of either, most of the buildings being storefronts or older brownstones.

The klaxon noise was growing louder.

"I hope they make it." Verkan looked around for supplies. He hadn't known what the situation would be beforehand and hadn't wanted to burden them with provisions and supplies they might not need.

"Maldar Dard and his squad will take care of your wife, Verkan. Dalla's a good distance from the city. It's us I'm worried about."

"Me, too. There's a shelter sign. Do you see that subway entrance?"

Ranthar nodded.

"Okay, Jard, you take that delicatessen there and I'll go through that sporting goods store on the next block. I'll meet you in the shelter. You've got, oh, maybe ten minutes, not much more, so move!"

Verkan knew the birds were at least halfway to their targets before they'd be spotted by NORAD. They didn't have a lot of time before all demons in the Pits of Kunargh broke loose on the City of New York.

They parted. Verkan Vall and his German Shepherd plunged into the small sporting goods store. Most of the merchandise was surplus, but some of the stock seemed to be intended for repeat customers rather than transients. The store was just far enough away from the downtown area of the city to carry quality goods as well as junk.

The proprietor, an overweight, pasty-faced man, looked up as the big man strode in.

"Just get out of the way," Verkan told him, as he grabbed a shopping cart. "I want one hell of a lot of your stock, I'll pick it. I'll pay for it in cash."

"Now just a minute, mister. I'm about to raise the prices here. You can't just barge your way…." his voice trailed off at the sight of the gun in Verkan's hand.

"Look, buddy, I don't want to rob you, but I don't have time to dicker. I suggest that you load up with what you want for down below, while I'll get what I need. Then everybody's happy. How are you fixed for food? Think you'll have enough?"

"I…uh…you'll be down in the shelter?"

"Yeah." Verkan handed him a wad of American currency. Then got busy gathering equipment and stuffing it into a sleeping bag. The shopkeeper stealthily moved toward a desk until he saw the gun in Verkan's hand suddenly come clear of the gear he was packing and point in his direction.

He quickly ran out the door. Verkan continued his systematic searching and packing. It took him longer than he liked, but soon he was wheeling the shopping basket out of the store and into the street.

As he was pulling the cart over the curb, he ran into Ranthar on the sidewalk where he was pushing two wire shopping carts overflowing with provisions. "I've got two more loaded, Vall. Can you help me shove these down the stairs? The breakables are in the others."

Verkan nodded, and he began pulling the carts down the stairs, one hand on each basket, while Ranthar shoved from behind. Goods spilled out and rolled around on the floor, collecting at the landing. Verkan kicked canned goods down the stairs as he pulled the carts around the bend. He left the dog to guard the carts at the station's turnstile. As he went back up, he passed Ranthar bringing down another cart. He reached the top and started working the other cart down the stairs.

It took him a few moments to prop open the blast door. He used one of the shopping baskets as a brace. Instead of bumping the carts down the stairs, Ranthar carried them, one at a time, down to the subway platform. It was three flights down and took several trips. Once they had all the baskets down at the platform, Verkan noticed there wasn't any station attendant selling tokens. He cursed.

"Where are the Transit Authority cops?" Verkan asked.

"Not sure. They probably got the early warning and were sent to protect the city notables and politicians. Not enough of them to guard the tunnels, anyway."

Verkan nodded.

Ranthar vaulted over the turnstile, saying: "Bring the baskets over to me. I'll take them over to our place one at a time."

Verkan said, "Good idea." He lifted the first shopping cart up and helped Ranthar muscle it over the turnstile. When Ranthar was down to the last cart, he made his way over the turnstile and Verkan helped him gather their goods in silence, then wheel them over to one corner of the large subway station.

The station was one of the older subway stations. The walls were tiled, but the grout was black with mold and there were condensation drops covering the tiles. The tunnel itself was moist with heat and too much moisture. Deserted, it seemed even larger than it was.

"Cigarette, Jard?" Verkan offered one to his companion.

"Thanks, Assistant Chief—"

"We're outtime, drop the title. I don't want to draw any more attention to the two of us than absolutely necessary."

"Sure, boss."

"Better, but it would be best if you called me Vall."

"Isn't that an unusual name for this time-line, boss?" Ranthar asked.

"In general, but not in New York City. There's a lot of foreigners coming and going or residing here; most of them have unusual sounding names."

"Gotcha."

Ranthar looked up and down the tunnel "A lot of the locals aren't taking this warning seriously, are they? Hardly anybody here. What's wrong with them?"

"There'll be more coming down in a minute. It might take them a while to believe it's for real. Too many false alarms on this time-line. Still, anyone smart who's been watching the news or reading papers lately will believe it."

"Yeah. Think this place will take a hit?"

"Not as bad as Washington D.C., but New York City's a symbol. And symbols make good targets. They'll probably take out Wall Street; that's the biggest symbol in this city to the communists."

"I hope their aim's good, then. I'll wish them a bulls-eye."

"We ought to be all right, the subway's three flights down."

"Yeah," Ranthar answered. "And don't I know it. I'm still breathing hard after moving those baskets. I've been spending too much time in the office—I'm getting soft."

"This'll toughen you up. I bet we're here at least three ten-days, maybe longer if the bombs take out that conveyer-head. What did you get for water?"

"Fruit juice. A lot of soft drinks. What'd you get, Vall?"

"The place I hit was a gold mine. The store had some hobby junk as well as sporting goods. I got a collection of guns I haven't counted yet, surplus stuff mostly, some good knives, a Geiger meant for prospectors, spare batteries, flashlights, razors, first aid kits, couple of sleeping bags—you'll like this, with air mattresses yet—and a whole mess of other stuff."

"Good, that puts us in pretty good shape, as long as we don't take a direct hit."

Verkan winced. "If we do, we'll never know it."

Ranthar nodded.

Verkan looked around. "Here comes company."

"Yeah. Some of them don't like us." Ranthar nodded over at a group of boys, dressed in tight trousers and leather jackets. "I bet we won't get along with them at all." He broke off, then whistled slowly. "Look at that." He pointed to a tall dark-haired girl, wearing a short dress and too much makeup, in her early twenties, just entering the shelter.

"Trouble," Verkan muttered.

The boys also whistled, and a couple of them made remarks which Verkan did not quite hear.

"I'm looking, Ranthar. You're right, there's trouble if I ever saw it."

The girl stood in the center of the station, a tall, pretty girl with an air of self-confidence just wearing thin at the moment. She looked around and saw that there were three distinct groups in the shelter. The two Paratimers, wearing khaki pants and blue work shirts, with no insignia, but still having an air of the military or police about them, were off to her left. The leather-jacketed boys were just behind her, near the base of the stairs, while across from the soldiers a small group of people were huddled together on the benches installed for waiting passengers.

She peered through the dim light of the station, then went over to join the group on the benches.

"That kind of trouble I'll take, Vall," Ranthar said.

"I don't think so, Jard. It's because of that kind of trouble we're here in the first place."

Ranthar grinned. "Yes, Dalla."

More people began streaming into the shelter, an elderly couple with four children, ranging in ages from a girl of eighteen to a boy about five years old. Another family of six came in, and Ranthar remarked, "They tell me outtime women can keep on producing kids until they die, but I didn't believe it until I went outtime for the first time."

A pompous man, dressed for the office, came in. Next, a young couple, clutching a tiny baby. Verkan shook his head, then stood up, strode rapidly over to them. "Excuse me," he said. "You, sir. Do you have enough milk for that child for an extended stay?"

The man shook his head. "This will all be over in an hour so."

Verkan shook his head. "No, I'm sorry. This is a real emergency. The first bombs will be hitting shortly."

The man, his hair brushed back and wearing an off-the-counter suit, said, "Are you sure?"

"Is your wife nursing?"

His wife turned her red face away, while the man stammered. "I…I… mean, no."

"I take it you don't have any milk for the baby."

The man was pale as a sheet, while his wife was clenching his hand like a drowning swimmer hanging onto a lifesaver's hand.

"Damn it, I just knew it."

He went back to Ranthar Jard. "How much canned milk did you get?"

"About ten cans, Vall. I didn't plan on feeding a baby. Look, there are lots of people here. Want me to go topside again?"

"No," Verkan said. "It won't be long before something bad happens, unless this was a false alarm. You'd better stay here."

"We're going to feel stupid if that kid starves while we're sitting here, if I could have gotten up there in time."

"You're right, Jard," Verkan said, shaking his head. "Get milk, cans of it. Baby formula, too—if you can find it. But make it fast, Jard, this is it. I'm sure of it."

The Shepherd was sitting down with its paws over its ears.

That animal is smarter than any of these people, Verkan thought.

Ranthar ran up the stairs, while Verkan waited nervously. Several minutes passed, and Verkan began to puff his cigarette, taking long drags, as he watched more people straggle into the shelter. A few of the people had shopping bags which he hoped were holding food, not gift items. One fellow, drinking a pint of whiskey with one hand, held tightly to a bag full of various spirits—probably stolen from the liquor store they'd passed—with the other hand. Then Verkan saw Ranthar coming back down the stairway, a heavy sack in each hand.

"Here's all I could find, Vall. Place was jammed. Onc of those small convenience markets, they call them here. There might have been more in back, but I'd of had to shoot everybody to get at it. Damn fools, they need to get out of there and in here. Time's running out; the guy who runs the place—he's gone. People are stuffing sacks like crazy."

"Looters," Verkan said. "They'll still be breaking into stores and stealing worthless gewgaws when the first strike hits."

"That's good for us," Jard replied. "Let them stay topside and die."

They sat, smoking and waiting. Verkan thoughtfully cupped his hand over the dog's eyes.

It came a full minute later, a flash of light, then silence, then a rumbling that built up to an unbearable sound—so loud that the walls vibrated like drum heads. Concussion came with the sound, then all the lights went out.

"Oh, no!" someone cried out.

The concussion had scarcely died away when another flash of light, then another, reflected even down into the subway pits, searing its way through closed eyes, burst into the room. There was a second of silence, and the noise following it was as if someone had lifted up the gates to Hell. To Verkan it sounded like the end of the world.

The ground began shaking and buckling as though they were going through a major earthquake. Tiles were falling off the subway walls and chunks of cement and other debris were falling down on the station platform. The subway tracks were humming and sparking as if a big train were coming. The earth itself gave up a terrible grinding noise.

After an interminable time, the noise came to a sudden stop. The subway tunnel was filled with a cloud of cement dust and the detritus of the last fifty years. Silence dropped over the station like a cloak, then suddenly every woman and child in the room began to cry and scream.

Then everything blacked out

SIX

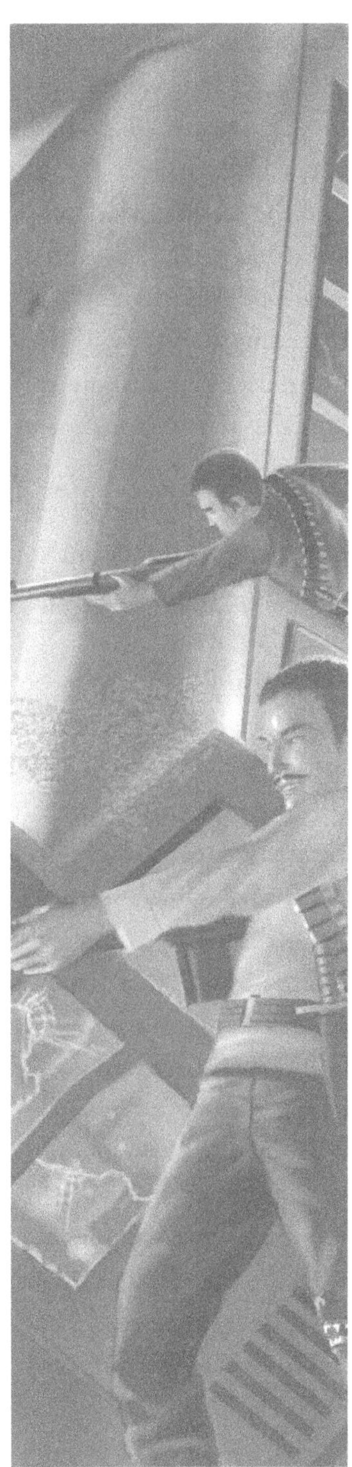

I

Dalla paced back and forth in the yellow kitchen with the black and white checkerboard linoleum floor. It was the only place where she could walk without bumping into a table, chair arm or knocking over some knickknack. Today was the Ides of October: Doomsday, if Jeane's prophecy held any truth. After spending weeks with the psychic, Dalla was a believer. This meant, at best, she was stuck here for a long time, and in deep trouble.

Even though it was mid-afternoon, Jeane was still in bed. She had awakened this morning with, as she put it: "The mother of all headaches!" Her husband James was attending to her now. Dalla had been surprised when James Dixon had arrived two days ago. But as he had told her: "I'm a believer. Jeane saved my life once before, when she warned me about a plane crash. Only a damn fool would ignore a warning like this one. I just wish my friends in D.C. had listened.... A bunch of damn fools!"

Verkan's not going to find this amusing, she decided. Although, she'd half-expected him to show up days ago. *Is he still outtime cleaning up that mess on the Fourth Level*

Pandyan Imperial Sector? Maybe I should have stuck around and helped him. I didn't take Dixon's prediction seriously enough....

The overhead light bulb flickered for a moment, and a chill ran up and down Dalla's spine. The blackout curtains, remnants of the last war, covered the kitchen windows so she was unable to see outside. Then a sudden scorching-bright light turned them translucent and she fell to the ground in a ball and closed her eyes as tightly as possible. Maybe a minute later, a deep rumbling sounded and the house began to shiver and shake as though in the midst of an earthquake.

New York or Boston? she wondered. The hairs on her arms were standing at attention and she could feel the warmth right through her bones as though she were standing in bright sunshine.

There were two more smaller shocks, then nothing. From the rear of the house, she heard Sylvia Crosthwaite's querulous voice call out. "Dolla, are you all right?"

She's still confusing me with her Chinese cook, Dalla thought wryly. "I'm okay, Sylvia," she shouted. "Stay where you are. There might be more incoming."

Dalla spent the next half hour on tenterhooks. No more blasts, but the electric was off. Nothing was working and the sky was covered with rumbling black clouds, some of them shooting forks of lightning, as though the god Thor was protesting man's latest actions. She was sitting in the living room in one of the overstuffed armchairs. The floor was covered with broken and crushed bric-a-brac, but the heavy furniture had hardly moved. Still, it was dark and dank—no one ever talked about the smell of mass destruction.

When she was sure it was over, Dalla used her lighter to light a candle she had found in a kitchen drawer. She used that to find her way back to where Jeane was resting. She and her husband were both clothed and intertwined on the four-poster bed quilt.

"Are you two okay?" Dalla asked.

"We lost everything," Jeane said, with tears streaming down her face. Then she gulped. "I don't mean that the way it sounds. Houses can be replaced, even jobs. But most of our friends were in D.C. That's where...."

She began sobbing, while her husband tried to comfort her.

Jeane reared up and cried out, "This is not a GIFT—IT'S A CURSE!"

Dalla choked up and left the bedroom, taking Sylvia with her.

"What's going to happen to us, now?" the old woman asked, her whole body trembling.

"I don't know, I don't know." Dalla repeated.

"What about your husband, dear?"

"I know he's safe. He's out on the west coast. He'll be looking for me soon."

Sylvia patted her on the arm. "Keep thinking that way, dear. It's for the best."

II

Verkan woke up to see Ranthar's profile in the dim light of a flashlight.

"Vall, come on, wake up, come on, wake up, will you," Ranthar was saying.

"Okay, Inspector, I'm awake. What's it like in here?"

"I haven't looked around yet," Ranthar replied. "From what I can see with the flashlight, this place is in good shape, saving about halfway across where a big beam collapsed and fell in. Don't know if it hit anybody."

There was a scurrying noise and Verkan turned on his flashlight and looked down to see about a dozen rats go skittering by. He slapped at one that tried to run up his leg.

The baby was still crying loudly, and other people were bawling or mewling. Someone was shouting, "Shut up! Shut the hell up!"

Verkan figured it was one of the gang members. One common method of channeling fear, for barbarians and other violence-prone outsiders, was to become enraged. Europo-American, for all its recent technological advances, had an abundance of yahoos and proto-barbarian types. The gangs that ruled the street turf here were little different from the street gangs in the Imperial Italian Belt. The Bureau of Psychological Hygiene would have a field day in this subsector.

Ranthar walked away and Verkan, using his flashlight, could see the fallen beam, an enormous supporting member was cracked and splintered, a fallen concrete pillar. The ceiling still looked solid above where it had fallen, but it was hard to tell in the poor light. Ranthar walked around the damaged area several times, running his flashlight over the debris, before returning.

"One of the kids in the black jackets and an old man, about seventy, were right under it when it fell," Ranthar reported. They're really done for. Nobody else that I can see, no other structural damage either. There's probably other casualties from the blast, though, if it knocked you out."

"You stayed conscious?" Verkan asked.

"Yes, although about that third or fourth blast just about did me in."

There was other activity around the subway station. Verkan realized the baby was still crying. Then he heard another voice that of the girl Ranthar had whistled at.

"Does anyone here know how to turn on the emergency shelter lights?" she asked, her voice surprisingly steady.

Some else cried out, "What's that running up my leg?"

Another voice, that of a man he couldn't identify answered. "Just a minute." There was the rasp of an unused metal cabinet being opened. "Here we go."

Nothing happened.

"The bulbs must be cracked. They're supposed to have spares over here. I was here during a civil defense demonstration, once. Never thought, at the time, it would ever come in handy."

Probably the electric grid is down, Verkan thought. He whispered to Ranthar: "Turn off that flashlight. We may need it later."

There was the sound of movement, feet moving across rubble and over concrete. "There are emergency lamps and spare bulbs in this cabinet." A man lit a match and worked on the cabinet for a minute.

There was more activity on the other side of the station, more matches flared, then a feeble light came on. Verkan took out a package of cigarettes. "Smoke?" he asked.

They lit their cigarettes and watched in the flickering light as a man of about thirty fussed with the miniature lights.

"Half the spares have been stolen, I think," the man said. "They sure aren't where they're supposed to be. But there's enough for a little light, anyway."

A dim glow illuminated the side of the room opposite the Paratimers.

"Must be some kind of emergency backup," Ranthar noted.

"I doubt it," Verkan said. "Most likely battery backup. It's a good thing he couldn't find any more bulbs; they'll last longer this way."

The tall girl stood in the center of the lighted area. "I'm Susan Majors," she announced. "Some of you know me, I'm the social worker for this borough. Come on, let's all come out here and introduce ourselves. We may be here for a while." She pointed to the man who had been replacing lights. "What's your name?"

"Bob Russell," the man said. He was on the bulky side, dressed in a blue off-the-rack suit; his face still had a dark beard shadow. "Say, before you all decide to stay here, we better check the radio." He reached back into the cabinet of Civil Defense supplies. Its small lock had been broken to allow him to get into it, as there wasn't a subway attendant present. New York subway trains had long since abandoned having a conductor on board to collect fares.

Russell got the radio connected, and all heard a shushing noise. "Nothing but static," he announced. "It'll probably take the authorities a while to get back on the air again. We can check the radiation levels here, though."

He took out a portable Geiger counter and began to read the instructions.

The young woman and an elderly man with a medical bag circulated through the shelter, examining the inhabitants. No one appeared injured, although many were dazed or stunned.

"Think we should help, Vall?"

"What for? They're doing just fine." Verkan continued to smoke.

"Should I take some of this milk over to the baby's mother?"

Verkan shook his head. "No."

Ranthar looked at him intently for a moment, then went back to his cigarette.

Bob Russell finally assembled the counter and turned it on. It clicked slowly, and he announced that the level in the station was safe. Then he started up the stairs. As he made the first turn, they heard the counter click more rapidly. Before he had rounded the third turn, it began to sing.

Verkan muttered, "That much this early. Must have been dirty bombs."

Ranthar shrugged. "They're pretty primitive, boss. I don't think the commies even know how to shield them. It's probably one of those three-stage thermonuclear weapons the Soviets just developed. Beria was in charge of that before he became Premier. *Tsar bomba*, that's what it was called."

Verkan nodded. "I remember that from my hypno-mech indoctrination. They're not terribly large, in the 50 to 100 megaton range, but dirty as an unwashed whore. We're going to be here for a while all right."

Susan Majors, the cute social worker, got to their corner on her rounds, looked at the two of them seated next to their mound of possessions. "Everything okay with you two? Anybody hurt?"

"No," Verkan answered.

"Well, come on over and join the others. If we stay together, maybe we can keep the rats at bay."

"You don't want us for anything, and we're doing just fine right here on our own," Verkan Vall told her. "You take care of the others, they need you. We're all right."

She looked at Ranthar, her dark eyes flashing. "Do you always let him speak for you?" she asked bitingly. "Don't you do any thinking for yourself?"

"Nope."

She turned back to Verkan. "Really now, this isn't so bad here. Come on out and meet all your new friends. We're all going to have to go through this together, so doesn't it make sense for us all to be friends? After all, we may be here for a day or two."

Talk about a dreamer, Verkan noted.

"We don't bite," she added.

Verkan shrugged. "Okay. When you get your little group assembled, we'll come and pay our respects." He watched her walk off, her high heels clicking against the concrete, a little less self-assured. As she walked away, shaking her head, he turned to his companion. "We'd better get our gear stowed away. Let's see what kind of formation we can get to this stuff, Jard." They began to arrange the groceries and supplies in their corner of the subway station.

III

Susan Majors' group meeting was finally arranged. The occupants of the shelter huddled against the walls, sitting in pools of light, or strode back and forth according to their temperaments. The group of boys with leather jackets stayed close together, talking softly amongst themselves.

She said loudly, "We will have to be here for a few days, maybe a week, maybe longer. Bob says you couldn't live an hour outside on the streets, and it's a mess anyway. That strong wind we all feel must be blowing toward a firestorm over on the other side of town, but here we have mostly stone buildings. I guess it's not too close, because I don't notice anything wrong with the air. Does anyone know about these things?"

Bob Russell put down his radiation monitor. "I think that we'll get all the air we need from the subway tunnels. This one leads all the way out of town, and it should bring in fresh air. The wind in the tunnel is getting stronger, do you notice?"

"Should we do anything?" she asked him.

"I don't know, does anyone else?"

Verkan spoke without looking up. "If we move that heavy bank of lockers and the other stuff that's big enough over there to the edge of the platform, it'll act as a windbreaker. There may be something like a hurricane in that tunnel in a few minutes, but if everyone stays near the wall they'll be safe enough."

Bob looked at him sharply. "Then we'd better get busy. Would you and your friend be kind enough to help us? And what about you boys?" he asked the gang members.

"We ain't boys," one of them said softly. There was a thin scar radiating out from the outside corner of his left eye down to his chin. "Don't call us that again."

Russell stepped back.

"Come on, you guys," he said to the others. "Maybe it needs doin'."

The leather jacketed crew stood up.

After the men in the station laboriously constructed a windbreak at the upstream end of the platform, they rejoined the meeting. The baby's mother managed to comfort the infant, and it stopped crying for the first time since the explosions.

Everyone looked at Susan Majors expectantly. "Perhaps we'd better elect a leader," she told them. "That's the best thing to do, I think."

No one said anything.

Now that the baby was quiet, they could hear sobs from an elderly woman against the wall.

"Well, I nominate Bob Russell here for group leader," she said. "Any seconds?"

The businessman seconded the motion in a dull voice. No one else spoke.

"Well, that's settled," Susan told Russell. "You're our new leader. Now, perhaps we should start with introductions. I think everyone should stand up, give their name and tell what they did before—before we came here."

Russell stood in the center of the room. "I can start it off. My name is Bob Russell, I'm forty-two years old and I'm an engineer with Eastern Metal Stamping. Maybe I still am, I don't know what things are going to be like outside—but I suspect the world as we know it will be in shambles for some time to come."

Verkan noticed that a number of people flinched at his words. One elderly man sagged down to the floor and cradled his white head in his arms.

"Before the rest of you introduce yourselves," Russell continued, "I think I'll begin by telling you what we've got here. There's quite a bit of water here, some food and a few batteries—not enough of them, I'm afraid. An old oil stove which I believe we can get going if we can find a smoke outlet. There's enough of everything to last if we're careful, especially since those gentlemen over there brought some supplies in with then." He pointed to Verkan and Ranthar, who did not answer. "Perhaps it would be better if you two brought your things over to the lockers. That way we can keep all our supplies in one place."

When the two Paratimers made no reply, Russell said more sharply, "Really, gentlemen, I must insist that we all share alike."

"Who are you, by the way?" Susan asked in what Verkan guessed was her professional friendly voice.

Verkan and Ranthar had prepared identities as South African mercenaries, which explained their unusual names; this cover also allowed them to go just about anywhere with a minimum of questions.

"I am Captain Verkan, and this is Sergeant Jard Ranthar." He spoke in an Afrikaner accent. "We're citizens of South Africa and what you probably call soldiers of fortune."

"Soldiers!? In what army?" Susan was still trying to be professional, but now there was a slight edge to her voice.

"Whatever army we like that will pay our price."

"Mercenaries!" she said incredulously. "It's people like yourselves who put the world into this mess. How can you admit it? Especially, here and now, after you can see the results of the kind of world *your type* have built. I'd be ashamed to show my face here if I were you."

"Good enough. Come on, Jard." Verkan went back to their corner of the platform. They heard the girl talking with Russell, then both addressed the group, but paid them no mind. After a few minutes, one of the leather jacket boys came over.

"Hi, I'm Joey Fish. War Leader of the Diablos. Or what's left of 'em, I guess. I'm in the same business you cats are." Fish sat down in front of Verkan, uninvited.

"You might be at that. So?"

"Just wonderin' what you dudes figure on doin'. You goin' along with this leader bit? This Russell cat? I ain't never seen him before. The Majors chick, she's been around our turf a lot, talks her freaking head off. She's all right, but ain't got any sense. You goin' along with this bit?"

Verkan looked down at the boy, well, young adult. He was probably between seventeen and nineteen, already shaving, from the heavy shadow, and was about six-two and well-built. He had his hair up in the high quiff style they called a pompadour or a water fall, with wings on the side leading back to a D.A. or Duck's Ass—as it was called. A greaser or JD or just plain trouble. The scars on his knuckles and the banged up nose said he was no stranger to street fighting. "Diablo" was spelled out on the back of his black leather jacket. A young warrior from a world Verkan Vall would never know.

"Maybe," he answered.

"Well, maybe we will, too. But we want to know if you're with us? To take over here."

"Take over?" Verkan asked. "What for?"

"No hassle, man; but what for? To run things, man. Take our share—you know. Be the top boys."

"I don't know. You mean you want to be the one who distributes the food and water? Takes care of the sick ones? Decides everything? That's more work than it's worth."

"Hell, sure, like that, man. That way we don't get the short end of the stick. We wanna get our share—of everything."

Verkan nodded. *I see,* he thought. "I don't think it's worth the trouble. I'm sure Mr. Russell will be fair about everything."

"Fair, my ass! He'll give the old ladies and children first choice, and tell us we're young and strong and better able to face it. Sure, it'll be fair—we do all the work and the old ladies get all the food. That's what's fair to that bastard. That's what fair always means, we work and they get it all. Fuck that bullshit! Now are you cats in or out? You come in with us, you'll get to keep most of your stuff."

"We haven't lost it," Ranthar growled. "And we aren't about to."

"You mean you're planning to keep all those goodies for yourselves?" the gang leader asked, his eyes boring in.

"I'm planning on keeping everything here, and using it any way I see fit," Verkan replied softly.

"We'll just see about that, Jack. At least, can you spare some smokes?"

"Sure," Verkan said. "Give him a pack, Jard."

"Sure, Captain." Ranthar took a package of cigarettes from a knapsack beside him and handed them to Joey Fish.

"Captain, huh. I've seen captains. Had my head busted open by a police captain once. Well, just don't forget and get in our way, cap'n. You stick to your side; we'll stick to our turf. You bug us, cap'n, and we'll take you apart."

Fish walked with a strut back to his gang, proudly displaying the pack of Lucky Strikes. The Diablos held another whispered conference.

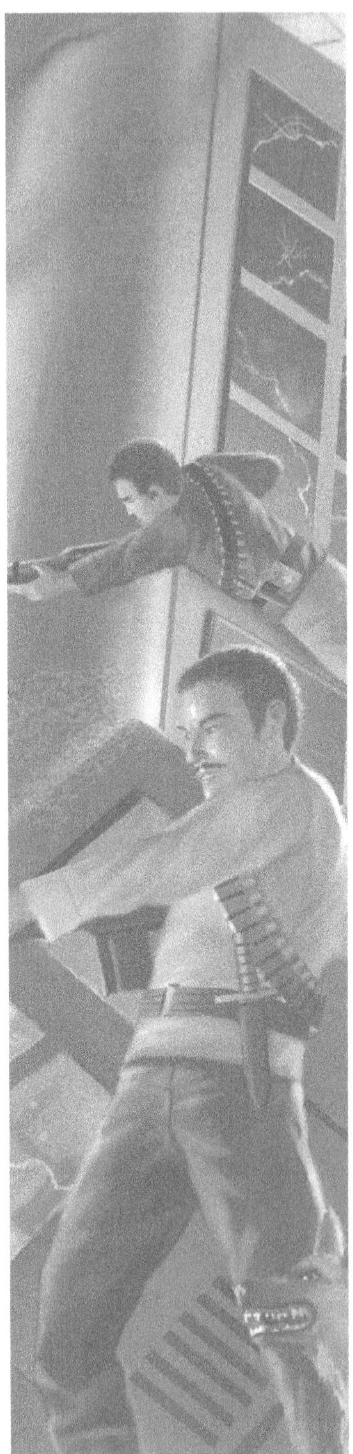

SEVEN

I

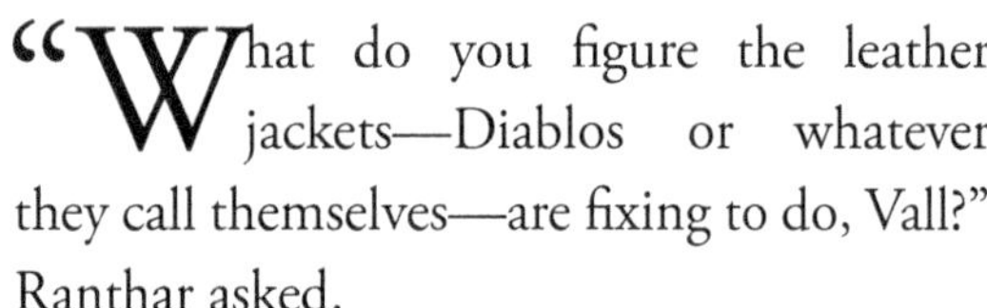

"What do you figure the leather jackets—Diablos or whatever they call themselves—are fixing to do, Vall?" Ranthar asked.

"I don't know. Probably something stupid. Right now they're still a little dazed. Wait until the penny drops and they realize there aren't any police, and the courts may never open again…then let's see what they do. Better get on full kit, Jard. Then start taking the pins out of those spare rifles. There's no point in having a lot of extra weapons around."

They carefully removed the bolts from each rifle, then began dismantling the extra pistols. "You know, Vall, if we move that poster there over this way a bit, then maybe that thing over there can be brought closer in and we'd have some privacy in our little corner.

They assembled screens made from recruiting posters and a large wallboard sign adverting Colgate Toothpaste. When they were finished, they had enclosed an area approximately ten feet square. They were just about halfway through disabling the guns and did not immediately notice when there was a knock on the walls of the cubicle.

The dog growled, but made no move when Verkan invited the caller in.

Bob Russell entered. "I'd like to talk to you two, if I may?"

"Sure. Why not?"

"Well, what I wanted to say was—well, I really think you should let us put those stores in the public lockers. I mean, well, there'll be less suspicion and all. We've all got to pull together in the face of this disaster, you know."

"I see. Thank you for your offer, but Sergeant Ranthar and I can take care of our own gear. You just go on running your end of the shelter, and we won't bother you at all—except when we go to the heads. I also suggest you encourage people to go ten or fifteen yards down the tunnel there, after you check it with your Geiger. You might even rig a light for them. That's a pressing need, to get proper latrines—"

"Can you show us how?" Russell interrupted.

"No, you just tend to your people, and we'll tend to ourselves. Okay?"

"Why no, it isn't, Mr. Verkan. It isn't fair for you to keep all those rations when all we have are the government supplies in the locker, and much of them are missing. It isn't fair at all."

"For Christ's sake, why not? Anybody else here think to bring anything in with them? Anything substantial, that is?"

Russell shook his head. "Most of the good people here don't make war and death their profession, Captain Verkan."

"I'm sure they didn't. Which is why we're down here in this hole instead of walking up there like free men."

"Why that's nonsense," Russell said, drawing back. "It's people like you that make wars, not us. If it weren't for your kind, nobody would ever fight. What was it Carl Sandburg said: 'Sometime they'll give a war and nobody will come.' But your kind always comes."

"I see. Nobody would ever fight. Not, that is, until someone slips up behind him and brains him with a cobblestone. Have it your way, Mr. Russell; I won't argue with you. You just assume that Sergeant Ranthar and I never entered this shelter. Act as if we weren't here, and dole out your rations on that basis. We'll make out just fine."

"I'm sure you will," Russell said, eyeing the piles of goods and the empty shopping carts. "It won't do, Mr. Verkan. As elected leader of this group, I really must insist that you give us those supplies and accept your share with the rest of us. Otherwise…" He let his voice trail off significantly.

"Otherwise, what? You'll get violent? You sound as if your ethics are wearing thin already, not to mention your survival instincts. Isn't that the sort of threat you'd expect out of someone like *me?* Isn't it? You put one hand on our things, and we'll tear your head off." Verkan smiled, but the smile did not appear to soften the impact of his words.

Russell looked past Verkan, to see Ranthar idly stroking a big .300 Magnum rifle.

"You can't do this, Mister Verkan," Russell demanded. "What right do you have?"

"About the same right as you do to take our stuff."

"Why, I have every right. I am the elected leader of this group. We had a completely free and open election."

"I see. You people want my things. You vote to take them. Instead of simply coming over and trying it, your group sends one man armed with the results of a vote to get my stuff. Like a tax collector. Well, Mister Russell, I don't give a damn about your election. There's only one way to get this gear, and that's over the dead bodies of Sergeant Ranthar and me—to put it a bit melodramatically."

Russell stood abruptly.

"And, Mister Russell," Verkan continued, "don't overestimate your authority here. The War Lord of that kids' outfit was just over here wanting to know if I'd like to join in, and help throw you out of office. I told him what I'm telling you: leave me alone and I'll mind my own business. But, you'd better watch your back. Those kids can get rough."

Outside their impromptu cubicle, people were stirring about, wandering aimlessly through their concrete prison. The leather jacketed boys disappeared into the men's room, as Susan and an elderly woman struggled with the kerosene cook stove.

Bob Russell fidgeted nervously, fingering his already loosened necktie. He was not a tall man, but Verkan noticed that he must have been strong once, and probably continued to exercise at infrequent intervals. "You'll just sit there while they kill me and take over all the food?" he asked incredulously. "You'll actually permit them to do this?"

"You have just told me that nobody in the world would fight if it weren't for people like Ranthar over there and me." Verkan took out a pipe and began to clean it. Although Russell was standing and Verkan reclined on the floor, there was little question as to who dominated the tiny recruiting poster and toothpaste advertisement cubicle. "Mr. Russell, you have your wish. As far as this shelter is concerned, there aren't any people like us. We aren't there. We'll stay out of our way. You got your damned wish—now get out of my corner!"

"But…but that's not right. That isn't fair at all. You should be, uh, you should help us, cooperate with us."

"Name me one good reason I should."

"Because it's to everybody's interest to have peace. Do you want that gang to take over?"

"Now there's a silly question. Good day, Mr. Russell."

"But…well, damnit man, what do you want? We need your skills. We need the supplies you brought, and more than that we need the kind of brains that it took to bring them. We probably need the fighting ability you have to defend ourselves. What's your price, Mr.…uh…Captain Verkan."

"Sorry, Mr. Russell, we aren't for hire this week. You can't hire us to fight for you. You never could, but I don't expect you knew that. Man needs some fighting done, he'd best do it himself, or at least be ready to back up the man who does. I'm sorry, Mr. Russell. Your elected authority doesn't impress me enough to make me give you my chow or fight for you."

Russell left the cubicle slowly.

"Kind of rough on him, weren't you, Verkan?" Ranthar asked.

"Maybe. I don't like him. I'm here for one thing, and one thing only—to rescue my wife. What does he want from me, anyway?"

"Blood, I'd reckon, Verkan."

"He can't afford the price."

II

They spent the next few hours straightening up their cubicle. Ranthar thoughtfully arranged some unpleasant surprises for uninvited guests who rummaged through their gear, and balanced cans on top of the partition, with strings which he could run out in several directions.

"It's Shpeegar's way of a tripwire, Vall," Ranthar noted. "But I reckon I can rig up something to keep things private. Do we want to sit guard, or will you trust the rest of it to the dog?"

Verkan chuckled. "With this crowd! I'll trust the dog."

The wind came up much stronger, and was whistling up the subway stairs as well as the tunnel. Russell led a small party of men into the stairwell, his radiation counter clicking loudly. After a few minutes, the wind ceased to blow across the platform, now it tore through the tunnel itself.

"They must have closed the fire doors, Vall," Ranthar said.

Verkan nodded, then continued to sharpen a small hunting knife he had bought from the sporting goods store. Anything to take his mind off Dalla and her predicament. At least she had the sense to get out of Washington, D. C., he decided. *Although, as a target, New York's not much better. Still, she's in a rural area and all they should have to worry about is fallout. Or looters, gangs of city folk desperate for food... Unless—don't even go there!*

Everyone had moved away from the subway tunnel as the almost gale-force wind was blowing its way through the passage. Russell tried to check the wind with his Geiger counter, but he had great difficulty remaining on his feet that close to the edge of the subway platform. He finally crawled along the edge, lying flat at the downwind end, where he used the counter to demonstrate that the wind, which came from the direction away from the center of the city, was not radioactive. He peered down the tunnel before crawling back to the light area.

"There's a lot of dead rats down by tracks," Russel observed.

Verkan shook his head. "I hope no one's stupid enough to try to eat them."

"Give them a few days. . . ." Ranthar noted.

While the subway station was far below ground, it did get a thin amount of diffused light from somewhere during the day. As night dropped, however, gloomy shadows crept into all the corners away from the civil defense lighting system. The Paratimers' cubicle was dimly lit by the alcohol stove on which Ranthar cooked their dinner. In the lighted area, Susan Majors managed to get the kerosene cooker burning and was cooking rice.

The Paratimers ate in silence, but the others attempted conversation, and even a current song or two. Few joined in, and their efforts trailed away.

The Civil Defense cabinet had also yielded three kerosene lanterns; Joey Fish simply walked up to the lanterns and took one of them, announcing that he was sure no one would mind if he borrowed it. There was no objection.

Using the lantern, the Diablos tore out the fixtures from the station's men's room and made themselves a cubbyhole. Bob Russell and Miss Majors loudly discussed whether it would not be better to let families use the private areas, but no one tried to stop the Diablos. After more discussion, some of the fixtures were torn out of the ladies' room, and families with children were installed in it.

By midnight, the wind had not abated and the shelter was growing chilly. Rather than waste fuel, Russell put the stove into the ladies' room, lit it for a few minutes, and invited those who were cold to huddle inside where their body temperature would help keep the room warm. The Diablos appeared comfortable in their quarters, and no one saw them for the rest of the night.

Verkan had a hard time sleeping, between his worries about Dalla and the hard cement floor. Finally, he asserted his First Level mental discipline and promptly fell asleep.

EIGHT

I

The wind died early in the morning. Without the civil defense lighting system it was difficult to read, but there was enough light for most activities. One of the Diablos emerged from their chamber, examined the radio set and determined that it was not working, or could not pick up any signal. It appeared there would be no communications from the outside.

Russell rested on the stairwell. "I'm sorry folks, but the second-level fallout is worse than it was the night before. We're not going to be leaving anytime soon."

He had not opened the fire doors, nor, when asked, did he think it would be wise to do so. No one wanted to test the tunnels, but finally Russell and a Diablo went down the subway tunnel towards downtown. They came back quickly, and went the other way before returning to the platform.

"There are ventilator openings about fifty yards off each way," Russell announced. "They don't come all the way through, at least I can't see direct light through them, but we do get some redirected daylight out of them. The radiation level gets very high under them. Not so much you couldn't go through it. But we didn't think that would be a good idea. No telling how high it might get closer to ground level. It's not the floor or the walls of the tunnel that get hot, it's the ventilator itself. The tunnel is safe until you get under there."

"What about that, Vall?" Ranthar asked.

"We won't be getting out for a while," Verkan replied. "Talk about bad timing. If we'd stayed on First Level, we could have waited until the radiation count dropped to safe levels."

"Sure, and watch you stomp around your office until it did! You wouldn't be happy at home, not with Dalla in danger."

Verkan shook his head. "It seems no matter where she goes, trouble is sure to follow."

Ranthar laughed. "That's what we call her, boss. Trouble, with a capital T."

"Still, even though she's away from the blast area, what if—"

"Let's keep our outlook positive, Vall. I'm sure she's fine; Dalla's like a cat, she always lands right side up."

"I hope you're right…."

"Besides, isn't Maldar Dard and his squad with her? He'd sacrifice his life before he'd let any harm come within a hair of Dalla."

Verkan nodded. "He's a good friend."

"She's probably a lot more comfortable and less hungry than we are."

"Speaking of hunger, what's for breakfast, Jard?"

"Coming up, Captain. Is it all right to light the Coleman stove?"

"Yes, but try to keep it out of sight. No point in irritating Russell and his crew any more than we have to."

Ranthar began cooking some of their more perishable goods, and soon they had a breakfast of sausages, eggs and coffee. He took the knife from Verkan after breakfast was over, and fell to honing it. When it was sharp enough to shave with, he handed it back to Verkan and started on another.

There had been no incidents during the night, but Ranthar noted that the baby had cried most of the evening, while the dog had prowled restlessly around the cubicle.

"I think it's time you went over with some canned milk for the baby," Verkan said. "Whatever supplies they brought with them are certainly low, if not out, by now."

Ranthar nodded. "How many?"

"Just a couple of cans. We'll give them milk as needed."

"Smart. Otherwise, the punks might horn in or some other citizen."

Verkan just smiled.

The last of their water was used for the breakfast coffee. Ranthar poured a cup, saying, "I hope you like it, Vall. We're down to the fruit juice, baring that bottled water you've got over there, and there isn't much of that. You know, fruit juice is fine, but I think I'll pass washing my face with it."

"Got it. Take a full can of juice and two of our empty bottles over to Russell and offer to trade. That's the deal, no haggling. Don't argue with him. If he puts up any objections at all, just leave."

II

Susan Majors was fixing breakfast for the group when Ranthar arrived with the juice. She appeared quite adept at using the oil stove which was now back on the platform. She did not object to the trade, but offered him regular water rations as well. He refused and took his two bottles of water back to the cubicle.

"Let's see how long we can make that last," was Verkan's only comment when told of her offer of rations.

Ranthar knew his superior and long-time friend was distracted by the way he spent most of his time staring at the posters. Dalla was Verkan's Achilles heel. Her safety and welfare came far above his own. The problem was that she didn't realize, or seem to care, that every time she got into one of these predicaments, it was Verkan who had to save the day. The wear and tear was mounting, especially this time when they were both trapped like rats in this subway station; out of touch of both the Paratime Police and Dalla and her minders.

The scary part was, Dalla was much more careful and considerate than she had been during their first marriage!

After coffee, Ranthar finished honing his knife, then went out on the platform where there was more room, and began sitting up exercises, softly counting cadence to himself. He was doing pushups when several of the Diablos came over to watch.

"Sock it to her, dad," one said happily. "Hey, look at the graceful form. Tryin' out for the Olympics, old man?"

The other two laughed.

Ranthar made no comment, continuing to count to himself. When the comments came faster, became more suggestive, he stopped and jumped to his feet. "Look punk, I don't know what you're looking for, but I reckon I could find some of it if I had to."

The other two Diablos straightened up and put their hands in their pockets. The one he'd challenged opened a switchblade and casually cleaned his nails.

"That's enough, Ranthar. Come inside," Verkan snapped.

"Captain, are you going to let—sorry." Ranthar went into the cubicle as Verkan stepped to the door.

III

Verkan walked out of the cubicle softly saying, "You fellows need to talk to Joey the Fish. He and I agreed to a truce last night. We agreed that we'd stay out of your corner and you'd stay out of ours."

"He's not my mom," the boy with the knife said. He was younger than the other Diablos, fifteen perhaps, but almost as large. He had big pimples all over his face, and two had been scratched until they bled. An older Diablo took a folding hunting knife out of his pocket, locked the blade open with a snap, and began lightly tapping the blade against the heel of his left hand.

Verkan noticed that it was a much better weapon than the switchblades the other boys carried.

"Yeah, man," the bigger Diablo taunted. "What's your haps? That cat's funny, doin' the horizontal bop like that. And I feel like laughing."

They all laughed.

"What is your name?" Verkan asked.

"Sam Raiffa, if it's any of your biz. What you want to know for, man. Wanna turn me into the cops?" They all laughed again. "There ain't no cops here, man. There ain't no fuzz at all. It's all gone, man. Gone, gone, gone. They're all gone. Splitzville, you dig?"

"Well, Mr. Raiffa, I can give you one reason why you shouldn't laugh at Sergeant Ranthar. He doesn't like it." Verkan turned to go back into the portioned area.

"Well, ain't that too goddamn bad," Raiffa snarled, rolling his shoulders. "We don't like you, tin soldier. Look at 'em. They think he's the man. Always with the orders, drinkin' coffee when we ain't got none. Say, funny man, give with the smokes. I wanna pack."

"Do you now. That's really a pity."

"You got plenty, man. Now, give!"

"No." Verkan walked back into the enclosure. There was a wrenching sound, then a section of their wall fell away as the three Diablos pulled it over.

Ranthar Jard had served with Verkan on numerous time-lines. And he had never backed down from a fight, nor had he ever lost one.

At Verkan's First Level command, Ranthar leaped forward. Raiffa, the nearest of the gang members, was holding his knife proudly in front of him, waving it gently from side to side.

Ranthar's shoe heel struck him in the pit of his stomach as the big man launched himself horizontally at the gang member. Raiffa and Ranthar fell together, and Raiffa received another kick in the stomach.

A second Diablo rushed forward stomping at Ranthar with his heavy combat boots, but hit only the concrete floor. Ranthar had bundled himself into a small package as he hit the floor with Raiffa, then sprang up at the next Diablo.

His shoulder caught the young man at the waist. Ranthar straightened up in one movement, tossing the Diablo back and over his shoulder. Then he reached across and behind his back, whipping out the sheathed knife he had worn there beneath his shirt tail.

The pimple-faced Diablo was the only one still standing. He shouted, "DIABLOS!" Then he fell into a crouch, his knife held with his thumb at the blade, his hand along his trouser seam—the classic pose of the inexperienced knife fighter. Several of the pack came running over, only to be halted by Verkan who was levering a shell into a Winchester rifle.

"Three armed foes against one is more than enough," Verkan said coldly. "Just stand still."

The youngest Diablo did not want to face Ranthar, but it was not in him to show fear. He stepped forward bravely, deftly slashing at Ranthar's face. Jard dodged, then lunged. His knife aimed at the boy's exposed arm. At the last instant, he let go of the knife, striking the boy's arm with the heel of his hand, following it up by burying four fingers of his left hand in the pit of his opponent's stomach.

Then, with one smooth motion, he scooped up his knife again and turned to face the other two Diablos.

Raiffa, who was still wheezing and coughing, was bent over the prostrate form of his partner who had been thrown over Ranthar's shoulder. Between coughs, he said, "Jesus, you've killed him—he's dead!"

Ranthar grabbed him by the shoulder, spun him around and smashed his fist into Raiffa's stomach.

He started to follow this with a blow to the face, when Verkan spoke up. "That'll do it, Sergeant."

"Yes, sir."

Verkan faced the other Diablos. "We had an agreement, or I thought we did. You have just seen some good reasons for not coming into our corner again. I suggest you keep the agreement we made earlier. If you want more reasons, I'm sure Sergeant Ranthar will be glad to oblige. In case you're wondering why I stopped the rest of you from interfering: it was because the only way he could have dealt with all of you would have been to play rough—very rough. Some more of you would have died. I don't think we need that. This time."

"You ever fight for yourself, tin soldier?" Joey Fish sneered. "Or does this cat do it all for you?"

Ranthar looked intently into the gang leader's eyes. "Kid, you better damn well hope if you have to fight one of us that it's me, and not the captain." He chuckled. "You just better pray to god it is."

Joey looked around at his gang members. The Diablo who had been tossed over Ranthar's shoulder was stirring, showing that despite Raiffa's pronouncement, he was not dead. The other Diablos looked to their War Leader.

"What's the matter, tin soldier? Chicken? Yellow? Gonna have this big guy do it all for you?"

He started to say something else, but Ranthar slapped him hard across the mouth, then hit him behind his left ear with the heel of his hand.

Joey swayed, but stayed on his feet.

"You don't get it, do you punk?" Ranthar asked. "Me, I can handle guys like you without anyone getting killed or maimed, barring a cracked rib or maybe a concussion—like on the one you thought was dead. But the Captain, he never learned that kind of playing around. Trooper strikes an officer, he's dead before a firing squad. Captain Verkan likes to save on the expense. You want to play games, play with me. You'll live longer."

Joey swallowed hard. It was no disgrace to be beaten in a fight. It had happened before, and probably would happen again. But he could not apologize or give up. No Diablo ever did.

Fish had not been part of the original trio lunging at Ranthar, and probably would have attempted to make the others live up to the treaty he'd negotiated with Verkan, if he had been aware that they were breaking it. Now, however, he had no choice.

He lashed out with his boot, intending to scrape it down Ranthar's shin and crush his instep.

Ranthar pivoted away, then swung his open hand to his temple. Joey shook his head, then tried to land a blow on his opponent.

Before it came close, Ranthar's open palm hit him again. Ranthar then proceeded to batter him systematically, with both fists and open hands, never landing a crippling blow, until Joey finally sagged to the ground.

"Okay, boys," Ranthar announced. "The fun is over. Beat it. All of you. I want to finish the rest of my exercises."

Still watching Verkan and the rifle, they began to edge away. Verkan called out to Joey. "You. Mr. Fish. If you can spare a moment, I'd like to see you inside. Ranthar, would you please get this wall back up again?"

NINE

I

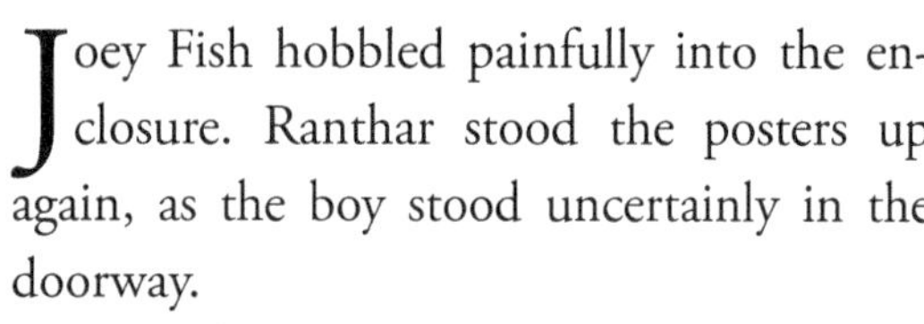

Joey Fish hobbled painfully into the enclosure. Ranthar stood the posters up again, as the boy stood uncertainly in the doorway.

"Sit down, Mr. Fish," Verkan invited. "Here, have a cigarette. Some coffee, perhaps?" As he spoke, Verkan lit a flame under the coffee pot. "It'll be hot in a minute."

Joey mumbled something through his bruised lips, accepting the cigarette. He lit it, then sat, saying nothing.

Verkan sat across from him. "I wanted to talk with you about our truce, Mr. Fish. We didn't spell it out in detail yesterday, but I thought it was understood that you would do what you wanted without interference from us. And that you would leave us alone. Perhaps you didn't understand it that way. We can begin again."

He turned to the stove. "Coffee's hot. Here, have a cup."

Verkan poured the boy a cup of coffee, then lit a cigarette for himself.

"Another thing, Mr. Fish. It's no disgrace to be knocked about by Sergeant Ranthar. He's been in this business a while. He's a professional at the use of controlled violence, and he's had a lot of experience—far more than your Diablos. You just might bring that up to the others. When you do—now, I don't know what kind of customs you have, but I want to make something very clear: Don't try to even up the score. If you do, some of you are going to get killed."

Verkan looked into the first aid kit. "Here, before I forget. Here's some tape for that big fellow's cracked ribs. If you don't know how to use it, I'm sure Miss Majors or one of her crew will be glad to do it. Otherwise, bring him over here and I'll wrap him up. And here's some pills for the lad that got the concussion. One every four hours until they run out."

"You a doc, or somethin'?" Joey asked.

"No. Do you expect a professional soldier not to know about taking care of the injured?"

Joey shook his head. "Where you guys been fightin'?"

"A lot of places." Verkan used his total recall to name off a number of recent Europo-American hot spots: "The African counter-revolutions, where they threw the communists out of those new African states. You'll remember some of those, I expect. We were in an anti-communist coup in South America, on the losing side of that one. Cuba, if you recall. Indo-China, there's always work there. Near East once. We get around."

"You get paid pretty good for that sort of thing?"

"Sometimes. We've also made some sound investments. Surprising how much you can make on the stock market when you know there are going to be uprisings in certain countries—things like that. We do all right."

"You mean you and that cat there?"

"And a few others. The reason I called you in, Mr. Fish, was to warn you that you'd best start making some plans about what to do when the radiation falls off. I suggest you start thinking about it, now."

"We'll do all right, tin soldier."

Ranthar spoke up without looking up from his work. "You talk like that to the Captain again and we'll have some more fun, kid."

"Well, what you gettin' at, man? You tryin' to get us to join your outfit?"

"No. You will all be better off after we get out, if you listen. That is if all of you are still alive. Mr. Fish, think about it for a moment. You see most people as weaklings. Civilization does that to people. You haven't any real skills except fighting. You haven't any real friends. There are going to be people a lot smarter than you left after the trouble dies away, and they can learn to fight if need be. They aren't that far away from their ancestors.

"You don't know much about making friends, and most of what you picked up on the streets is going to be useless. The more of your Diablos who live through this shelter period, the more chances all of you will have to survive afterwards. The best way for that to happen is to keep out of our way. Make a truce with me, and keep it. A formal truce. I'll go further and suggest you ought to make one with Russell and his people, but you won't take that advice, I'm sure. You'd better damn well not try anything else with us."

"I have to talk to the Leader first."

"I thought that was you."

"Naw. I'm War Leader. El Toro's the leader. You didn't see him yet, man. He came in last night through the tunnel. Got trapped up the line with some of the other Diablos, had to fight his way back to our turf. Lost some of our boys."

"Is he all right?" Verkan asked.

"What do you mean, 'all right?' Sure he is. Little beat up from taking out four of them Jokers. Man, you just wait. Toro'll fix that cat of yours, soon as he's back on his feet. He's just beat up something bad right now."

"I wasn't asking about his health. Did you say he came from uptown?"

Joey the Fish nodded. "Didn't feel a thing. Toro's all right, man, just tired and beat up. Nothing hurts El Toro."

"What's it like uptown?" Verkan asked.

"The Jokers and the Imperial Lords—a spade gang out of Harlem—joined up and took over. Got a court set up, with their own judge. First guy they tried was a cop. Even gave him an attorney for the defense. Let the trial go on for an hour before they cut 'im." Fish rubbed his bruised arms, then glanced significantly at Ranthar and Verkan.

"How many of them are there?" Verkan asked.

"I don't know, maybe twenty-five…maybe more. They got the whole station. Run it *their* way. It's the next station up the line."

Blocking our way out of here, Verkan noted.

Fish stretched. “You got any more questions, man?”

“Not if you’re in a hurry.”

“Okay, man.” Joey stood, then grimaced as he discovered his bruised muscles had stiffened, and turned to leave.

“Oh, by the way, Mr. Fish—” Verkan started.

“Yeah,” he said with a sneer.

“Here. Take a package of cigarettes to your troops. Be sure to give one to Mr. Raiffa.”

“Look, Daddy-O, this gets you nowhere. Dig it, nowhere. We don’t need your handouts!”

“Remember what I said, Mr. Fish. Leave us alone and more of you will walk out of here alive. Otherwise....”

Verkan pocketed the cigarettes and turned back to the cubicle. Joey Fish limped across the station platform and disappeared into the washroom the Diablos were using for their headquarters.

“There’s going to be trouble, Vall,” Ranthar told him. “Those kids are tough. You got to hand it to them, they kept going on even when they knew they couldn’t win. That’s trouble on the wing.”

“Yes, Jard. Maybe not for us.”

“Are you kidding, Verkan? Those kids will knock over Bob Russell, and then we’re next. See the look on Fish’s face when he told us about the others trying that cop? I’m sure they’d love to do that to us right now.”

“All right, Ranthar. What do you suggest?”

“Wade in there and take them all before they get ready to take us.”

“That’s the direct approach. Well, we’ll see. Your way ensures that we have to kill most of them, and I’d rather not do that if I don’t have to. They might even be useful when it comes to getting out of here, if Joey’s information about the next station up the line is accurate.”

II

After repairing the cubicle walls, there was nothing to do but wait. At Verkan's suggestion, Ranthar supplied more milk to the couple with the baby, and helped Russell organize a screened-off area in the downtown arm of the tunnel for latrine use. Then they took turns catnapping for half-hour stretches, falling easily into the routine of soldiers on duty in a quiet area.

Susan Majors attended to the wounded Diablos, then talked with them for over an hour before she approached the corner where Verkan and Ranthar had their area. She strode into the cubicle without knocking and stood directly over Verkan before she noticed Ranthar's weapon aimed in her direction. "Just what I might have expected. Put that thing down. I won't hurt you. Or, if you won't do that, point it at me and be done with it."

"Lady, when I point a gun at somebody, I'm likely to use it. Next time, though, you might knock. It's more polite." With that being said, Ranthar grounded the butt of his rifle but did not set it down.

"Your paranoid excuses don't work for me. Just what do you think you're doing?" she stormed. "Everything you do confirms my worst opinion of you. You beat up those children, you defy Mr. Russell, you won't have anything to do with us.... What are you afraid of, that you might have to join the human race?"

Verkan casually waved toward a wooden grocery box which Ranthar had reinforced and said, "Please, sit down, Miss Majors. You are a tall girl and—if we are going to talk—I'm tired of looking up at you."

She sat down in a huff, radiating displeasure at both the surroundings and her companions.

"Now, am I correct in understanding that you object to our treatment of those 'children,' as you call them?"

"Object?! You've cracked one boy's ribs, fractured the skull of another and beat the life half out of Joey Fish. You're damn straight I object."

"Lady," Ranthar said, "those *children* were after me with knives. Three of them at once."

"They told me about it. You provoked them. Oh, I don't object to your defending yourself, but you overdid it—and you know it. Captain Verkan, this may be the way you do things in South Africa, but it doesn't wash here in the States. I will thank you to keep this brute of yours from harming them further. You have guns, you even menaced them with one. You could have stopped that fight without beating those boys to a pulp. Next, I suppose, you'll set your attack dog on them."

She sat on the offered box and arranged her skirt. Verkan noticed, that besides a nice pair of legs, she had managed to keep her light wool outfit reasonably intact despite having to sleep in it. However, her blouse was stained with blood on the right sleeve. She had taken her stockings off, and the effect of the fashionable skirt and heels combined with bare legs was mildly disturbing. He already had one attractive bundle of trouble to rescue and he didn't need another one.

Verkan also thought she was a very pretty girl and regretted that she didn't seem to be at all sensible. "We have every intention of leaving them alone, provided that they will do the same. I have offered them a treaty, or truce, or whatever it is they call these agreements. Now, you are a pretty lady, and I don't at all mind looking at you, but I don't care to have you shout at me any longer. If you can't come up with something better to talk about, get out of here."

"I will not leave until I have finished. Or will you have this beast of yours throw me out?"

"I might. Oh, the devil with it. Have some coffee, Miss Majors, and tell me what's on your mind. Surely you didn't come in here just to accuse me of brutality toward the Diablos."

"No. But I didn't come to be menaced with guns, either." She ran her fingers through her short hair, tried again to arrange her skirt.

Ranthar handed her a partly filled cup of coffee which she accepted with an automatic smile of thanks. "I came to see if I could get you to help Bob Russell and me work out a plan of what of do when it's safe to leave the station. We didn't get off to a very good start, I'm afraid. I can't pretend that I like you, Captain Verkan, but we do need your help. I can at least be polite to you."

Verkan decided that his initial estimate of her age, early twenties, was correct, probably not more than a year out of college. Outtimers in more primitive cultures grew up quickly, while those in civilized ones frequently took a lot longer to mature and were often quite naïve. That would mean that she'd been in the field of social work just long enough to get over the initial shock of the contrast between the actual job and the things she was taught in school. But not long enough to become cynical about it. She would have made friends in her district by trying very hard to understand her clients. Of course, she wouldn't see them as clients or herself as a patron, but the intelligent ones would treat her that way. They would continue to do so until she stopped being a soft touch, after which they would switch to other methods of winnowing the bounty her office dispensed.

Now, she was trying to be charming, but it was obvious that her self-control was wearing a bit thin. This was hardly surprising, and Verkan thought she was doing well to remain as collected as she appeared. Susan Majors was, after all, a very young girl—and way over her head in this situation.

"Where are you from, Miss Majors?" he asked.

"New Hampshire. A very small town I'm sure you've never heard of."

"That wouldn't be surprising, I can't think of many towns I know here in America. I haven't traveled in my own country as much as I would like." Verkan shifted his weight and settled in, sitting up against the wall of the subway station. "How did you come to social work in New York City? It's a long way from a small New England town."

"My professors in college interested me in the field. We studied the urban unrest and poverty in the ghettos and what caused all of this. I thought maybe I should do something to help stop that."

"I see. Do you think what you're doing has been effective?"

"I haven't been in the field that long. I don't know; this city is different from the places we studied. It always seems to take so long to understand these people." She drained her coffee. "But, that isn't what I came to talk with you about, Captain Verkan. I've heard terrible stories about how you treat minorities in *your* country, but enough of that. I meant it when I said we need your help. I wish you wouldn't just sit over here and ignore us."

"What do you have in mind?"

"Well, you could come out and talk with us about the future, help us plan what we'll do when we get out of these tunnels. Or how. And there's all this food you have here. It should be used for the benefit of all. You can't use it all yourselves, and there's a real need out there. Why, you even feed that dog, when the food is needed for the children."

"Want some of his chow, Missy?" Ranthar said, holding up a handful of dry pellets. "You're welcome to it, that is, if you can get it down."

"What is all this about food, anyway, Miss Majors?" Verkan asked. "This bomb shelter was designed for a hundred people. There aren't more than sixty or so here, counting Sergeant Ranthar and myself. You can't be running low already."

"But we are. Vandals destroyed one of the Civil Defense lockers; it must have been quite a long time ago. Not all of the shelter equipment and stores are here. And...and...last night, someone stole quite a lot more of our food stocks. We don't know how to get it back, and...well...we're going to be short before long."

"I see." Verkan stood, looking down at her. "Didn't Mr. Russell think to post a guard?"

"No. Neither he nor I have...well, what you would call a military mind. We didn't think of it." Although she continued to try to be charming, it was obvious that she felt some pride in not being possessed of a military mind.

"How much food is left?"

"Well, it's not that bad. There's still plenty of water, flour, soy bean mash, buckets of lard and dried peas. Lots of vitamin pills. But someone took all the fruit juices and chocolate; all the things that make the staples seem a little less unpleasant. And you have *all* this bounty, and I think you should share it."

"In other words, due to your incompetence—excuse me, because you haven't a 'military mind'—someone got away with your things, but not ours. So, now, you think we should share ours with you. What happens when ours is stolen as well?"

"But it wouldn't be, Captain. We can guard the stores; we just didn't think of it in time. We know to do it, now."

"What good would that do? How could you people stop a determined effort to take the stuff away from you? Or do you fancy fighting the Diablos? No, Miss Majors, I'm afraid I can't help you. Besides, you don't want me. Your Mr. Russell has as much as told me that, and your first words when you came in here made it quite plain that you wouldn't approve of me or even consider my advice if I joined your council."

"I thought you'd say something like that." She stood up. "Thank you for the coffee. I won't waste any more of your time." Instead of turning to go, she stood in front of Verkan, her left hand clutched tightly in her right. She was quite tall, her head just below the level of Verkan's eyes. She continued to stand, not moving, but not saying anything."

"Was there something else?" Verkan asked.

"Yes. I...well, Bob Russell asked me to ask you. He wants one of your guns. He thinks he will need it."

"I expect he will. And he wouldn't ask for it himself, not after our last conversation. This is really rather interesting, Miss Majors. First, you decent people wish the earth clean of me and my kind. Then you want things from me. Food, now a gun. You are upset when Ranthar is armed, but you want your Mr. Russell armed, as well. Tell your Mr. Russell that I really have but one objection to giving him a weapon, but that one is insurmountable: he'd probably point it at me, and get himself killed. No, there's a second objection. He wouldn't keep it an hour, because I don't think he has the guts to use it. And somebody who does would take it away from him. Either way, I would be arming an enemy. I think I had better keep the weapons."

She nodded. "I may even agree with you. Captain, those boys—they're just children. They weren't so bad, up there"—she paused to point up the stairwell—"before all this happened, I could trust them, at least when they were sober. There were others, how can I put this, well, there were others much worse; but the Diablos weren't hopeless. But now I'm afraid of them. They're going to be very anxious now, especially after Sergeant Ranthar humiliated them this morning. They have to prove themselves men. They kept talking about how things are going to be very different soon. I think it's you they're really mad at, but...well...they worry me. If you won't help us yourself, won't you give us a weapon?"

"I've already explained why not, Miss Majors. No."

"And you and the Sergeant are just going to sit there and let whatever happens to us happen? I'm not sorry I was angry with you. There really isn't much humanity to you, is there Captain Verkan?"

She turned and strode rapidly across the platform, her head held high.

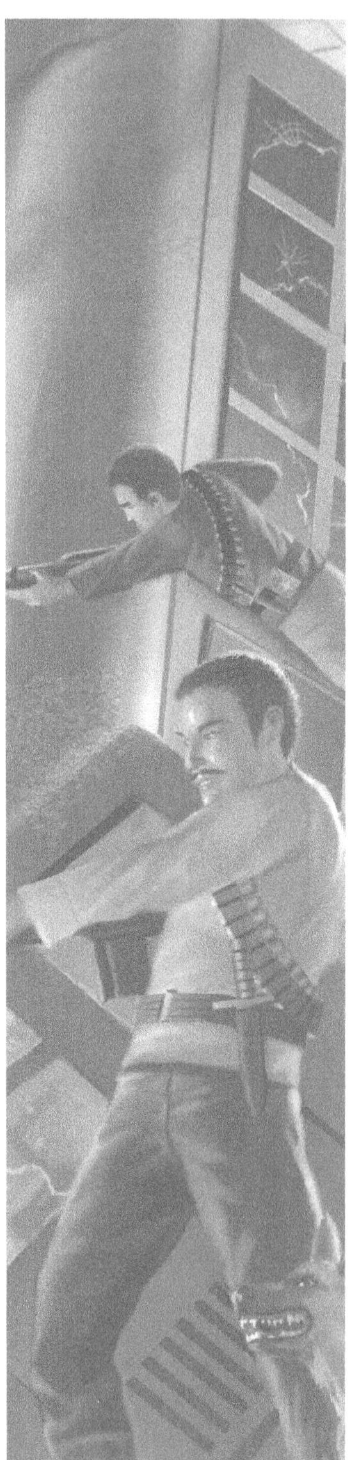

TEN

I

The first revolution took place during the noon food distribution, but it died stillborn. The Diablos, led by Joey Fish, came to the food line in a body and pushed themselves to the stove without waiting. After they served themselves whatever they wanted, while taking extra portions for those who remained in the stronghold, they elaborately but insultingly apologized to Bob Russell before retiring. Susan looked intently at the soldiers in their corner, then went back to serving rations to the others.

"What do you make of that, Vall," Ranthar asked.

"What do you think? They've shown everyone they do as they please. They don't really know what they want to do yet. It's a stupid strategy on their part to warn the others of their intentions, but I guess they're counting on nobody organizing to stop them. They were also testing to see what we might do about it. You notice that there's been nothing from them about a truce. They want to see if we interfere when there isn't a treaty."

Verkan idly scratched his dog's ears. "Tonight, I rather expect they'll try to get our guns. They don't really trust us not to interfere, not if they actually take over and start raping women and carving up people for fun."

"Would we, Vall?"

"Why should we interfere? The closest anyone's come to asking us for help was the Majors girl, and she really doesn't want us—she wants somebody to put things back the way they were before the bombs fell. I can't do that, Jard, and they aren't ready for what we can do for them. By the Fangs of Fasif, I'm no expert on government."

"When do you think the boys in khaki will be back?"

Verkan shook his head. "Right now, they've got more important things to do, people to kill and places to protect, like Washington D.C. If things are really bad, it could be months before the army comes in. The National Guard, maybe sooner. I don't see any Transit Authority police, either."

"So we're all on our own," Ranthar said.

"That's how I see it. But we have a mission—to rescue Dalla. And that comes first. I don't know what it's like in the rural areas, but they will quickly be flooded with refugees from New York, Boston and other large cities."

"Dalla's pretty handy with a firearm, and she can take care of herself. Plus, she's got Maldar."

"He won't do much good if they run into a big pack of looters and marauders. Civilization is just a thin veneer, and that surface has just been ripped away. It just depends upon how disrupted the local constabulary and National Guard are. And how determined the looters and criminals are. The one thing I know for sure is we need to get Dalla off this time-line as soon as possible."

Ranthar nodded. "Well, we have our own problems here. What should I do about tonight?"

Verkan looked around the station. There wasn't much in it. He thought that there would be tool lockers somewhere in the subway system, but they would be off in the tunnels, not in the station itself. He regretted that the hypno-mech had not contained any in-depth information on subways: but why would it have? From what Sardrath Darn said, on this time-line they might be completely different from Survey's records. As he thought of it, he didn't even know the geography of the New York City subway system other than the rough map which hung on the station wall. The tunnel leading to Manhattan he was convinced was devastated. The city map he had and the wall maps showed that it led uptown for several miles, came out in the open for a short stretch, then burrowed under the water before coming to the surface again. From there, it would be open country to Jeane Dixon's hideaway and grounds, across fairly open and not well-populated rural areas with lots of trees and farms.

The station itself was not well-equipped for warlike preparation. As he looked at the equipment he and Ranthar had brought it, Verkan said, "You can rig up that hunter's floodlight so that we can turn it on from a distance. That'll help."

"Sure, Chief's Assistant, but what do I use for wire?"

"Rip out some of that telephone wire over there. I don't think that those booths will be getting any more calls after the electro-magnetic bursts."

"Sir, I believe this time-line is primitive enough that they might still depend upon operator-manned mechanical phone switches."

Verkan nodded. "In that case, leave one phone in working order, just in case someone topside does repair the system. There may be somebody in Civil Defense headquarters, and they just might get around to calling all the stations in a week or so."

"Yes, sir. Where do you figure the city took hits? I saw flashes and it seemed to me they came right up the tunnel, or one of them anyway. The sounds came from all over."

"Hard to figure. The firestorm was definitely downtown from here. It's like that finished off much of the city that way. I'm sure Manhattan was a prime target, Wall Street and all being such heinous symbols to the communists." Verkan paused to shake his head. "It was a dumb move, too. From our intelligence, the American nuclear arsenal outnumbers the Soviet's stockpile by at least three to one. Let's thank our lucky stars that we weren't in Moscow!"

"Yeah, boss, but you're thinking of Europo-American prime," Ranthar noted. "The Soviets on this Beria branch have a lot more bombs than the primary. Plus, the Soviets have fewer major cities and their missile-range is much shorter. Most would have been intercepted over Canada. Still, I doubt their missiles went much past the northeast corridor, which of course doesn't do us any damn good."

"You're right. I doubt there's a building standing anywhere within a hundred-mile radius of Moscow and Leningrad. What worries me is there are not very many people coming into these subway tunnels. If many had lived through the nuclear blast and firestorm, there would be some coming in—even now.

"The radiation's not so bad you'd drop dead just from walking around in it, but anyone who comes in now is probably a walking dead man. Of course, every school has a shelter and all of those big parking lots underground were supposed to be stocked, but from the evidence here, I think we can see just how seriously people in New York City took the Civil Defense Act. Stock stolen or ruined by vandals, and not replaced…I just don't know."

Ranthar retrieved the wire and worked quietly out of sight behind the partitions of the cubicle. "How do you figure the Diablos will try and take us?"

"I wouldn't underestimate them. They probably have one or two pistols or zip guns, I think that's what they call them. Single-shot guns made from coffee pot percolator tubing…not real effective. But deadly if they get lucky. And they'll have knives, with experience in fighting with them. You surprised them this morning, but now they'll be ready for you. They can fashion other weapons out of what's at hand, clubs from pipes out of the washroom. Slings, maybe some kind of bow, throwing sticks…My guess is they're making an arsenal in that stronghold of theirs right now."

"I wish we had thought of one of those rooms."

"So do I, Jard. I must admit I didn't think of it until it was too late."

"Anything else you want me to do?" Ranthar asked.

"No. We'll wait for them to make the first move. I don't want to sit guard on them for two or three weeks. Even if we could get the drop on them and capture all of them, the others wouldn't help us if we simply overwhelmed the kids. We'd have to kill two or three, at the very least. Then listen to a sermon a day from the social worker and whatever other bleeding hearts—a very useful Europo-American term—she has on her side."

"They'll take casualties if they attack us, too," Ranthar noted.

"I'm not worried about the solid citizens, just the leather jackets. In this half-light, good shooting is going to be difficult. Well, we'll just wait for them."

Ranthar grunted. "Verkan, what about if we just take off up the tunnel? You could take the Geiger counter from the sheep and we could check the radiation count, and maybe there's a maintenance room where we can hole up for a while."

"I thought of that. But I don't want either of us alone for any length of time, and I'd hate to set out without a thorough investigation of where we're headed. The next station, according to Joey, is in much worse shape than this one. And I don't relish being cooped up in that tunnel for a couple of weeks."

"I'll go look for something better if you want me to, Vall," Ranthar offered. "I'm going to get cabin fever just sitting here anyway."

"No. I don't want to have to stand guard over the stuff by myself. There are more than a dozen Diablos, more if their leader is of any use or if he brought others along with him. That's big odds."

Ranthar nodded. "It's a cinch we can't go off and leave this stuff by itself."

"Exactly," Verkan said. "Of course, we could pack up the stuff in carts and wheel it along with us. If we don't find anything, we could always come back. I'd rather not leave without somewhere to go, though. I think our best plan is to wait for the radiation levels to die away a bit."

"Hell, you won't leave anyway, Vall. You aren't going to leave all these defenseless civilians to the kids and we both know it."

"Would you give me one good reason why I shouldn't?"

"You won't do it, Vall. Not you."

"But I'm not responsible for them."

"Yeah, sure. Cover me while I go to the head."

Verkan nodded.

ELEVEN

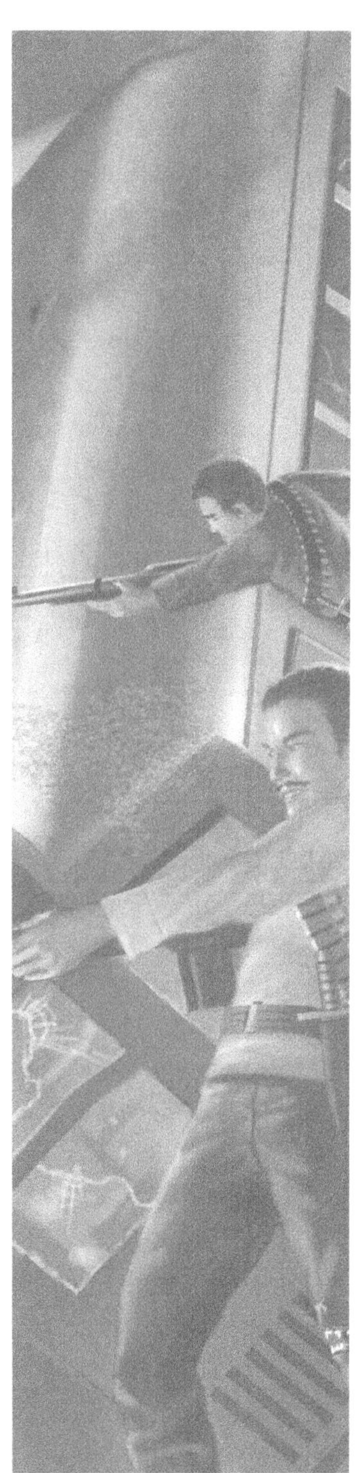

Shortly before dark, an elderly man with a bald head and a tonsure of white hair knocked on the cubicle wall. Verkan noticed he was carrying a black medical bag. He had noticed him earlier, attending to the family with the baby. But, since he hadn't said anything and took no part in the shelter activities, Verkan hadn't paid him any attention. He was in his sixties, at least. A small man who looked as if he had once been strong and active, but was now quite thin. As he examined him more closely, Verkan thought of the term, 'wasted.'

"May I come in, gentlemen?" the elderly man asked.

"Certainly," Verkan replied. "Quiet, dog. What can I do for you, sir?"

"I am Dr. Pearson, James Pearson, a former Lieutenant Colonel in the Medical Corps. Retired some years ago, more years than I'd care to say. Haven't practiced in a long time, but when I heard the alarms I brought my bag. Not much in it, I'm afraid. I'd like to talk to you, Captain, is it?"

"That's right, Captain Verkan Vall, sir. Have a seat. Sergeant, would you get Colonel Pearson some coffee?" He turned back to the doctor. "The seat is only an old box, and coffee is about all I can offer in the way of refreshments, but you're welcome to what we have."

"Thank you, Captain. I want to ask you what you plan to do. That is, just what do you propose doing about the Diablos?"

"I don't propose to do much of anything unless they interfere with us."

"Miss Majors said as much. I'll tell you frankly, Captain, it is your duty to restrain them. They have in mind to seize control of this shelter, and if they do, they will undoubtedly institute a reign of terror. I am convinced it is only your presence here that has kept them from giving us more than a token demonstration of their power. One of the new ones, one that came in last night, has been telling the others how their rivals—I believe he called them the Imperials—up the line are in absolute command of their shelter and how much fun it would be if they did the same here. Are you really going to let that happen here, Captain?"

Dr. Pearson looked at Verkan intently.

"Yes. I expect you're right. But, Dr. Pearson, it isn't my duty. I have been told by the elected leader of this group that my presence isn't wanted here. And, that in fact, it is people like me who are responsible for everyone being forced into here in the first place. He and Miss Majors told me to mind my own business. It isn't the first time these people and their friends have told me that. Well, I'm going to take their advice. I intend to mind my own business, and let them mind theirs."

"I see. And what will you do about the war itself?"

"In my experience," Verkan said, having seen this attack play out on more than one Europo-American time-line, "the Strategic Air people on both sides will fight it out until they have no more resources. That shouldn't take too long, all things considered. You people have a clear superiority in nuclear weapons—"

"What do you mean, you people?" Pearson interrupted.

"I'm a South African citizen, doctor. It's sheer happenstance that I got caught up in all of this."

The doctor nodded. "That's true, your country has its own problems."

"Anyway, the Soviet smaller reserve is already played out. Knowing how vengeful you Americans can be, I suspect that there isn't a standing city with a population of over a hundred thousand that hasn't been hit. Of course, the subsequent fallout will make tough going for your European allies, especially the Germans. Still, everyone has atomic weapons these days: the English, the French, the Indians, the Chinese…and probably a few we don't know about. And, they all have enemies they will fire them at. It wouldn't surprise me to learn there isn't a country left on earth that hasn't been hit by at least one nuke, perhaps more.

"Fallout will disrupt the rest. The war will just lie dormant until somebody has rebuilt enough industrial potential to prosecute it again. That could take years, or it could take centuries. Until then, I can't think of anything I can do about it."

Pearson nodded. "I would agree to that, I suppose. Let me ask you something else: What are your plans when you leave this shelter?"

"Sergeant Ranthar and myself will make our way north, since that portion of the state is less built-up and therefore probably untouched. Other than a miss by one of their birds, there's nothing much there for the Soviets to have targeted."

"There are the sub plants in New London and the Grumman plants on Long Island or the old Suffolk air force base on Long Island."

Verkan shrugged. "We'll have to take our chances."

"And, what will you do when you get there?"

"First, I will try to determine the extent of this war. After that, Sergeant Ranthar and I will do our best to get back to South Africa and find out how my wife is doing."

"What if you learn that South Africa has also been nuked and is not in any better shape than the east coast of America, what will you do then?"

"A good question, doctor. Once I get there, I can find out if there is still a government, and whether or not it is the kind of government that I would be willing to offer my resources to. If not, I'll do for my own and build a secure compound."

"And try to rebuild civilization?" Pearson asked.

"I suppose. Something like that, Colonel Pearson. If not civilization, at least something more comfortable than this shelter."

"You will need help getting out of these tunnels, Captain. There's at least one gang, and probably more, between you and freedom. You will not be able to do it by yourself. Why not these people?" Pearson indicated the inhabitants of the shelter with a sweep of his hand. The veins stood out prominently on his skin's chalk-white surface.

Verkan shook his head. "From what I've seen, the only ones I'd really want with me are the Diablos, and they're not interested. Your people won't stay alive long enough to get out. Besides, they wouldn't care much for my leadership. I'm not much for elected councils and democratic government, Colonel Pearson. It may have been great for the United States, but it won't work here and now, and it never worked that well from what I've seen as a foreigner, or outsider."

"But surely you will admit some obligation to those weaker than yourself. I don't know anything about the South African Army, but it is based on the British military model—to a large degree. Do you agree?"

"Yes, doctor. To that much I will agree."

"Then you must surely admit some obligation to your fellow man. Some small feeling of a debt owed. These people, for the most part, are innocents. It follows that your duty is to them. To us, to put it crudely."

He shook his head. "Colonel, I have some feeling of kinship, as a fellow military officer, to you. To those who wore the uniform. I may even feel a bit of obligation to you because you at least understand my profession. But to them? To a foreign country? I did not swear an oath to protect this country."

Verkan stood abruptly and paced around the cubicle. "And I will be hanged if I feel any duty toward *them*," he said, indicating the people in the shelter with the same gesture Pearson had used. "I don't need them. More importantly, they don't want me. But they now expect me to bail them out of troubles they got themselves into. So-called 'advanced societies' always do that, you know. They get themselves into trouble because they get rid of the warriors and all the warrior feelings that 'my kind' have. Then, when the trouble gets too big for them, they want us to help them again. Not much, just enough to get their heads above water again. Then they start kicking us in the teeth to make up for lost time.

"Right now, all they want from me is a gun, some food and perhaps some advice. Then they'll learn they can't use the gun. They'll want me to use it for them. After I've killed those kids, they'll be grateful for a full day before they start with the 'ruthless barbarian' routine again and throw us out. Colonel, they don't want me, and I don't want them. There's the end to it."

"Coffee's ready," Jard said. "Had to use some fruit juice in making it, as we're out of water."

"Now, there's something they can do for me, Colonel. They can give me water so I can have coffee that doesn't taste of pineapple." Verkan sipped the coffee, grimacing. Then sipped again. "But the price is too high. I'd rather get used to pineapple flavored coffee, or do without."

"I wish I could be more persuasive, Captain Verkan. Unfortunately, I understand your point all too well. After I retired from the service and went into private practice, I worked in a small socialized clinic. Forever treating people for things they had no business getting, but who wouldn't take my advice because it was free. Besides, why take preventative measures if treatment costs nothing? But it was still my duty as a medical man to do whatever I could for anyone who asked for my help. Old-fashioned as I am, I even believe in the Hippocratic Oath. Didn't you take an oath once, Captain? Haven't you an obligation as an officer?"

Verkan stopped pacing and stared out into the gloomy subway station. It was getting darker again, and as he watched Russell switched on the Civil Defense lighting system. They had disconnected most of the lights, so that only a small area around the cook stove was lit. The tiny pool of light made the rest of the station appear even darker.

The German Shepherd growled as one of the Diablos passed close by the cubicle, on his way back from where the men had set up heads. Already a faint stench was coming back up the tunnel from the latrine area. The Diablo nodded at Verkan as he passed.

Verkan turned back to Dr. Pearson. "As an officer? My rank is a courtesy title, as I'm sure you know. I'm not even a South African citizen. In my last service, I had to give up my citizen rights in order to fight the battles that the South African government ought to be fighting herself. True, They don't know about it, but they ordered any mercenary who fought against the insurgents in Mbwangli stripped of their citizenship. It appears that it was all right to join the rebels, though."

Pearson stood beside Vall, and said softly, "Then as a human being you still have an obligation. You can't escape your duty, Captain Verkan."

"Why not? Their fathers took their pleasure with their mothers without my consent. I didn't share in the fun, and I don't see why I have to pay the consequences."

Pearson said nothing, but sat again, picking up his cup of pineapple-flavored coffee. "There isn't much left to say, is there, Captain?" Doctor Pearson climbed wearily to his feet, looking older than when he entered the cubicle. It was quite dark now, the only light in their compartment being a penlight which Ranthar had covered with a handkerchief to diffuse the beam softly around the closed area.

"No, sir, there is not. If you'd care for a game of chess tomorrow, we have pencils and paper and we can make a set."

"Perhaps later, Captain. If there is a later. For either of us. Thank you for the coffee." He limped out of the area. Ranthar looked at Verkan, who nodded. He silently walked with Pearson to the other side of the station, lighting his way.

TWELVE

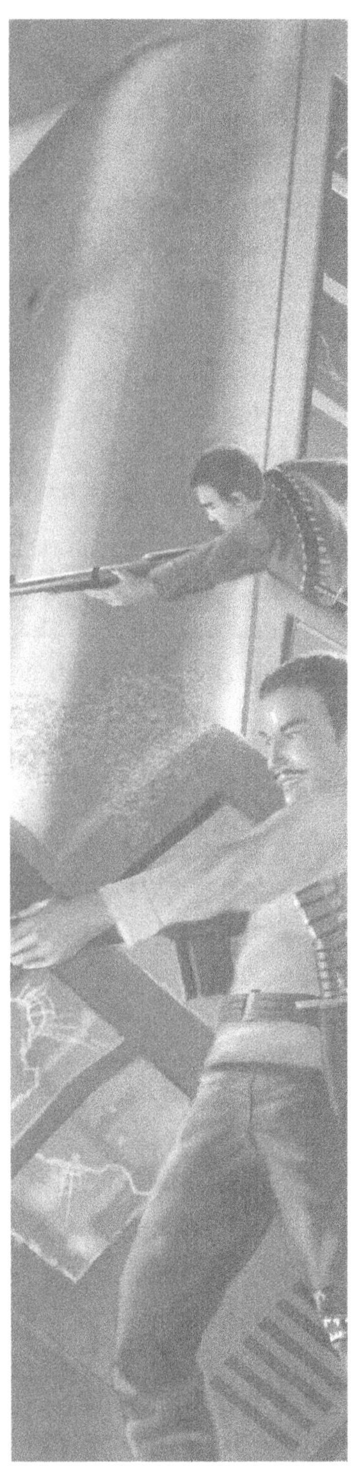

I

The evening meal was late. Susan Majors was using the cook stove to make a kind of fried bread with the flour, powdered eggs, cornmeal and lard from the CD locker. It took longer than she had expected to cook it, so that the meal was not only late but served in bits and pieces. As she sat down to eat her own portion, the Diablos announced the complete takeover of the shelter. Their leader, El Toro, made his first appearance outside the Diablo stronghold, leaning heavily on another boy for support as he hobbled out into the lighted area.

He made a short speech which Verkan and Ranthar could not quite hear, but the outline was quite clear: no one would get hurt if they did what they were told. Other Diablos flanked him as he spoke, idly displaying their knives.

After the takeover was announced, another Diablo from the stronghold joined the group. She proved to be a girl, dressed exactly as the boys in jeans and leather jacket, her hair concealed under a beret. Verkan watched as the Diablos forced a young mother to go into the ladies' room with the Diablo girl, coming out later dressed in the girl's trousers and a shirt the boys had tossed in to her. The husband stood, raging furiously, but two Diablos lounged near him and he said nothing.

Susan Majors was set to cooking larger portions of food for seconds for the Diablos, while the others searched everyone for valuables and weapons. The search was thorough, but without incident; the Diablos collecting nothing of real value, and returning almost everything they found. Two of them stood watching the Paratimers' cubicle, which was totally dark, but they did not approach it. After the search, the occupants of the shelter were permitted to resume their places on and around the benches.

"Verkan are you going to let them get away with this?" Ranthar asked.

"Why not?"

"It just doesn't seem right, pardon me for saying so, boss."

"Want to try to take them all, Ranthar?"

"We could cut down most of them. They have those spears, but I don't see any pistols or rifles. We could make a good go of it before they could get us."

"Not as good as you think, Jard. I've been watching. There's a man with a rifle, a .22 caliber, I believe, behind the barricade they have in front of their stronghold. They've been careful not to let us see it, but the last time they changed guards they slipped. They keep the same two men behind the barricade in turns, which suggests they are the best shots. They've kept them spaced out, too, ever since the fight this morning. It won't be easy, even if we want to do something about them."

"Think they'll come after us next, Verkan?"

"Perhaps. I noticed something else: They've got a new number two. Have you seen Joey Fish at all in the last half hour?"

"No, I haven't."

"From what I can see, they've made Raiffa their new War Lord. It figures. Joey fixed up this defense plan of theirs, and maybe even the shelter takeover, but I'll bet he was too smart to go along with attacking us. Or rather, planning the attack. He'll come along if they order him to. The Raiffa kid wants to even up the score for this morning, and I think he's got the others to go along."

"Vall," Ranthar said, "they didn't strike me as crazy mean. They're tough, but I didn't think they were too bad. We've seen way worse."

"Yes, but don't forget their pride, Jard. You beat them up as though they were wayward children. They were humiliated. Now they've got to show everyone they're better men than you are. Probably some of them are scared after the beating you handed out, but they can't help it. I can see how it worked. They're typical barbarians and saving face is everything. Raiffa and the crew you stomped this morning probably told the others they'd do it alone if the rest were chicken, and they fell right into place."

"Should I have come at them differently?" Ranthar asked.

"No, if we would have backed down, they'd be all over us now."

"You're probably right. It's a damn good thing those gang members weren't organized enough to bring in some liquor. If there was a lot of booze floating around, things would be a lot worse than they are now. Look at that!"

One of the Diablos advanced toward Susan Majors, making obscene gestures. She stood her ground bravely enough, but then glanced toward the cubicle. When it appeared she saw nothing but darkness, she stepped back away from the boy with a big pompadour. He moved in closer. El Toro said something which the Paratimers couldn't hear. The Diablo protested loudly. "Hell, Toro, I got this coming."

"Later, man," El Toro barked. "She ain't goin' nowheres. Now move away, or I'll kick your ass!"

As the pompadoured Diablo walked away from Susan, Verkan heard the click of Ranthar's rifle, as the Inspector slipped the safety back in place.

Verkan glanced at his companion, but said nothing.

"Verkan," Ranthar said, "that girl isn't safe with those leather jackets around. None of these gals are."

"So? We don't intend to harm them."

Ranthar shook his head. "No, sir." He watched in silence for a moment. "Want something else to eat?"

"No."

"Mind if I get back inside? I want to make sure we're ready for tonight."

II

An hour later, Ranthar relieved his superior. "Sir, are we really going to just watch if those boys get serious about the gals? They aren't going to hold off much longer."

"Inspector, you know this isn't our business. There are injustices, some much worse than what's going to happen to those women, going on all over this Subsector—hell, all over this Level. And think about some of the horrors we've witnessed on Second Level and elsewhere. Our job is to keep a low profile and take what we want without attracting any attention; that's the Paratime Code. We're not here to right wrongs, or prevent them from happening.

"Things would already be worse for those people if we weren't here. The Diablos are unsure of us enough to keep themselves in check—for now. The only obligation we have here is to our people stranded on this time-line, which just happens to be my wife and her guard. And they're a hundred miles away. I intend to get to them, alive, and I intend that you get back with me. I don't have anything to spare for a random collection of outtimers I never met. Now, that's the end of it."

"Yes, sir."

They sat at the entrance to their cubicle in silence, watching the lighted area. The Diablos were quiet now, and the station seemed normal. Once every few minutes, one of the leather jackets would slip into the men's room stronghold, and another would come out. After one such exchange, Sam Raiffa walked across the platform towards their cubicle.

"Soldier," he called out. "I want to talk."

"Come ahead. You can stop right out there, though."

"We want some guns, soldier."

"Where do you expect to find them?" Verkan asked.

"Right in there."

The heavy rifle Verkan was holding filled the station with sound as he fired. Raiffa winced as he heard the bullet snap past his head. He looked at the cubicle, "You bastards!" he called out. Then he turned and walked away.

"Tonight, right?" Ranthar inquired.

"Yes. Okay, Inspector. Total dark. Silent routine."

"Shall we use our needlers?"

"Sure, for close-up work. After the bombs, we don't have any reason to worry about Paratime Contamination. Use the rifle first for shock value, though."

A few minutes later, the Diablos turned out the Civil Defense lights. There was a low buzzing of sound from the bench area where the other people in the shelter were huddled, but that soon fell silent. It was completely dark in the station.

Verkan and Ranthar crept out of their cubicle, separated and found places out in the station itself. The Shepherd was left inside the walled-off area.

Time passed slowly in the night. The dog whimpered once, then walked around the cubicle, his nails clicking loudly on the concrete floor. There were no other sounds except for restless stirring near the bench area. Occasionally one of the Diablos shined a light on the cubicle, but could see nothing. When they swept the light around the station, people stirred, muttered and attempted to fall back asleep again.

Suddenly, there was a growl from inside, then a sharp bark. Light crashed into the room as Ranthar closed the switch on his hunting light. Lashed atop the cubicle walls, it illuminated the Diablos creeping toward the Paratimers' cubicle, Raiffa in the lead.

The gunner behind the barricade was good. His first shot put out Ranthar's light, but there was no other target.

Verkan shouted, his voice echoing in the subway tunnels on either side. "Drop your weapons and stand still!"

The gunner fired at the sound of Verkan's voice. Another shot, strange and hollow, came from a Diablo on the floor.

Raiffa yelled from within the cubicle. "There's nobody here!" He flashed a light and swept it around the station. Before he could switch it off, Verkan shot carefully through the light and they heard him scream. The light fell to the floor, stayed on, shining across the station platform.

Verkan's rifle flash came from across the tracks. The gunner behind the barricade fired at the flash, and suddenly the chamber was filled with a deafening sound as Ranthar fired his big .300 rifle, working the pump like a madman, firing again and again. Four shots crashed into the barricade, and in the light of the flashlight on the floor, everyone could see the boy thrown against the station wall, dancing like an insane marionette as the slugs tore him and the barricade to bits.

There was the sound of a shot from the floor as one of the Diablos fired at the flash of Ranthar's rifle. The big inspector had snap-rolled from his prone position, but the bullet hit him in the fleshy part of the leg. Verkan's rifle flared again, and there was a clatter as the Diablo dropped his rifle.

Ranthar's rifle roared again as someone moved near the washroom headquarters. A Diablo screamed, which mingled with the echoes of the gun, the crying baby and the whimpers of women and children.

Verkan whistled once, softly, and the Shepherd's nails clicked through the sudden silence as the dog came to heel. Then Verkan called out: "If you want us to clean you all out, we can. If you don't, turn on some light so I can see all of you. Or we will pour it on. NOW MOVE IT!"

THIRTEEN

I

A flash came on at the washroom door, then moved across the room as whoever carried it ran to the Civil Defense light switch. The lights came on, and the Diablo girl was seen standing at the switch, screaming and screaming.

"Jesus Christ! Make them stop. God, don't let them shoot anymore!"

Verkan shouted again. "You've got one minute to get where I can see you. Move or die!"

"God, Toro, call them in, please," the girl cried. From somewhere in the station, El Toro shouted at his men. "Do like the man says, Diablos. He's got us."

Someone ran across the platform, down one of the tunnels. "Take him, boy!" Verkan shouted.

The dog leaped forward, ran in a long, loping stride, moving through the darkness. They heard a low growl, then a human scream. Someone fell to the ground and the dog growled viciously. "Call him off!" someone in the tunnel shouted.

"I'll see to it, Verkan," Ranthar said

loudly from one side of the platform.

Verkan heard the Inspector run, his steps falling unevenly, and knew for the first time his companion was wounded. A light flashed down in the tunnel. "Back, dog!" Ranthar called. Then he said, "Okay, son. Get up and come with me."

Other Diablos moved into the circle of light, El Toro leaning on one of his cohorts. From behind the protection of the platform, Ranthar swept his light across the subway station so Verkan could see without exposing himself. Three boys were stretched out on the concrete. The rest were standing stiffly in the lit area.

"I think that's the crop, Jard," Verkan called out. "Cover me while I check. If any of them moves, kill him."

"Yes, sir." Ranthar moved back into the darkness across the tracks. Verkan and his dog circled the room, looked into the stairwell and the restrooms, and walked through the excited crowd huddling around the benches. He found the .22 caliber rifle and picked it up.

"That's it, Sergeant," he called.

They rigged up more lights and gathered the population of the shelter around them, the Diablos herded into one corner under the eyes of Ranthar and the German Shepard.

Doctor Pearson examined the boys. Three were dead, another's hand was smashed; Sam Raiffa was lying on the concrete by the entrance to Verkan's cubicle, clutching his stomach and moaning.

Verkan gave Pearson a searching look, but the doctor shook his head. "Too much internal bleeding, I give him an hour—maybe. Not a lot more."

"Get a priest," Raiffa groaned.

"There isn't one, son," Pearson said softly. "You'll have to make your own confession."

"Doc, Ranthar took one in the leg. Will you see to that when you get a chance?"

"Yes, of course." The two of them went to examine Ranthar. Pearson looked at the wound and said, "This isn't very serious. Captain, do you mind if I perform my amputation before I get at it?"

"Do what you think is best, Colonel Pearson," Verkan told him. "I haven't assumed command of this shelter. I can take care of Ranthar's leg if I have to, but I'd rather you probed for the bullet than me."

"Then I'll see him in half an hour." Pearson took out instruments from his kit and examined them, shaking his head. "Not much here to work with, I'm afraid."

"The kid's hand has to go?" Verkan asked.

"Yes, that bullet turned it into hamburger. If I had proper facilities and a surgical nurse, I might be able to save it. Anyway, there's no question about it here. The kid's lucky nothing else was hit. Those soft-nosed slugs of yours tore the other three boys apart." Pearson went back to the benches where Susan Majors was tending the injured Diablo. She was boiling water on the cook stove.

"You cats are mean, aren't you?" a Diablo cried out. "Rough bastards. Dum dum bullets, yet. Wow."

Verkan looked at the boy for a second. "I couldn't use full jacketed ammunition here, even if I had any. Soft slugs break apart when they hit concrete. A jacketed bullet would have bounced around in here like a handball. We didn't need to hit anybody we didn't aim at."

Verkan left the Diablos guarded by Ranthar and the dog, and went back to the cook stove.

II

Dr. Pearson's amputation was successful. A small amount of morphine helped the Diablo, while Verkan held his arm immobile. The boy was seventeen, Verkan guessed, and took the amputation of his hand better than other soldiers he had known. His name was Raymond Espinoza, he had lived with his mother over a family grocery store she operated; he wouldn't be much use in helping with the store anymore. He probably never had been. Besides, the store and Mrs. Espinoza were cinders at this point.

After the boy had fallen asleep, Verkan sat near the stove and lit a cigarette. In a moment he would have to guard the Diablos while Ranthar had the .22 bullet removed from his leg, but he wanted to examine the people of the shelter first. A few had offered to help during the operation, but most just sat staring dully at the walls or each other. The young couple were fussing with their baby, attempting to quiet it.

Bob Russell sat on the bench next to him, accepted a cigarette and smoked in silence for a few minutes. "We all want to thank you, Captain, for rescuing us, although I know it wasn't the main purpose you had in stopping the leather jackets. Well, it worked out the same, anyway. If you would like, I'll take charge of them now. Or would you rather wait until morning when I can impanel a jury?"

"Impanel a jury?" Verkan was astounded. "For what purpose?"

"Why? To try the Diablos. Theft. Attempted murder. Kidnapping. I could think of other charges without even trying. They held all of us prisoners for five or six hours, then they tried to kill you. God only knows what they would have done if you hadn't been here."

Verkan shook his head. "I don't think you really understand the situation, Mr. Russell. Thank you, but I'll keep charge of my prisoners. There's not a lot of point in trials and juries, now is there?"

"Well, yes there is," Russell said. "We have to establish that the normal rules of civilized behavior apply right here and now, just as they did before. If we don't, this whole situation will degenerate into anarchy. Yes, those young men should be tried and punished."

Verkan looked around the room, glancing at people sleeping on the benches, huddled against walls, at the oil cook stove with its eerie orange glow, at the dim bulbs of the Civil Defense lighting system. Over by the stairwell, Ranthar Jard, his leg bandaged, cradled a shotgun against his hip as he sat on the station's only chair. The Diablos sat stiffly against the wall in front of him, while the German Shepherd prowled restlessly between them and Ranthar.

"I'm afraid the normal rules of civilized behavior just don't apply here, Mr. Russell. I'm not sure they ever did for those boys. You didn't do a hell of a good job enforcing them before the blast."

"That wasn't my fault, Captain," Russell protested. "I worked for better law enforcement. And I don't see why they can't be made to apply now. Yes, things have changed. Yes, there's going to have to be a new order now that the war has temporarily smashed the old one. But it should be a decent order, where we can at least be safe from one another; the only way to do that is to start here and now with these hoodlums. Show everybody we mean business. You said something like that yourself, earlier."

"Perhaps I did. I'll think over your request, Mr. Russell, but I'm inclined to think you've missed some points. Those kids did nothing that you and Miss Majors and all the rest haven't been encouraging them to do for years. Oh, hold your protest. Maybe you personally opposed the way we treated criminals, especially so-called juvenile delinquents. But all in all, the United States made a complete mess of things."

"Have you and your compatriots done any better in South Africa with your apartheid and separate and unequal laws?"

"We're not in South Africa, and true, we've made some mistakes. However, that doesn't excuse yours."

He stood up, watched Susan Majors dozing near Espinoza, the boy's good hand in her lap, and turned back to Russell. "Nobody believed much in your country anyway, Mr. Russell. It's not much of a system if you can't hold it against the barbarians."

"Are you telling me that if those thugs could get away with taking over here, that would make it right? That only force makes things right?"

"No. But they couldn't have taken over if all of you had told them to go to hell when they started giving orders. Their method of establishing a leader had about as much meaning as the stupid little vote you people took. Elections only work if everyone agrees in advance to accept them. It should have been fairly obvious to everyone here that neither the Diablos nor Sergeant Ranthar and I would accept the results of your vote. That made it the wrong way to select a leader."

"Did you have a better solution? Captain Verkan, your ability to fight is beyond doubt. I'll even concede that you ought to be the leader of this enclave. But you won't do that, will you? I don't have much choice in the matter, since nobody else wants the job, and they do seem to want me."

"No, I don't. They wouldn't fight for you when the chips were down.

Nobody defended your right to rule, not even you. Maybe you didn't realize it, but your people expected me to defend your order, just as you always expected someone else, professional soldiers, conscripts, the National Guard—but not yourselves—to defend the republic. And you wanted it done at low cost, so that you could go on with the swimming pools, barbecue pits, multiple cars per family, and all the rest of it. It didn't work."

Russell looked up at him intently. "Are you trying to tell me that the amount of violence a country can accomplish is a measure of its justice?"

"I don't think I said that. It is a measure of a country's power. Come to think of it, what kind of justice do you have if nobody will rise to its defense? If a nation isn't worth dying for, is it worth living for?"

On the bench behind them, Sam Raiffa gave a long groan, then began rocking from side to side his hands clasped tightly across his belly. Susan Majors quickly disengaged her hand from Espinoza's, and went to stand beside Raiffa. There were tiny glints in the corners of her eyes, which she wiped away so they would not see her tears.

Verkan looked down at the lad. "That kid had more guts than a lot of you did. He had a club he'd defend with his life. You didn't think much of the Diablos, but he did. But this time he ran into somebody who meant what he said. It might have been the first time in his life that kid ever found out that what he did had real consequences. Good God, man, if you people were so proud of your system before, why didn't you knock his head in the first time he tried to mess up? What you did was send Lady Bountiful here to *understand* him. He didn't need understanding, he needed lumps. You could have stopped the street gangs and crime and all the rest of it—but you didn't. You people killed that boy the first time you let him walk out of a police station. If you loved your country so much, you should have made it clear to the barbarians that you wouldn't put up with them."

Verkan started to walk away, then turned back. "So finally I had to kill him. A policeman would have had to do it one day...."

FOURTEEN

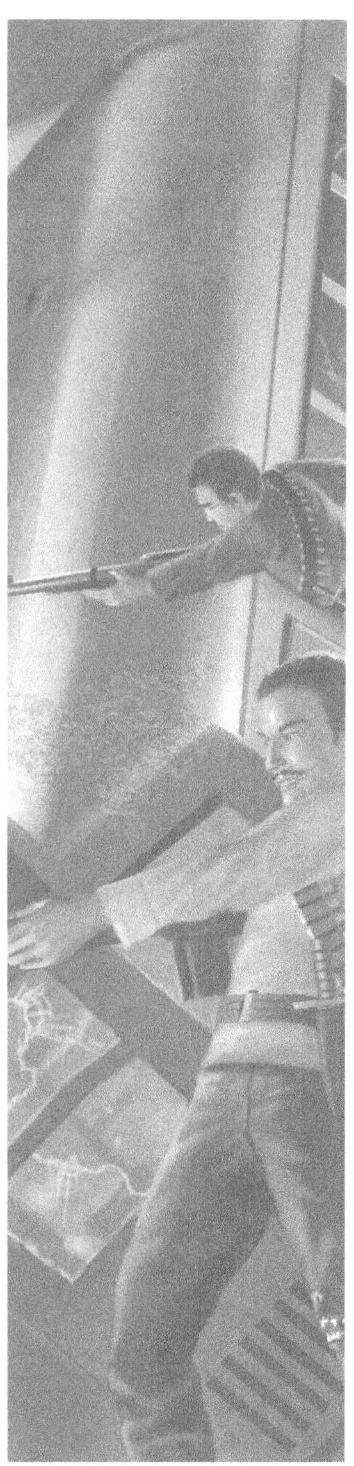

I

Verkan looked down at the luminous dial of his watch: it was 0214, scarcely half an hour after the gunfight. He had examined Ranthar's leg and stopped the bleeding, but he was anxious to get it attended to. He found Pearson resting in a corner.

"The leg will wait a while," Pearson told him. "I've got a couple of people helping Susan rig up some better lights before I start probing." He paused to catch his breath. "And, I need a bit of rest. Not as young as I'd like to be. Probing for a bullet near the knee is a little more delicate than whacking off a hand."

"Let me know when you're ready," Verkan told him. "I'll be in my area getting my gear straightened out." He went back to his corner.

The young father of the baby found him in the cubicle, working by the light of one of the kerosene lanterns. Verkan looked up as the man knocked on the wall.

"Yeah, what do you want?"

"May I come in?"

"Why not? I won't offer you any coffee, because there's none made."

"That's not what I came after. I…I'm David Mills, Captain. That's my wife Shirley over there, and the baby is our son, Andrew."

Mills extended his hand, and after a pause, Verkan took it, noticing the firm grip. "I just wanted to thank you," Mills continued, "for saving us tonight, and for the milk you've been giving us."

"Thanks for what? I just took care of my own that's all. As for the milk, thank Sergeant Ranthar. He went back out for it."

"I will," Mills said. "I should have seen to that myself. We heard that these shelters were completely stocked, but nobody ever paid any attention to what was in them. After I heard the air raid sirens, I was so glad to get Shirley and my son to safety, I didn't think of anything else. I guess, deep down, I thought it was just another false alarm. I mean, everybody knew there couldn't be another war. I just didn't believe it was really happening.

"Our only defense was mutually assured destruction. We didn't want a real defense system because that might anger our enemies. We didn't want real bomb shelters, even though the commies have them, for the same reason. Don't think about it and it goes away. Yeah."

Verkan nodded in agreement.

"Captain, I was a student. Political science at Columbia. But we never truly thought *this* would ever happen. Uh, do you know what's happening outside?"

Verkan brushed his hair back. "No more than you do. My radio won't pick up anything but static. I haven't heard any more explosions, we haven't heard any low-flying aircraft flying over so I expect everything of value here was wiped out. All the military stuff anyway. If the blast was close enough to shatter that concrete beam down here, it must have done a hell of a lot more topside."

"What will happen now, Captain? Will the war go on?"

"I don't know, Mr. Mills. I wouldn't worry about invasions. All we had to do to end this war was clobber the Soviets' central administration machinery, then their whole empire falls apart. I'm sure we managed that."

"But why would they do it?"

"Who knows? The top people over there were desperate men. They didn't want to back down over their missiles in Cuba because they didn't dare show any weakness. It might encourage political dissent, something they can't afford. Premier Beria has been on shaky ground; not everyone in the Presidium favors the NKVD. And he made a lot of enemies under Stalin. A lot of high ranking officials 'disappeared' after he took the top spot. Or maybe somebody decided the whole thing was absurd and wanted to prove it all over the world. Maybe anything. Why did Hitler want to destroy everything in Germany once he realized the war was lost? I'm busy, Mr. Mills and I don't have time for idle speculations. We do know somebody started it, and as far as I can tell it was pretty thorough."

Verkan turned back to checking his supplies.

Mills stood at the entranceway, unwilling to leave. "I—yes, I suppose you're right. I still want to thank you for everything you've done. If you had seen the way they looked at my wife…they would have killed me. I don't know what would have happened to Shirley then, or the baby. We both owe you a lot…."

"Okay. You thanked me. Anything else?"

"Yes, sir. How does somebody get to be one of 'your own' as you called it?"

"I don't understand," Verkan replied.

"You said you took care of your own, just now. Well, I'd like to be in on that. Not just me, I need help to take care of Shirley and Andrew. I'll do anything you say if…if I can join you. Or if we can hire you."

"Hire me? What in the hell can you pay with?"

"Nothing, really. Anything worth having here, you already own. But you don't fight just for money. How can I earn my way into your outfit?"

"I haven't thought about it, Mr. Mills. It's likely to get you killed, anyway. Ranthar and I have a lot of miles to cross, and I don't know what we'll find out there."

David Mills turned to go, then looked back. The lantern picked up a firmness in Mills' eyes that Verkan hadn't seen there before. "If I do get myself killed, what happens to Shirley and Andy? It's likely to happen anyway—out there." He pointed up toward the ceiling. "I'd rather they were with you when it does. I can't be you, Captain, but if you've got any openings, I'll enlist."

Verkan straightened, took out a cigarette and lit it before replying. "Okay, Dave. I understand you. Now get back to your wife."

II

Pearson found Verkan in the cubicle entranceway looking across the platform while he finished his cigarette. "Captain, I have the bench and lights rigged up for your man's leg. Need that lantern, though."

Verkan picked up the lantern and walked out with the doctor. "Raiffa's dead," Pearson continued. "The Espinoza kid will probably live, but I don't know what to give him to replace that hand. I suspect there won't be any prosthetics available topside for some time. I couldn't even save one finger."

They walked toward the stairwell where Ranthar was guarding the Diablos. Verkan halted in the middle of the station floor and turned to Pearson. "Colonel, what was it you told me yesterday?"

"About what, Captain? We talked for quite a while."

"About my obligations to protect these people," Verkan replied.

"Yes, I said that you have a plain duty to the Western civilization that produced you. Your country may have rejected you, but the civilization didn't. It couldn't. You can reject it, but how can it reject you? It's a part of you; it made you what you are. And these people in here are the only examples of it around, whether you like it or not."

"What kind of people are they?" Verkan asked.

"They're all right. Stunned, shocked, terrified, but still, they're pretty good people. Like that father you were talking to. And Mr. Patterson, he was a bookbinder up there. He offered to cut his rations in half to make sure everybody got enough. We have all kinds here, as you would have anywhere, I guess. But they're all right."

Verkan took another step, then halted again. The last thing he wanted—with Dalla on the loose—was to get involved in these outtimers' problems. Still, they weren't as contemptible as many of the Home Timeliners that he ran into outtime. "I haven't had much to do with ordinary people, you know. I joined the 11th Armored Brigade in 1949 and stayed until it was disbanded in 1953. For a short period, I joined the Commandos, but many units were disbanded for lack of recruits. I started freelance mercenary work, mostly in Africa, although I did spend some time in East Asia and the Middle East. Most of the time working against Communist insurgents. I've fought all over the world and know the barracks better than the streets. The only people I know are soldiers and soldiers' girls. These folks here seem so stupid."

"Why shouldn't they be, Captain? They're stupefied. They never believed this would happen. I didn't myself, and I was career Army. It takes time to get used to the idea that the unthinkable has happened—a nuclear attack on American soil. They never believed this would happen; in fact, their political leaders told them so. Now, they're having trouble accepting the idea that we're not just going to go back up those stairs in a day or two and find out that everything will be normal again, that there's more to being down here than just waiting. Most of them are doing just that, you know, waiting for things to get back to what they understand."

Verkan nodded. "That will take some doing."

"Oh, it never will go back for them, and they're beginning to realize it. Look, Captain, they hadn't given much thought to anything affecting their lives for quite a while. How could they? They had cradle to grave security. They didn't have to make decisions for themselves. Give them time. I'll wager a lot of them will get back to being men again. That Mills man for one."

Verkan lit another cigarette; there was no point in saving them. He wished he'd brought another pouch of tobacco along. *I would have, if I'd have known I'd be cooped up somewhere for a few ten-days.* "Doc, there's so much to do, and I can't take time out to explain everything. I'm a soldier, not a teacher. Do you realize what we have to do here?"

"Not really, Captain. But I know you do. And you know you have to do it, don't you? You can't turn these people down when they ask for help. You can't even abandon your enemies: how can you say no to your friends?"

"They aren't my friends," Verkan snapped. *This old coot is beginning to get under my skin. The problem is: I like him. He's a good man, but I don't owe these outtimers anything.* "I have no friends, Colonel Pearson. I have comrades, I have employers, but I have no friends. And my comrades are men."

"Isn't Sergeant Ranthar a friend? After all, he risked his life to secure your safety. If the Diablos had linked up with the other gang, no telling what might have happened. You would've had trouble on the inside and trouble coming from the outside."

Verkan smiled sheepishly. "Yeah, Ranthar is much more than a comrade. Even a friend, I'll admit that much."

"And these people aren't? That's what you are implying. But they might be. Most of them are just realizing what it means to be a man. And a lot would like to be your friend as well—"

"Enough talk, Doctor. Let's get Ranthar's leg looked after."

III

As Ranthar Jard hobbled away with Dr. Pearson, Verkan laid the inspector's shotgun in front of his chair, sitting with his own rifle resting across his knees. He watched Ranthar being led to the crude dispensary Dr. Pearson had set up, then faced the Diablos. "Okay, boys. I don't know what the sergeant told you, but this is the way it is from now on. If you want to make any sort of movement, you will raise both—and notice I said both—hands above your head and ask permission. If you want to talk, you will talk loud enough for me to hear you."

"Can we belch quiet, soldier man?" one asked.

"You're Big Ed, aren't you?"

"That's right, tin man, Big Ed Bone."

"Mister Bone, you and your people will address me as 'sir' from now on, and you will be respectful when you do it. I haven't decided what to do with you at present. For the moment, I'll treat you as prisoners of war, but only on the condition that you act like POWs. If you want to act like common criminals, I can treat you that way, too. Is that clear?"

Big Ed said, "Yes."

Verkan said nothing in return. There was a long pause.

"Yes, sir."

"Now. You may pass these around." He tossed them one of his rapidly diminishing supply of cigarettes, then another, then a third. "Make them last. There aren't many left."

The Diablos lit the cigarettes and passed them among themselves hungrily.

Bone asked, "What do you figure on doing with us? Sir."

Verkan thought for a moment. "I don't really know, Mr. Bone. What do you suggest? What should I do with all of you?"

"Let us go up the stairs."

"You'd never live to see the outside again if you went up that stairway."

"You kidding? Uh—sir. I came down 'em."

"That was forty hours ago, before the fallout had a chance to really come down. It rained in the afternoon yesterday; didn't you hear it? A hundred feet up those stairs, it's likely to be as hot as a firecracker. Deadly."

"Well, you can't watch us alla time."

"Alla time, what?"

"Sir."

"No, but I don't have to watch you all of the time. I can tie you up good and go to sleep. Or I can strip you naked, and lock all of you except the girl in the men's room. I'm sure I can find someone here who'll be glad to shoot the first one who looks out."

"Yeah, you could at that. That Russell cat wants to try us."

"I know. I wouldn't let him." Verkan shifted his chair slightly, lit another cigarette, and prepared to relax.

"You're a funny one, aren't you—sir? I mean, I never met anybody like you two cats." Bone turned toward Verkan, thought better of it, and resumed his position facing the stairwell. "I mean, you two don't act like no squares I ever seen. I don't get you."

Verkan didn't answer. He sat, staring across the Diablos, smoking quietly until the cigarette burned down to the nub before tossing it away. Then he stretched his feet out and leaned back in the chair.

After fifteen minutes, one of the Diablos thought he was lost in thought, and began to slowly gather his legs underneath, intending to spring to the shotgun which lay invitingly at Verkan's feet. Inch by inch, he drew his feet under him, putting more and more weight on his hands which were flat on the floor on either side. A poster in the stairwell was covered with Plexiglas, and in its dim reflection he could make out Verkan, the rifle laying idly across his knees, his feet stretched out before him, not looking at the Diablos but staring above them.

The Diablo started to spring—

The heavy rifle crashed, echoes sounding from the tunnels on either side of the station platform.

The Diablo heard the bullet whip past his ear.

"I told you to raise both hands and ask permission if you wanted to move," Verkan said. "I won't tell you again. Do you understand that, mister?"

"Yes, sir," the Diablo said, swallowing hard. "Of course, sir. I understand sir. It won't happen again sir."

Verkan leaned back in the chair again, cradling the rifle across his knees.

The Diablo glanced at his reflections in the Plexiglas again, remembered the snap of the bullet past his head, and looked away.

Marie, the girl Diablo, was crying softly. She sat close to El Toro, but not touching him. As she began to sob, he put his hand gently on her shoulder, then stroked her hair. She turned to him and buried her head against his shoulder, and he quickly looked around at Verkan.

He glanced at them and said nothing.

El Toro stroked her hair again, slowly, trying to look at Verkan without turning his head. The girl cried softly.

"Eddie," she sobbed. "Eddie, why? Why is it always like this for us, Eddie. Why?"

"It's just the breaks, kitten. Just the way the crud flies."

FIFTEEN

I

"I'll take over now, Captain," Sergeant Ranthar said.

"How's your leg?"

"Okay. It'll be sore for a while, but the bullet didn't hit any bone. Doc says it's no worse than a deep cut."

"Stay off it, Jard. Okay, you watch. Dog, you stay here."

The dog looked up as Verkan walked away, stood, stretched and then rested at Ranthar's feet.

Dr. Pearson entered the cubicle as Verkan sat down. "Made your decision yet, Captain?"

"I'm still thinking it over. It begins to look as if the only way to keep this place from falling apart is to take over. I wonder what it's like in the next subway station?" Verkan sat down on the air mattress. "Mostly, I'm just tired, Doc. Tired and maybe a little disgusted. I don't want to command a lot of slaves, and that's what they'd be if I told them I was in charge, whether they liked it or not."

"Found out there's something to this election business after all?" Pearson asked.

“Don’t get me wrong, Doc— I never said there wasn’t something to it, I just said that there were other factors involved. If people elect the right man, there’s no better way to run an outfit. The problem is they usually won’t elect anyone who will make it rough on them. And it doesn’t get any rougher than our situation down in this station.”

“I believe they’d elect you, right now.”

Verkan looked up at him. “Yes, probably. But, then when things got tough, they’d have another election. Or they’d want to vote on every unpopular order I gave. No, Doc, I don’t want any part of this outfit. Let them keep Russell.”

“What is it that you have against these people, Captain?”

“It’s the contrast. Sergeant Ranthar and I have been to places where the people didn’t have anything at all, but they knew what the score was. Some people in Southeast Asia fought for twenty years— Hell, are still fighting now. Twenty years on campaign, Doc. Not here. Bunch of damned sheep here.”

“You may be surprised. Get some sleep, Captain; I think I’ll do some election campaigning.”

“Don’t bother. Say, you going to be up? Not sleeping?”

“No, I’m not tired.”

“Then wake me in two hours so I can relieve the Sergeant.”

“I can do better than that. I’m a little old, but my grandson could stand guard for you.” When Verkan started to protest, Pearson continued, “Give him a rifle with one bullet. I won’t guarantee he will shoot anybody, but he can make a lot of noise. That way both you and your sergeant can get some rest.”

Verkan thought it over. “Why, not. There’s no place the Diablos can go. If they escape up the tunnel, we’re well rid of them. One bullet won’t do them much good if they do manage to rush him. They won’t, anyway. They’ve got more sense.”

Doctor Pearson’s grandson was thirteen years old. Verkan seated him in the chair and gave him the rifle, placing him a dozen yards from the Diablos.

“Jimmy,” he said, “I don’t want you to try and shoot anybody. If there’s any trouble at all, any at all; just fire this rifle. We'll take care of the rest. You just be sure to pull the trigger and not fall asleep. If you get sleepy, call your grandfather. Okay?"

"Sure, Captain Verkan," the boy replied. "I already got some sleep tonight, and granddaddy made me take a nap this afternoon. I won't go to sleep, I promise." The boy looked up at Verkan seriously. "Do you think there's anyone else alive in the city, sir?"

"Eh? Oh, sure, Jimmy. There are shelters all over New York City. We know there are people in the next station up the line, too. No question about it."

Verkan turned to the Diablos, who were sullenly watching them, and trying to listen in. "You can have it easy or hard. If you want to stretch out on the floor and try to sleep, that's fine. If you try to escape, I'll make every one of you sorry. Got that?"

Heads bobbed up and down among the now ragged and slovenly gang members, several had scrapes from hitting walls and floors during Verkan's fire attack. Others, never well-dressed to begin with, were beginning to show real wear and tear.

"El Toro, I'll hold you personally responsible for the conduct of your group. Will you promise me you'll stay quiet until morning, or shall I have you all tied up? You won't be comfortably tied, either."

"We'll be good, tin sold—, uh, sir." El Toro stretched elaborately. "We could use some sleep, too."

Verkan and Ranthar went back to the cubicle, leaving the dog to stand watch outside.

"Do you think it's okay to leave that kid there, Vall?" Ranthar questioned.

Verkan shrugged. "What are they going to do? The kid runs away if they get up in a body. He can fire that rifle, and we come out armed. Even if he goes to sleep, and they get his gun: what can they do? The dog will let us know if they come this way, and out there are more people than the Pearsons who want the Diablos under control."

II

It was two hours later by Verkan's chronometer that they were awakened by the blast of the rifle. The Paratimers leapt up, armed. Verkan pushed over a section of the cubicle wall rather than use the entrance way. They dashed to the stairwell.

The Diablos were still lying on the floor, having just been awakened, but Russell and another man, armed with hatchets, were in the area where Jimmy Pearson had been stationed. The boy dashed out of the shadows, still clutching the rifle, to speak to Verkan.

"Sir, sir, it wasn't them," he cried, pointing to the Diablos. "They were asleep. But Mr. Russell and this man came over and said they'd take charge. He said he was really the elected leader here, and I should do what he said. I didn't know what to do...but when they reached for the rifle, I fired it. You said I should shoot if anything happened."

"Good man," Ranthar growled.

Verkan looked straight at Russell. "What do you think you're doing, Mr. Russell?" he demanded.

There was no reply.

"Sergeant," Verkan snapped, "disarm those men."

As Ranthar steeped toward them, Russell's companion raised his hatchet.

"This has gone far enough, Mister Verkan," Russell said. "I have been thinking about your sermon on government. I do have authority here, and I intend to use it."

There was a loud growl, then a yelp, from the cubicle. Two men rushed from it, holding rifles.

Russell smirked. "You see, Captain. Drop your weapons. I intend to assert my command here. You can't manage all of us."

His companion with the hatchet nodded, as the men with the rifles pointed them at Ranthar and Verkan. Verkan saw his dog lying on the concrete, a blanket covering his head. He saw red.

Jimmy Pearson swung his empty rifle like a baseball bat, directly into the ribs of Russell's hatchet wielding companion. As he did so, Ranthar lunged with his rifle at Russell, jabbing the barrel into the pit of his stomach.

Russell doubled with pain, dropping the hatchet, as Verkan whirled to face the men with rifles.

"Don't try it," he warned. "They're not operative, anyway. But if I hear a click, if you pull a trigger, I'll cut you both down. Lay them down, now! Gently. You bend one of those pieces, you're dead. They're worth more than you anyway."

Ranthar had completed disarming the man Jimmy had attacked, and backed away to a point where he could cover the entire group, including the watching Diablos.

The two men grounded their rifles. "We didn't want to do this. It was Russell who said we had to."

The man Jimmy had struck was clutching his ribs, white with pain. Verkan calmly called out to Dr. Pearson, "Would you come with me, please? I want to examine my dog."

Verkan pulled the blanket from the Shepherd's head.

"He's still breathing," Pearson reported. "I'm not much of a vet, but I'd say he'll be all right." He ran his hands over the dog. "Looks like they kicked him. Here's a fair-sized lump on his head, but he'll recover from that easily enough."

"So these are your good people, Doctor Pearson? The ones who are competent to manage their own affairs," Verkan muttered.

"Don't judge everyone by four men, Captain."

III

Russell's hatchet-wielding companion had a cracked rib from Jimmy's homerun. His name was George Farris; he had been an automobile salesman in a suburban agency. Pearson taped his ribs as Verkan watched.

"Just what in the name of Hell did you think you were doing?" he asked.

"Protecting ourselves from you," Farris replied. "Russell told me that you and that sergeant of yours intended to take over this place and make us do whatever you wanted. It's true, isn't it?"

Verkan did not answer. Bob Russell was bent double on the floor, nursing his bruised abdomen. Pearson said that he would recover within an hour or so, but would be sore for a week.

Verkan thought it served him right. "That does it, Sergeant. We either get out of here, or we get some discipline into this place right now. I can't take much more of this crap!"

"No, sir. Shall I assemble all of them right here?"

"Please do. While you're at it, send Mills by—he's the father of the baby—over to my quarters. Round up the rest of these characters and assemble them in the lighted area."

"What about the prisoners, Captain?"

"Set the Diablos to watch Russell and his idiots, and Russell to watch the Diablos. That will do for now."

Verkan returned to their cubicle as Ranthar efficiently gathered the shelter occupants onto the benches in the lighted area.

David Mills knocked on the wall.

"Come in, Mr. Mills," Verkan told him. "Help me get this thing set back up, will you?"

"Sure." Together they righted the fallen poster and quickly restored the cubicle's borders.

"You wanted to see me?"

"Yes. Still want to be a recruit?"

"Absolutely, sir. Provided the offer includes Shirley and Andy."

"It does. Very well, Mr. Mills, you can consider yourself a member of Verkan's Company. Your family is under our protection to the best of our ability, and you will take orders from your superiors. I don't think you have a clue as to what you're getting yourself into."

"I know enough to realize that it's you or nothing, Captain," Mills said, looking outside the cubicle around the subway station.

When he breathed hard, Verkan caught the stench of the latrines and the two dead men who had been carried as far down the tunnel as Ranthar cared to go. It was so pervasive that he had lost conscious awareness of it.

"The world's not going to be anything I understand, not for a long time, sir. You'll be able to help keep Shirley and little Andy alive much better than I can. There might even be a chance with me."

"Face it, Mills. There's not much chance for any of us," Verkan said quietly.

The young man nodded. "You said my superiors. That's you and Sergeant Ranthar, right?"

"For the moment. I don't know how long this outfit will last. I've got friends up north, but we've got to get there first. And I may appoint someone here to rank you, you realize."

"Yes, sir."

"That's all, private. Go see if Ranthar needs any help. You'll get your lessons tomorrow."

"Yes, sir." Mills stood awkwardly, his hands moving slightly, then raised his right hand in a clumsy salute.

Verkan returned it crisply and went back to packing canned goods.

SIXTEEN

I

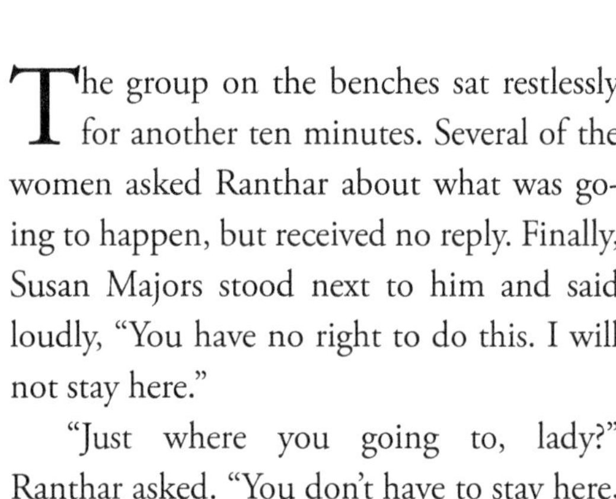

The group on the benches sat restlessly for another ten minutes. Several of the women asked Ranthar about what was going to happen, but received no reply. Finally, Susan Majors stood next to him and said loudly, "You have no right to do this. I will not stay here."

"Just where you going to, lady?" Ranthar asked. "You don't have to stay here, but there aren't a hell of a lot of places to go. The Captain said he wanted to talk to everybody. You don't want to listen to him, you don't have to."

"Well, where is he now?"

"Lady, for all I know he's asleep. I'm not in the habit of asking him why he wants me to do something. He said round you people up, and I did."

Susan walked away, looked around the shelter, and went back to the benches. Ranthar continued to stand in front of the group, his shotgun held carelessly across his chest, glancing from time to time at the Diablos and Russell's small group seated on the floor at the edge of the lighted area.

David Mills stood just behind Ranthar, uncertain as to what to do, but unwilling to leave the sergeant's side.

Verkan came out five minutes later. He motioned to Ranthar to join him at the edge of the subway platform, far enough away that they could have a private conversation.

"How's the leg?" Verkan asked.

"I've had worse," he said laconically. "What's with the new recruit?"

Verkan shook his head wearily. "It's obvious that we can't hold all these people indefinitely and, with the radiation levels, we can't leave. So we're going to come to an accommodation. We're going to take them with us."

Ranthar reared back. "We can't take them back to Home Time Line, or were you thinking of Police Terminal? What would we do with them there? They're not barbarians we can drop off on some Fifth Level uninhabited world. They'd starve to death within a ten-day."

"Agreed. No, I have no intentions of taking anyone but us off this time-line. My plan, if you can call it that, is to take them with us upstate. It should be safer up there, and we can drop them off there. But until then, we're going to have to turn them into a real outfit."

"That's going to be a feat of legerdemain, Assistant Chief. It'll be like herding kittens—"

"Yes, yes, I know. But I've come to respect Pearson and that grandson of his. The Mills kid isn't too bad either. I'm sure, once they get some training, some of the others will shape up. If not, none of us may make it out of this tunnel."

"Well, when you put it like that...."

II

They returned to the main body of refugees. Verkan walked up to them as if he were on a parade ground. He looked intently at the group. Shirley Mills was cradling her baby in her arms, gently rocking him to keep little Andy quiet. Jimmy Pearson, with another boy around his age, sat quietly in the background. Dr. Pearson and Susan Majors were in the front row. The others were a meaningless group, random people whom he did not know.

"I'm not used to making speeches, so I'll keep this short," he said loudly. "And this isn't much of a speech, anyway. Let me tell you how I see this situation. When we took shelter in this subway station, it was as individuals or families. I gather that, with the exception of the Diablos, very few of you knew each other. It was more or less an accident that you found your way to this shelter, since not too many people live in the immediate area. So we were a collection of individuals.

"It can't stay that way. You elected—and please, I know the circumstances, you voted because the man stood out—but you elected a leader who didn't even know to put a guard on the stores, but who did want me to turn over my supplies to the common stock. If I give him half a chance, he'll arrest me right now. Furthermore, you let these boys take everything you had without a fight; and yes, I know, they were armed and you weren't. But I had to bail you out of that to protect myself. Now this business with Mr. Russell using his elected authority to assert his control. All right, it was a good try. At least he did something—for once. But it failed.

"We can't keep this up. I won't submit myself to Mr. Russell's authority, for reasons I won't bother to explain. I will not run for election to take Mr. Russell's job, because I don't know how to be some kind of constitutional leader, and I'm not about to learn now. However, I will make you an offer."

Verkan paced back and forth. He was hesitant to commit himself; he had enough responsibility trying to keep himself and Ranthar alive so they could rescue Dalla. On the other hand, they were not going to be able to do it by themselves. Not with high levels of radiation blocking one end of the tunnel and a large gang holding the next station at the other end. Then he returned to the center of the lighted area.

"Verkan's Company is open to recruits. Anyone who wants to join, without regard to age, or sex, or what's happened here in the last couple of days, I'll accept. You won't like it. You'll train hard, you'll work hard, you'll obey orders. You'll do as I tell you, without question and you'll be subject to the kind of justice I decide to administer.

"In return, I make you one promise. The Company will do its damnedest to take care of its own and we'll find you something outside that'll give you all half a chance at survival. You may get killed, I may even order you to get killed, but the Company will go on and your family, if you have one here, will still be under its protection.

"Those that join, we'll do our best for. The rest of you—we'll leave you your share of the rations in the locker there, and you'll keep out of our way. Any questions?"

Susan Majors stood up. "Yes, I certainly have questions. How do we know you'll keep your word to us once we've submitted to your discipline? How do we know you'll be fair?"

"You don't."

"Under what authority are you acting?" she asked.

"Some of it is in Ranthar's magazine. You're looking at the rest of it."

An elderly gentleman whom Verkan had not noticed before stood. When he came out into the light, he saw that the man wasn't so old at all, not more than forty-five, but he had deep lines in his face and his shoulders were bent in a permanent slump.

"My name is Cranston, Captain. I've got a wife out there somewhere in the suburbs, and two kids. They may have gotten to the shelter under the school in our neighborhood, and they may not. Can you help me get them back?"

"It depends upon where the school is, Mr. Cranston. It depends on how much chance there is of the place being intact, and where it is in relation to where we are when we finally get out of this tunnel maze."

"If I join you, and you decide you can't go after my kids when it's possible, what happens?"

"I give you whatever I can spare, and wish you well."

"Thank you." Cranston sat on the bench in the front row, and put his head in his hands.

Another man about Cranston's age but not as old in appearance stood. "Can you give us some idea of the regulations you expect us to live by if we join you?" he asked. "You don't expect us to live like slaves, do you? Is that what you're asking for?"

"I'm not asking for anything. I'm not even sure I want the responsibilities that go with recruiting you people into my Company. But it's a fair question. If you recall the old Articles of War, that's the code. And this is a time of war. It's harsh, but it's fair and it makes sense. Don't kid yourselves, the discipline is severe. If you think you can find easier terms do so."

"I see. My name is Herbert Saperstein, Captain. Another question if I may: How long does this last? I'm not sure I understand the necessity in any event, and I want to know the length of time that I am going to be under this code of yours."

"It lasts as long as I think necessary, and that's likely to be a long time. I won't track down deserters unless they steal something, but if you join and then quit, you leave when I say to leave with what I say you can take."

"There—uh—those aren't very attractive terms, Captain. I don't much care for them."

"That's a pity, Mr. Saperstein. It isn't a very attractive world up there right now. I don't think you realize just how unattractive it is going to be. Out there will be bands of brigands, gangs, outlaws, killers on the loose, madmen, fanatics of every stripe—you name it. There will be some decent and orderly communities, but they won't trust strangers. Our civilization is gone, sir. It may be revived, or it may not be. But I'll be damned if I promise you all the rights of the US Constitution. I won't guarantee your survival if you join, and all I really promise you is that the Company will do the best it can for its own."

"But why you? And why this way?" Susan interrupted. "Why must you be in command all by yourself? Can't we have a council, a committee, something like that?"

"Surely. But without me. I won't take orders from any committee or council you put together. If you don't want me, form any kind of government you like."

"But as absolute dictator? Why should we gratify your desire to order people around?"

Verkan regarded the girl. *She really believes this*, he decided. She's been told there are people who have this craving for absolute power, and she's applying her school lessons. "This has gone far enough," Verkan announced. "Think anything you like about me and decide anything you want to decide. You can hold another election, you can even elect Mr. Russell again. In fact, I recommend you do so. But do it without me. I won't work for anyone you select. I'll not risk the lives of myself, my sergeant, and the others who choose to join the Company by taking orders from you. Your election does not bind the Company. Anyone who wants to join, I'll be in my quarters. You can see me whenever you like."

He turned smartly and strode away. Verkan had not reached his cubicle when Harold Saperstein caught up to him.

III

The family men were among the first volunteers. Verkan gave Mills the shotgun and ordered him to guard the prisoners, then let Ranthar take down the details on the new recruits to the Company. He was trying to sleep when Susan Majors knocked on the cubicle wall.

"It seems, Captain, that you have sympathizers," she began. "You may even have a majority."

"Miss Majors, I don't think you can envision our situation exactly as it is. I neither want nor need a majority."

"You'll just take the food and stores from the lockers?"

"Correct."

"And you'll leave behind those others, all of those who won't join your Company when you go?"

"Yes," Verkan said wearily. He was beginning to feel as if he were watching a debate in the Executive Council between Management and the Opposition Party. "Why not?"

She looked at him coldly. "So we either become your slaves, or else we are abandoned?"

Verkan slowly crawled from his sleeping place and sat against the wall. "Putting it roughly, that's right, Miss Majors. You once said you didn't have a military mind. Well, I do. I don't consider private soldiers slaves, and I don't consider outsiders my business or my responsibility. Those of you that don't join the Company will keep—or best be kept—out of my way, but beyond that they can do as they please."

She sputtered incoherently.

He looked up at her. "Please sit down or get out, Miss Majors. I've told you before that I don't like looking up at you."

She sat on the box-chair Ranthar had prepared.

When she was settled, Verkan continued, "Don't you get it, Miss Majors? You appear intelligent, and you're certainly well-educated. There is no government left, or if there is it's in total disarray. Certainly not, at least, as you understand government, a big sugar daddy to deal out food and sympathy for everyone. That's gone, dead—kaput. Maybe we could have once carried the dead weight, but not now. Everyone pulls together. We work and we die together, but we don't carry dead weight."

"Hah. Then why are you talking about protecting children, the Mills' baby for example? He can't help you."

"Because, Miss Majors, I wouldn't want a man in my Company who wasn't concerned about his family. What do you think it's all about, Lady Bountiful? You do-gooders seem to let your love of the masses get in the way of understanding real obligations, like families. What in the hell did they teach you at that college of yours, anyway?"

She looked at him pettishly. "There's no need to be insulting, Captain Verkan. And I still don't see why everyone has to follow your orders without question."

"Because, the world as you know it—is gone. What we have now is a place where you are lucky just to survive. You might just live by following orders, but not any other way. You can count on it."

"If it takes all that," she declared, "just to survive—if you have to throw away all that's beautiful and noble—I don't want to survive. I don't think I want to live in your world, Captain Verkan."

"Then don't."

"You—you're horrible," she said. Then, suddenly sobbing, she rushed out of the cubicle.

IV

Ranthar told his captain later, "I've got a feeling that's going to be more woman than you think, Vall."

Verkan snorted. "You can keep that opinion, Inspector. Now, bed those recruits who joined us over in that area, and keep them separated from the ones that didn't join. Families in a separate area from the men. Fix up some lights for the troops, and see if you can get a supply corporal out of them. Maybe one of the women can help with that. Let's get some order into this system."

"Is this it, Verkan? We play at being soldiers."

"Yes, for now."

"Very good, sir." Ranthar snapped to attention and saluted. When the salute was returned, he went out to help the recruits set up their new quarters area.

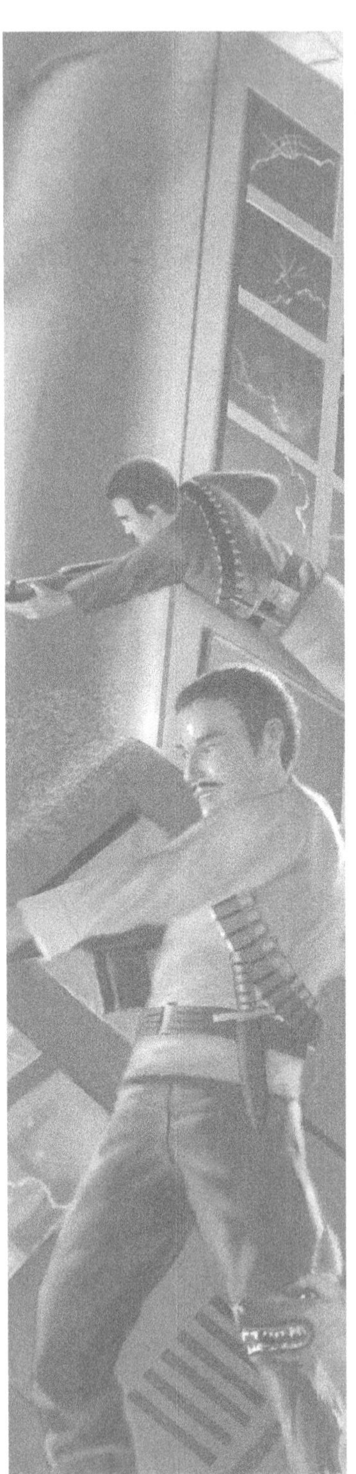

SEVENTEEN

I

It was almost noon of the following day before Colonel Pearson came to talk with Verkan. He entered the cubicle and sat down without a word. Verkan offered coffee, but Pearson merely shook his head, looking intently at him. Finally he spoke, "Why, Verkan? Not that I'm not glad for it, but why? I thought you had about decided you could manage nicely without us."

"Too many prisoners for just two of us to guard," Verkan said laconically.

"Not true. You could have been more selective about who you let into the Company. The Mills boy would have done anything to protect his family. You weren't just insuring your own hide."

"All right, so I'm not. Next item?"

"I wanted to make you say it, that's all."

"Now, I said it. You a holdout?"

"Yes and no," Pearson said. "I'll join you, Captain. You're a good man, and I want to watch out for Jimmy. I'm sure my son and the boy's mother are dead. They're in Florida on vacation—or were. It's unlikely I'll ever see them again. I need you to help Jimmy."

"He's a good lad," Verkan said. "No problem. What did you mean by yes and no?"

"As long as there are others, they need me more than you do. I have to stay with them."

"Okay, doc. I'll take Jimmy without you. You'll be along when I need you, anyway. Now, there's one thing you can do right now. Keep that Majors girl out of my hair. I won't put up with another lecture from her."

The doctor chuckled. "That's simple enough, isn't it? Tell your big sergeant to keep her away from you."

"Won't do any good. He likes her. I've seen the symptoms before. Somehow, he'll do his best, but she'll slip past him."

Pearson laughed. "Now, what can I do to help—seriously?"

"Get the medical department organized. You can have whatever you need, people, stores, whatever. Ranthar will help you with that. The Mills girl looks like a good bet to assist."

"Will you have to fight to get out of here?"

"I expect to. I hope not, but at the next station, it's a pretty sure thing. Beyond that, who knows? People are going to be getting hungry, there'll be walking dead men, radiation dead who haven't been buried yet. Some may turn homicidal. There's street gangs like the Diablos, only maybe not caught out of their home turf and will have their arsenals with them… I sure as hell expect to fight, and what's more I intend to win."

"What do you intend to do with the prisoners?" Pearson asked. "You have almost everyone here with you; I think the rest will fall in when they see how lonely they're going to be by themselves. But what about Russell and the Diablos?"

"Russell and his group are no problem. They didn't hurt anything much, now that I see my dog's all right. I figure to let them join."

"Russell, too?"

"If he wants to."

"What about the leather jacket boys?"

"They're another problem entirely," Verkan said. "They just took one big shock. They're due for another, I suppose."

"What do you mean?" Pearson asked, his forehead furrowed.

"Well, they lost one battle. Lost it completely, and now find themselves at the mercy of somebody they don't understand and who by their code has every reason and every right to use them like dirt."

"You know, that surprises me. Why did they collapse so quickly? I would have thought they would give you a lot more trouble. Maybe they weren't so tough after all."

Verkan shook his head. "You got it wrong there, Doc. They're tough all right. But what happened to them was something else. Look—here are these boys: They've been in street fights, stomps, gang wars; they're vicious and they're mean. But it's all been man to man. It's been a demonstration of courage as much as a battle. Then they try us. And we're not even there. They've been in gunfights, or so they think. But those were little affairs, pistols popping off, but here it's different. The gun doesn't go pop, then somebody yells 'I'm hit' and maybe groans a little.

"There's a noise like hell opening up, and a flame out of the dark, and somebody's very very dead. They're lonesome out there in the dark. They can't see one another. There's more shots. Who knows how many are hurt. There's never been one of their friends pounded to pieces against a wall, and boys who are never going to get up again. The fight goes on, and on, and on, and they can't get anywhere, and they never see anything to fight. What would you do?"

The Doctor nodded. "I see."

Verkan stood. "If you don't want some coffee, Doc, I'll take some. I've got to ration the stuff, but there's quite a lot of water here if we're careful." He poured half a cup. "Battles are different from neighborhood brawls. There's nothing like one to make you the loneliest guy in the world. They had a face saver, too; the girl cracked first. That helped them decide."

"I suppose the other shock you think they have coming is El Toro?"

"Yes. He's a walking dead man, isn't he?"

"I think so," Pearson told him. "He doesn't seem to be getting over his beating. The bruises are getting larger, if anything. I give him a week, perhaps."

"When he goes, I'll enlist the whole Diablo force. I may get them earlier, if he'll help."

"An elite. As your internal security force?"

"More or less," Verkan agreed. "The others keep an eye on them, and they serve me as a guard. I think you'll find it works."

"Oh, I wasn't questioning the effectiveness of the arrangement. I just wonder what kind of leader we have here."

"You, too? I never saw a crew for wanting their cake and eating it, too."

"Oh, don't get me wrong, Captain. I'm with you. Until I decide that you're more dangerous than the outside. When I do that...you'll have fair warning."

"I don't need it, Doc. If my volunteers are half the men I hope they are, you won't be the only one who feels that way."

II

Training exercises went on all morning. Ranthar began with military courtesy and foot drills. When a couple of recruits objected to some of the sergeant's instructions, they found themselves lying on the concrete platform without quite realizing how. He did not report the incidents, and although Verkan saw one of them, he never mentioned it to the recruit.

During a break, a recruit asked, "Sergeant, why this drill? We aren't going to fight in some kind of formation like they did in the eighteenth century when this was developed."

"No, but you're going to have to make forced marches, in step if need be. Besides, the Captain said you learn it. That's enough for me. How about you?"

Russell and his men, as well as the Diablos, remained prisoners after the noon meal. At 1500 hours, Verkan sent for El Toro and Joey the Fish. When the gang president and newly reinstated War Lord of the Diablos were seated on the floor of the cubicle, Verkan offered them coffee and cigarettes, then waited for them to recover from the unexpected treatment.

"Thanks, Sir." Joey said. El Toro mumbled something which might have been a thank you. The two sat in silence, looking at Verkan wearily.

"There's a point to your being here," Verkan said. "I'll permit you and your men to join my Company. Without prejudice. We'll forget what happened in the last couple of days. You join, you're in. But don't do it unless you mean it. You cross me, you die."

"You mean come in with you?" El Toro asked. "Why should we? Other than being turned loose from the guards. Man, sitting or lying on that floor, going to the can in step under guard—that's harsh, man! I'd do just about anything to get out of that."

"There are other reasons," Verkan replied. "What can you and your boys do when we get out of here? Know anything about farming? Cottage industries? Handicraft? What can you do except fight? And you don't know how to do that very well. I'm offering you a chance to be of some use to yourselves, even have a chance at a future. It isn't much of a chance, but it's a hell of a lot more than you have right now. Or had yesterday, when you thought you ran this shelter, for that matter."

"You goin' to teach us how to fight?" Joey asked.

"Some."

"You trust us?" El Toro asked.

"Not much. But then, I don't trust anyone very much. I intend to show you that you're better off with me than you are without me, so there won't be much reason for you to cross me."

"He knows his business, El Toro," Joey said. "If we'd had him with us last stomp with the Roman Lords, wow, we'd have creamed those bastards."

El Toro smoked his cigarette in silence for a moment, then looked intently at Verkan. "Sir. Will you tell me the truth about something? Give it to me straight, like it is?"

"I may. What?"

"How long have I got? Sir."

"What do you mean?" he asked.

"I'm finished, and you know it. Don't bullshit me, man. I've been beat up before, but it never took this long to get over it. And you said that tunnel was deadly…it was killing me when I came through it, wasn't it? Sir?"

"You want it straight, El Toro?"

"Yeah. Sir."

"Doc Pearson says you've got about a week. It was the beating…you're young and strong, and if you'd had your full, healthy constitution, you probably would have survived the radiation. But now, I don't know. It looks this way: your bruises will get larger and larger, your hair will start to fall out, your gums will get sore. One day you'll start to bleed somewhere. It won't ever stop."

"It don't sound pretty," El Toro said stoically.

"It won't be," Verkan told him. "You wanted it straight, right?"

Joey looked at his president. "Jeez, Toro, what we goin' to do? There ain't no better leader, if you go."

"I ain't been a very good one, Fish. Too many dead Diablos. Your turn, I guess."

"Me? But God, El Toro, I ain't…Naw, I can't. They won't listen to me."

"Yeah." He turned to Verkan. "Captain, what you want me to do? There's nobody can keep the Diablos together, if I'm dead. They're my gang, and if I can't look after them no more—will you give them a break? Can you keep that Russell cat off their backs?"

Verkan did not answer.

El Toro looked at him for a minute, then said, "Yeah. You already did. And you won't take any conditions for us joinin' up with you." He thought for a moment, then turned to Fish. "We got to trust this man, Joey. There ain't nobody else."

"That's right," Verkan said softly. "Not here, anyway, and you won't get your gang outside without my help. What you find out there isn't likely to be much better, either."

"Don't matter. Okay, Captain, what you want us to do?"

"I'll accept your enlistments on the same basis as the others here," Verkan told him. "You discuss it with your Diablos. But warn them, El Toro. They're better off as prisoners than they will be if they join me and then get funny. The first shot you people take at me is cut rate, but I charge full price for the rest of them. You already had your cheap shot. Understood?"

"Yeah, sir," El Toro said. "*Yo comprende.*"

"And you, Mr. Fish?"

"I dig it, sir. We'll join your Company, and we'll—yeah, you'll be the new leader." Joey appeared relieved.

"Very well. El Toro, first, what's your real name?"

The big man seemed to collapse in on himself. "Eduardo Gonzalez, sir."

"Very well. Gonzalez, you are now a lance corporal in the Company. You are responsible to Sergeant Ranthar; he will explain the articles to you and your men tomorrow, or perhaps this evening. You start training tomorrow and I'll withdraw the guard as soon as you've had your discussion with our troops."

Verkan stood, ending the interview. Joey Fish, still smarting from the beating Ranthar had given him, rose uneasily to his feet, but had to help Lance Corporal Gonzalez. When Gonzalez was erect, he leaned slightly on Fish, and said, "Captain…don't tell anybody about me? Huh? And you, Fish, keep an eye on Marie for me. When you think everybody'll know about me, Captain?"

"Again, I don't know for sure. Doc Pearson may be able to tell you. You may even live, you know. It isn't likely, but you may."

"Yeah. Martians may land outside tonight, too. I know, man. I've been beat up before, but never like this… There's something wrong inside, I know it."

"All right, Corporal. You may join your men. I'll tell the guard to let you have a conference. Dismissed."

They limped away, Gonzalez still leaning on Fish. Verkan watched them go, shook his head slightly, then returned to the inventory of shelter supplies Shirley Mills had made for him.

EIGHTEEN

I

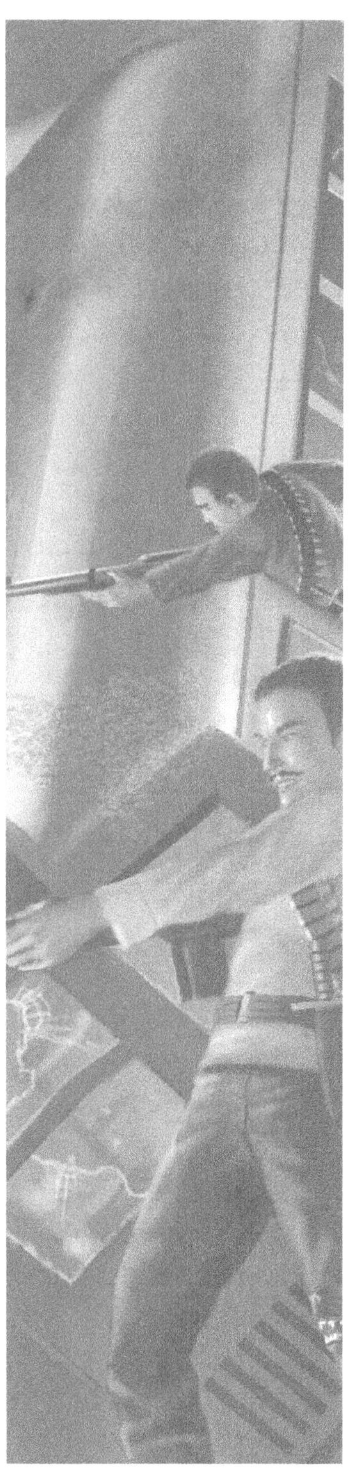

That evening, the Diablos and Russell and his men were released from guard. The Diablos joined the Company in a body, swearing allegiance in a ceremony obviously adapted from their own club rituals. Russell's men also joined, although Russell himself did not. He spent the rest of the evening talking to the other shelter inhabitants before asking Ranthar, the next morning, if he too could enlist. He was accepted without comment.

That day, Doctor Pearson took blood specimens from everyone, mixing them to find possible donors for Gonzalez and the Diablo who had lost his hand. He gave Gonzalez a transfusion from another former gang member. When he finished, Verkan asked, "Think that will do any good?"

"No. I can't get enough blood, nor can I even type the blood accurately. I may be killing him for all I know. I don't have the proper equipment for accurate typing, I can't do anything about Rh factors...I know some types from Civil Defense cards. That Diablo boy had his, and he's a universal donor. Most of these people don't have cards."

"Yeah, they were too smart to carry them," Verkan growled "Gonzalez is a good man, Doc. I wish there was something you could do."

"Don't get your hopes up. I haven't enough donors, and even so I think things have gone too far. He's in worse shape every time I look at him."

After Pearson left, Verkan connected his radio, which he knew to be working, to the outside antenna of the Civil Defense set. They both received nothing but static. It was possible that the antenna was faulty, but Verkan couldn't even get his own set to work. He'd been out of contact with the Beria Study Team, based in Washington, D.C., since the bombing. There weren't going to be any outside rescue efforts; they were going to have to make it on their own.

He didn't want to even think about how Dalla was doing in Upstate New York. *I know she's resourceful; she's proved that many times. But she's also foolhardy and thinks she's invulnerable.* Verkan had to use First Level mental discipline to force his mind back onto his own problems; he wouldn't be doing anyone any good if he sat and stewed about his wife and the danger she was in.

Jimmy Pearson and the other twelve year-old boy were set to listening to the CD radio in relays, to make sure they did not miss any messages.

II

By the third day after the Company was formed, there were only a few holdouts. Susan Majors cooperated with the Company, and acted as if she were a part of Verkan's group, but she never said anything about enlisting. The Company fell into a routine of training and exercises, dry firing weapons, learning hand signals and unarmed combat. The listlessness which had characterized the group earlier began to disappear. Some of them even dared hope for some kind of life after their emergence from the tunnel.

It was on the evening of the eighth day in the shelter that a man staggered in from the uptown tunnel. He was a mass of sores, his hair falling out in patches. A trickle of blood oozed form his lips, and he bled constantly from other tiny wounds.

Eduardo Gonzalez saw him and turned his face to the wall.

The man staggered into the center of the shelter, helped by the tunnel guards. He gasped for breath. Verkan and Pearson put him on an air mattress, covered him with a blanket and gave him some fruit juice before they allowed him to talk. He asked for a cigarette, and was given one out of the last of the supply.

"My name's Avery Matheson," the man gasped. "I was in the shelter up the tunnel for a while. It's awful up there."

He paused, gulping air. Then Matheson continued talking, the words bursting out in short staccato phrases. "There's about fifty kids in it…and they're running wild. Some of us managed to bash their guard…we tried to get away down the tunnel…but they caught us. Beat me…left me for dead. Don't know how long ago. Days…I think. I didn't even know which way to walk…when I could stand up. Walked back to where they were at first…they didn't see me….thank God."

Verkan asked, "Mr. Matheson, do they have guns?"

"Yes…a lot of them. They made one man go out and loot a pawn shop…kept his wife and daughter hostage. He came back…tried to shoot them. They killed him…his family, too. Oh God…what they did to them. Then they sent out another family man…he came back with the guns. A lot of them…I don't know how many. He had to make two trips."

"You leave family back there?" Verkan asked.

"Dead…lying in the tunnel next to me when I woke up…"

Avery Matheson was obviously in both physical and mental shock. He spoke in a flat even tone, as if he were telling about something that happened far away and to other people. When he mentioned his family, there was a slight catch in his voice, but then he returned to the emotionless tone he had used previously.

"Do they have a radio that works?" David Mills asked. "Do you know what it's like upstairs? In the outside?"

"They have a CD radio…but they're not getting anything on it. They told us once…but wouldn't say what it was…I didn't believe them. Outside, above the shelter, a lot of buildings burned down…It was very hot in the shelter, the first day after the winds died away. Some of the concrete buildings are still standing…the man they sent up told us. He said there were lots of dead people in the streets, thrown against walls in heaps…others burned to a crisp. Don't know anything about other shelters…there were supposed to be several nearby. We could have gone to one of them…but I thought it was safer in the subway, lower…underground. Safer…I thought." He choked out a laugh, then gasped for air.

Pearson knelt next to him, then stepped away, taking Verkan's arm.

When they were out of earshot, the Doctor spoke to him in a low voice. "Half his chest is crushed, sir. I'm amazed he's still alive. Should I use a little of the morphine? We are almost out, but the man's in pain. Or maybe somebody could be kind enough to clip him alongside the ear. He'd never wake up."

"Yeah, But we can't do that, can we." Verkan swore under his breath. "Give him a shot, Doc. What'll we use for Gonzalez?"

"I don't know, Captain. I hate to use what few drugs I have left to ease the dying, Captain— I have enough problems keeping the living in reasonable shape."

"I know," Verkan said, patting him on the shoulder.

As they approached Matheson, the man suddenly began to cry. The crowd of onlookers pulled back. "They killed her!" he sobbed. "And they killed me, too. Didn't they?"

No one said a word.

"Answer me!" he shouted.

"Yeah. They killed you, too."

Matheson painfully sat up, put his hands on the ground and tried to push himself erect.

"Here, here!" Pearson cried out. "What are you doing?"

"I'm going back up there," he cried, his breath coming in huge gulps. "I've warned you about what's there…now I have to go back. You couldn't let me have a gun…could you?"

Verkan shook his head.

"I didn't think so," Matheson gasped. "Any kind of weapon…anything that will kill?"

"You'll never get up there alive," Pearson told him. "Lie down, Mr. Matheson." He took the man's arm.

"Let him be, Doc," Verkan quietly ordered. "Sergeant, get Mr. Matheson one of those spears the men have been working on. He can lean on it when he tries to get back up the tunnel. Mills, you help him until you get to the first vent, then come back."

"Yes, sir."

"Captain, I can't allow this man to go in his condition," Pearson said.

"Yes, you can. Get out of the way, Doc. That's an order."

Pearson stared at Verkan, then turned and walked away without a word. Avery Matheson took the spear and used it as a staff to stagger from the platform, leaning heavily on David Mills. They vanished into the darkness, Mills returning shortly.

"He's still on his feet, sir," Mills reported. "Only God knows how...?"

Verkan found Doctor Pearson. "Sorry, Doc, I didn't like to get rough, but the man's got his rights. It had to be."

"You've killed that man," Pearson said quietly.

"You said he wouldn't last the night."

"He might have. You had no right."

"He was a man, Doc. If it was me, I'd far rather be headed back with a weapon after the scum that killed my family, rather than lying on a bed waiting to die. Wouldn't you?"

The Doctor pushed his hands through his hair, then clenched his fists. "As a doctor, I have to say you were wrong. But—well, yes, I would, too."

"Okay. I didn't send him. But I sure wasn't going to keep him here if he wanted to go. That was a man, Doc, a real man."

III

Verkan noticed a real change in the atmosphere around the camp after the departure of Matheson. The new recruits were working out harder, with more enthusiasm. There was little of the listlessness of the days before. Suddenly, it was as if a veil had been lifted from over the little group. They realized just how dangerous their world had become and how fortunate they were to have a leader who understood those perils.

"How are they doing, Sergeant?" Verkan asked after one strenuous workout.

"Better!" Ranthar exclaimed. "Much better than I'd ever expected. Matheson and his story lit a fire in their bellies. Even Russell's doing what he's told without any eye rolls. The Diablos are working as hard as they have in their entire lives. Each one is trying to best his neighbor. They're not going to be first rate troops, but for a gang of civilians, they'll do."

Which was high praise indeed from Inspector Ranthar, Verkan knew. "How long before they're ready?"

Ranthar shook his head. "Hard to tell, Verkan. Another couple of weeks—if our rations last that long—should see the bunch of them ready for action."

"Good. We need to leave the moment the radiation danger has passed. I can't imagine what's going on in the rural areas, but I bet they're inundated with refugees. And, knowing Dalla, she'll be in the middle of things. I wish our communicators worked; I'd like to give Maldar some instructions."

"Wouldn't do any good, Captain, knowing Dalla as I do. She's going to do whatever she's bound and determined to do. But, she's not stupid about it; and neither is the man she's with. If things get too bad, they'll bug out."

"I agree, to a point. Dalla's problem is that she acts like she's immortal, not a woman with a few hundred years left to live. I wish I would have been there to talk her out of this assignment...."

"Good luck, Verkan. Dalla was determined to visit this Dixon psychic, and on this time-line where her predictions were uncannily accurate. Not even a resolution by the Executive Council could have kept her on First Level, once the Institute told her about Dixon's predictions."

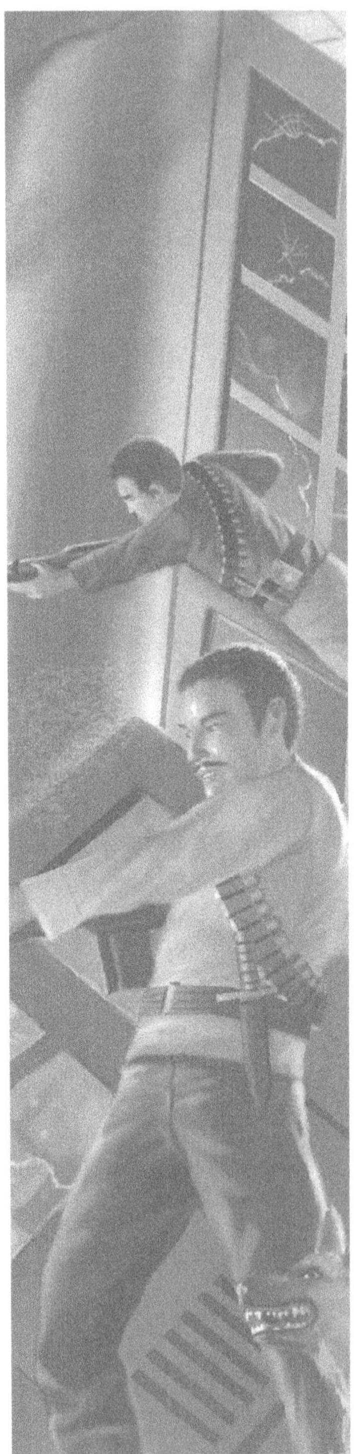

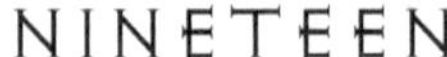

NINETEEN

I

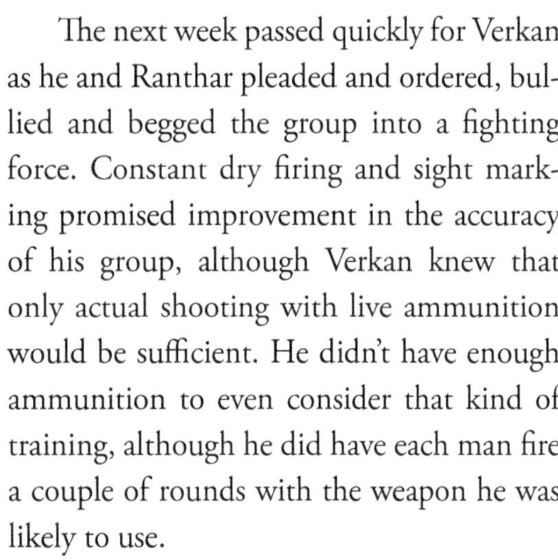

The next week passed quickly for Verkan as he and Ranthar pleaded and ordered, bullied and begged the group into a fighting force. Constant dry firing and sight marking promised improvement in the accuracy of his group, although Verkan knew that only actual shooting with live ammunition would be sufficient. He didn't have enough ammunition to even consider that kind of training, although he did have each man fire a couple of rounds with the weapon he was likely to use.

They also constructed spears and clubs from the ticket booth railings and any other pieces of the station they could take apart. One of the shopping carts was broken up to furnish spearheads and short knives, its wheelbase preserved for a cart on which to carry the rapidly dwindling supplies of the Company.

When it became apparent that Verkan had no intention of reducing his men to slaves, the last holdouts joined the Company. They really had no choice, as they watched the others train, saw the new spirit of it—if not hope—then at least something better than the resignation of previous days, served as a powerful recruiting force.

In theory, Verkan commanded a reasonably disciplined and dedicated force, but he knew that many of these members had joined only because there seemed to be little else to do and would desert at the earliest opportunity. There were still those who could not accept the fact the world was changed—although there were less of those since Matheson's brief visit. Although intellectually they might know better, emotionally they expected everything to return to normal someday. They yearned for a life much as it had been before the bombs fell, with reduced comforts, but not fundamentally different. While Avery Matheson's visit had shocked a few out of their dreams, others preferred to think of the incident as something apart from their lives.

II

It had been weeks since the nuclear attack, but here in their isolated hamlet it was almost as if nothing had happened. Maldar Dard had convinced the locals to band together to form a watch to protect the village from outsiders. His squad was busy training them to prepare for the onslaught sure to come. So far, there had been only a few bands of roving displaced persons, mostly looking for shelter and food; isolated families fleeing from the Danbury, Connecticut suburbs. The locals had taken them in with welcome arms, but Dalla knew that would change when the first flood of refugees appeared, or food stocks started to grow short. Fortunately, it was late enough in the year that most of the apples, pears and cranberries had been harvested. The beef cattle were tended carefully, never out of sight of one of the local farmers.

Their own party was in good shape as far as food stocks were concerned; thanks to Jeane's prediction they had filled two storage sheds and the back of the barn with provisions. Maldar had been busy, with the help of a few locals, building a defensive perimeter around the farm, using and adding to the old stone walls around the old farmhouse and barn. He had also helped to train and organize the local watch. The radios and televisions were still broadcasting nothing but static so there was no information on the outside world. Fortunately, the locals were more realistic than their citified cousins and went along with Maldar's suggestions. He wore the uniform of the local Connecticut National Guard and the villagers treated him like a hero.

Dalla wondered how things were going in the big cities, like New York and Boston. There was talk of looters and bandits; one straggler told of gangs roaming the Hartford suburbs, looting homes and killing and raping homeowners. By this time, it was every man for himself or herself, Dalla suspected. Sooner or later food would begin to run out and, like rats fleeing from a sinking ship, the big migrations from the damaged cities to the rural areas would begin in earnest.

Things, however, were not going well inside the farmhouse. Jeane Dixon was still confined to bed; against all logic, she blamed herself for the attack and kept second-guessing herself, as if she had any responsibility for what the madmen in Moscow had done. Sylvia, sprung from old New England stock, had proved stronger than Dalla had expected and had taken full charge of Jeane's care. Meanwhile, James Dixon had been helpful in organizing the villagers. He was a natural leader, but smart enough to know when he was out of his element and gave full support to Sergeant Maldar.

With James and Maldar's help, Dalla had them clear out about half of the unnecessary furniture in the parlor. There was nothing to be done about the overstuffed furniture, but at least she had some breathing room. She was thinking about Verkan and what her husband might be doing to rescue them—*What's taking him so long?*—when she heard a polite cough.

"Dalla…" Sylvia said haltingly.

She looked up. "Yes?"

"It's Jeane," Sylvia said with a tremble in her voice. "She wants to talk with you. She had another vision."

Uh-oh, Dalla thought. *What now?* "Okay, Sylvia, I'll go speak with her."

She made her way to the back bedroom where Jeane was laid out on the quilt like a dead body. Her formerly well-coiffured chestnut hair was hanging limply and there were dark circles around her eyes. With one of her limp hands, she patted the bed. "Please come closer, Dalla."

She moved right up to the bedside.

"I know, I know—I'm a mess. I should be out there helping you and Sylvia, but my mind's on fire. I keep thinking all of this is my fault, that I should have made more of an effort to warn—"

"Hush," Dalla replied. "You're blaming yourself for something that was absolutely beyond your control. Don't blame the messenger for the message. There's no possible way you could have warned anyone about the attack; other than a few believers, everyone else would have deemed you a madwoman, publicity whore, or at best a Cassandra."

Jeane nodded. "That's what Jim tells me. And maybe you're both right, but I can't help what I feel. Why did God give me this message when there was nothing for me to do? I keep asking myself that question over and over."

"Some questions don't have answers. Just accept that you and your husband are still alive; if you hadn't had your vision, you both would be dead now."

Jeane jerked her head as is if she'd just been slapped. "Maybe you're right," she said in a little girl voice.

"What's this about another vision?" Dalla asked.

Jeane's face turned even paler, which didn't seem possible. "I saw a band of riders coming from the east. The leaders are driving jeeps and pickups, but most of them are on horseback. There were several hundred of them, badly dressed and many wounded. They're looters and murderers. And they're on their way here. You have to stop them!"

Dalla took her vision as seriously as she took the daybreak. "I'll warn Sergeant Maldar and the town watch. Meanwhile, stop blaming yourself and get up and help around the house." She gave the last like an order, hoping it might jerk Jeane out of her well of self-pity.

III

On the third Sunday in the shelter, fifteen days after they entered, Verkan allowed chapel services. Jewish members of the Company had held their service on Saturday. The service was brief, led by Colonel Pearson, who was convinced it was good for morale. Verkan saw no reason to object; he knew most Europo-Americans were religious to one degree or another. He was completely indifferent; religion was viewed as a contagion on First Level, but he could see no danger from it within his small community.

After it was over, Joey Fish reported to Verkan. "Two things, Captain. El Toro's still no worse—no better, but he don't seem no worse either."

"I know." Verkan was seated in the shelter's only chair, behind a makeshift desk which had been fashioned for him. "Doctor Pearson tells me he doesn't know what's keeping him alive, but maybe the massive blood transfusions are doing it. The doctor thinks that if he can hold out for another two weeks, he may live after all. What's the other thing?"

"We heard this mornin' that it's safe to go up the tunnel, now, sir. That recruit, Russell, said he'd measured it last night. The other Diablos asked me to see if it's true, sir. If it is, could we please get moving. They're tired of rations—uh, sir, that don't mean nothing, but they thought anyway we could ask...."

"Okay. You've asked. Anything else?"

Fish gave his formal report on the training status of the Diablos. With Gonzalez on the sick list, Verkan had appointed Joey as Lance Corporal in charge of the Diablos. El Toro holding the same rank but relieved of duty. The Diablos had adopted surprisingly well to the new regime. They stayed together as a unit, under their original leaders, and were genuinely interested in the combat training they received.

Marie was proving quite useful in assisting Susan Majors as quartermaster, although she spent much of her time taking care of Eduardo Gonzalez. Jimmy Pearson and his companion, Martin Guliksen, also drifted over to the Diablos' portion of the shelter whenever possible, much to the disapproval of Mrs. Guliksen. She proved to be a cheerful soul, recovering her disposition after her husband joined the Company and became the chief cook of the little band.

Susan Majors' quartermaster report was next. She had been given the job when it had become more responsibility than Shirley Mills could handle with a baby to take care of. When she entered, he noticed that she had managed to keep her appearance surprisingly neat, considering that laundry facilities were almost non-existent. Everyone in the shelter was now accustomed to the smell of people without deodorants and toothpaste. For morale purposes, Verkan allowed shaving every three days, the men taking turns using a community pot of water. The women were also given a small quantity of water for personal use.

Susan did not salute, but she stood respectfully before Verkan's desk. "The report is not encouraging, Captain. We have quite a lot of water, although most of it is not potable. There is probably enough for another three weeks at the rate at which we are using it. However, there isn't much more than five days' food supply, even with what you and Sergeant Ranthar contributed."

Verkan leaned back in his chair. He had reached the same conclusion days earlier. "Anything else?"

"We have five on the sick list, including Lance Corporal Gonzalez. They probably wouldn't make it a long way in the subway tunnel, although they might be able to walk, I wouldn't want to walk them far. Recruit Espinoza can be returned to light duty any time you want him to. I would suggest you get something to replace his hand. Could one of the men bend a hook from pieces of the shopping cart?"

"That's a good idea," Verkan told her. "I'll have someone see to it. Sit down, Miss Majors. I don't exactly know what your status is here, but you've certainly earned the right to sit down when you report to me. I'll have to make you some kind of warrant officer or civilian consultant, I guess. You're too useful for me to throw out, and too stubborn to be a regular member of the Company."

She sat on the converted grocery box Verkan reserved for visitors. "Thank you, Captain. I'm not stubborn. I've said I'd submit to your orders, but I don't understand these military formalities. I don't think much of them, either."

"But you do practice them when required."

"I said I'd obey your orders, didn't I?"

They discussed the food situation, the morale of the women of whom Susan was the unofficial spokesman, and other matters pertaining to supply and nursing. When they had finished, she stood in front of his desk, smiled, and saluted crisply as she had seen Ranthar teach the others.

Sergeant Ranthar was next. He had no unusual matters to report.

Verkan said, "I need three volunteers to go up the stairs and check the street level out. Private Baker can handle the Geiger counter; he seems to be pretty good with it. I need young healthy people, or old healthy ones. No family men. If radiation levels are too high, they will come right back. All I really need is a peek out to see if anything that might have some food in it is still standing."

Ranthar nodded. "Good call."

"You can also let the Diablos know that while it would be safe for the healthiest of our troops to go up the tunnel now, it would definitely be harmful to those who have already taken a dose of radiation. That includes Gonzalez. Fish asked me in their name if we could move out."

"I know. He talked with me first; I told him he could ask you."

"Good, as long as they're talking to me, we don't have to worry about them. And, Jard—make sure the guard in the tunnel is alert. There has to be a reason nobody has come down it since Matheson. If the radiation level is falling at their end, and that's a reasonable assumption, maybe they'll come after us next. They must be low on supplies as well. We have to get out of here ourselves pretty soon, you know."

"I agree, Captain. Anything else?"

"No, that's all." Verkan returned to his contemplation of the morning reports.

The situation was not good. If the radiation continued to fall at the rate it had been subsiding, the party would definitely be better off in several days. That did not leave much margin, however, for fighting their way past the next station. And possibly the stations after that one. He was concerned about what they might find beyond that. He wanted ample food supplies for the trip, but given the radiation levels, leaving immediately was not a good idea. He had little hope that the expedition up the stairs would even be able to get out onto the streets, much less find any significant additions to their food supply.

Fifteen minutes later, Ranthar reported again.

"It's hot as hell up those stairs, Verkan. I wouldn't let anybody stay up there more than two minutes. That was Doc's estimate of what was safe. Baker wanted to go, but I let Private Mendez, that Diablo kid who's so full of piss and vinegar, go instead. If Baker's going to be working the radiation counter, he's likely to be in hotter places than the rest of us."

Verkan nodded. Paratimers had adapted to high radiation levels long ago so he knew that Ranthar had led the party and was the last to leave the surface. "What did you find?"

"It's bad up there, Vall. There was fire all though the block, although there wasn't much to burn. The buildings are still standing, sort of, but most of them are pushed out of shape. A few look like they partially melted. Even if there was food up there, only a dead man would bring it back. If I'd thought there were any uncontaminated foodstuffs I would have stayed longer, but I don't think there's any edible food on the surface within a circumference of twenty miles."

Verkan nodded. "Just as I suspected."

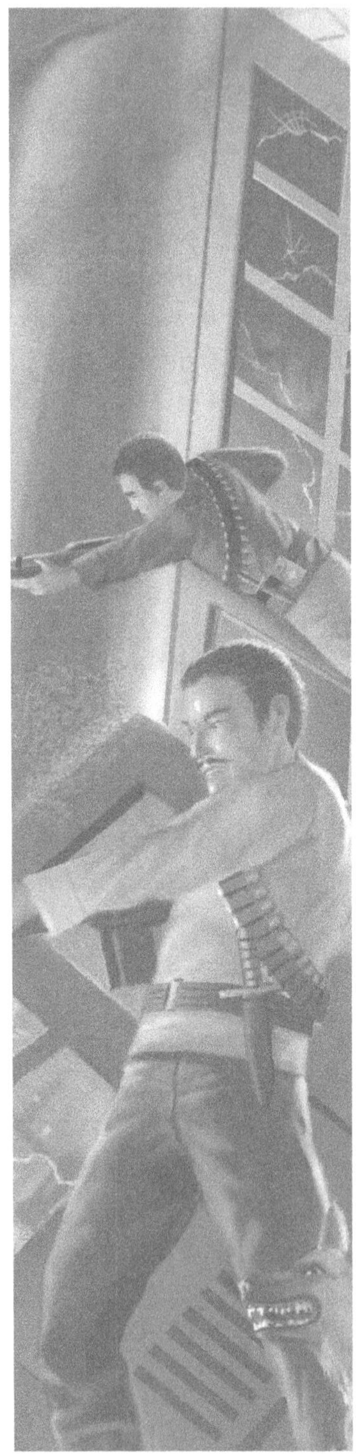

TWENTY

I

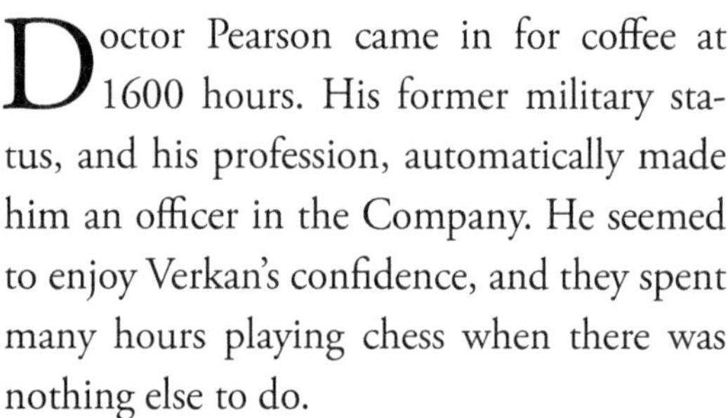

Doctor Pearson came in for coffee at 1600 hours. His former military status, and his profession, automatically made him an officer in the Company. He seemed to enjoy Verkan's confidence, and they spent many hours playing chess when there was nothing else to do.

"What's the story?" Pearson asked. "You have a worried look, Vall. Are we going to start marching soon?"

"To tell you the truth, Doc, I don't know what to do. Yes, we're going to have to start marching soon. But I'd sure as hell like to know what the situation is beyond the next station, but I'll be damned if I'll risk sending a scout to try to get around it in this tunnel. If I get this crew going in the tunnel, there's no telling how long they'll be in it before we find a spot as safe as this one."

Pearson sipped his coffee. "Yes, and we're running out of food. I'm damn glad I don't have to make that decision."

"Yeah." Verkan shook his head. "And like a damned fool I let myself be responsible for all these people. They're all waiting for me to tell them what to do." He poured another cup of coffee, looked at his tiny stores of cigarettes and decided not to light one, chewing his empty pipe instead.

"I could make a suggestion," Pearson offered. "You won't like it, though."

"What's that?"

"Call a council of war, tell them what the situation is and let the Company have a hand in the decision."

"No, Doc. I took on the job, I'll see it through. The only purpose to a council would be to collectivize the decision, so that if it turned out wrong, I'd still be popular. But I can't do that, and besides, if it turns out wrong—we're all dead. By definition: anything that keeps us alive was the right decision."

Pearson moved one of the paper chess pieces. The board was the back of a poster, alternate squares painstakingly shaded in pencil by Jimmy Pearson as he sat before the radio set with nothing else to do. It was quite a nice chessboard, although the pieces, being irregular pieces of cardboard torn from another poster, left something to be desired.

"I suppose you're right, Captain."

"I will call a kind of council, though," Verkan said. "I have to get some of them used to the idea that sometimes there's no best policy, just the least worst."

Pearson looked up at him. "You know, you really didn't ask for this and we didn't give you the right to decide something that you're no better at than anyone else. They aren't slaves, you said yourself. I think you could use some advice."

"Maybe. Let's get the best ones over here and see what happens. This won't be put off much longer."

II

The commanders assembled in Verkan's cubicle, now used as an orderly room. Eduardo Gonzalez was carried in on a litter. Verkan invited them all to be seated on the long bench which now stood along one wall of the cubicle. He sat down on the chair.

"This will be short," he began. "We have to pool whatever knowledge we have about conditions farther up the line, and decide what we'll do. There is no question about one thing: we have to get moving soon. Food is running out, there is no possible replacement and there is no way of surviving on the surface of the city. The outgoing tunnel offers a chance to get further out of New York City, where the radiation may—notice I said may—be less. There is a reasonable chance of that. The wind was from out of town the night of the bombardment, and appears to have been blowing steadily towards the ocean ever since.

"We know that the next station is occupied by hostiles. How many after that are occupied at all, or by what, I can't say. In any event, we have up to twelve miles of tunnel to go through, and about twenty stations."

"Eighteen exactly, according to the subway map," Susan Majors said.

Verkan nodded.

"That's about two days march for this crew," he said. "Certainly, no less, if we are to carry the sick. And there will be wounded after we fight our way past the next station, have no doubts about that. But the radiation level is higher than I like anyone to be in for more than two days. It's dropped, but not far enough. Doctor Pearson informs me that one day is more like a safe dose."

Pearson nodded.

"I'm not putting this to a vote," Verkan said. "But I'm open to discussing the best methods of getting the Company out of here. We have two choices. March now, tonight, or wait until tomorrow night. Beyond that is cutting it too fine."

"I'm glad to hear you say you aren't omniscient," Susan Majors said.

There was a murmur from the others, and she glanced around before turning to Verkan. "I'm sorry, Captain. I don't want to…it seems that everything we can do is horrible. But I think we ought to wait; it will be better for the sick."

David Mills said quietly, "Yes, but it just leaves everyone who isn't sick—and the sick too, since they can't survive without us—in dire straits if things don't turn out well up the line, doesn't it, sir?"

"Captain, leave us here," Gonzalez interrupted. "It won't matter much, and hell, some of you guys can get out." He spoke defiantly. "Not that I give a damn about you clods, but my Diablos are going to make it. Yeah, get out and leave us behind."

"I have thought about it," Verkan said quietly. "I can leave the non-combatants here while we clear the way ahead. I won't send anyone back down that tunnel to fetch you, though. You will have to get up to the next station, or wherever it is that we will halt, by yourselves."

"Will someone stay to guard us?" Mrs. Guliksen asked.

"It won't be necessary," Verkan told her. "The tunnel appears to be absolutely safe in the downtown direction. No one has come up it since we've been here; the radiation is very high in that direction. The main force will be between you and anything up the line. Nothing hostile will get past us. Or, if that does happen, we won't be any protection for you, anyway. I will leave you and Dr. Pearson one pistol. I will not further divide my combat force."

"What about rations?" Susan asked.

"Good question. You and the other women and children will have to get them up the tunnel. Again, I can't spare any soldiers for porterage. Some of my combat force can carry a light load with them, but I can't take carts and litters on an attack."

"Do we know anything about the radiation levels around the bend of the tunnel?" Guliksen asked.

"No. We don't know a damn thing. The next station is right in the crook of that bend and it's held by hostiles. We take our chances after we force passage. I'll have to play that by ear, too. It's one thing to take an armed force past that station and quite another to cover non-combatants and a supply train getting past. We may have to clean out that station even though they outnumber us in combat effectives."

Susan Majors looked up at Verkan. "You have a lot to worry about, don't you? We'll stay behind, Captain, and when you signal, we'll get the sick and the supplies up the tunnel. That you can stop worrying about. There are enough of us who can carry or push carts."

Mrs. Guliksen nodded in agreement. "Yes, you men stop thinking about us. We'll get there, you just clear the way." She laughed. "And God help those savages in the next station. Verkan's Company is coming through."

The others murmured in agreement and the meeting broke up in good spirits. Outside, the Diablos gave a loud cheer, something like the old rebel yell, when they heard that the Company was moving now. "Now, we'll show those damn mooks who's boss!" one shouted.

III

It was agreed that Doctor Pearson and Susan Majors would be in charge of the women, children and injured who were to be left behind. Susan aided Ranthar and the combat troops by packing up supplies, parceling them out to the men who would carry, while loading the others into carts or packages for the women and children to bring up later.

Pearson sat across from Verkan in the makeshift office.

"Hadn't I better go with you?" he asked.

"No," Verkan replied. "You aren't that good a combat troop, Doc. We need you alive and in one piece. There'll be work for you after the battle, you can bet your life on it."

"Okay, okay," Pearson replied. "How will you signal the 'All Right?'"

"I hate to waste ammunition, but I can't think of anything else. Have Jimmy watch for flashlight signals, and give him a strong light to answer back with. I'll try to do it that way, but in case I can't we'll use a pistol. Eight shots, in a pattern of three-two-three if you are supposed to advance. One-three-three-one means we've run into something we can't handle and you're on your own. I'll try to signal when there's no fighting going on"

They arranged other signals. Jimmy Pearson was a Boy Scout and understood Morse code, but they also agreed that the gunshot signals could be sent by flashlight.

"We can signal you, too," Pearson said. "But I don't think we'll have any trouble."

"Nor do I," Verkan replied. Nobody is going to come up the line from downstream, not even walking dead men. The tunnel might be blocked, or everybody down that way is dead, but it may mean there's something stopping people. If it is, they could send an expedition up here as easily as we can go uptown ourselves. I don't like this much, Doc, but I like dividing my forces when I know I've got to face superior numbers a lot less."

Pearson left and Verkan began copying his notes on what would be taken with them and what would be left behind. As he was writing, Susan Majors came into the orderly room.

"I meant it when I said I didn't want to fight with you anymore," she said. "I still don't like mercenaries much, and you were perfectly horrid at first, but...but, thank you, Captain Verkan. Truce?"

She held out her hand.

"Okay, truce." He took her hand, shaking it as he would have shook a man's. Then turned back to his papers.

"Can I help?" she asked. "I was a pretty fair secretary working through college, and social work has a lot of reporting to type and forms to fill...there's no typewriter, but I can take shorthand and I have neat handwriting."

"No, but thanks. I expect Doctor Pearson will need some help, though."

Susan smiled. "Well, I just wanted to make up a little for all the fights we've had. I know you don't like me, but you can use some help. Do you really expect anyone to be able to read those notes you're making?"

"I'll manage," he grunted. "If you want to help, you can go make a final check on where each and every item in the quartermaster list is. Now, I don't want to be impolite, Miss Majors, but I have work to do. I need to plan an attack."

"All right," she said, still smiling. "Truce but no peace, right Captain."

She left, and he heard Ranthar chuckling outside before he came in to discuss the battle plan.

TWENTY-ONE

I

Verkan had his battle force rest until 0400 hours. Even though it was dark most of the time—the period right before dawn and before the body starts waking up and was most sluggish—was the best time for a night action. He assembled them in the dark. The Civil Defense lighting system was dismantled and packed to be carried up with the other gear, and his men sat just outside the circle of light cast by the kerosene lantern.

"For the first part of the march," Verkan said, "Baker will be point man. He'll be carrying the radiation counter with the volume turned down low so that only he can hear it. Be alert for his signals, if we have to halt. This is a total darkness operation. You've each got a small cord attached to your shoulder. The man behind you takes the cord and keeps it taut. We walk with one hand against the left side wall, and we move quietly.

"When we get to where you can see light from the station ahead, we'll chance it with the Geiger counter. We'll take our battle stations then. Ranthar and his handpicked

Diablos go first, to scout around if they can and to take out any guards. That's garrote work. Don't get cute and try to use knives, you're not good enough with them in the dark."

The Diablos, their faces streaked with soot from the cook stove, nodded, grinning evilly.

"There's a good chance they won't be able to get anywhere. I'll be with the next group, close behind them. Corporal Fish will bring up the rear, and he'll be in command of the rear group."

Verkan looked his force over. They weren't well trained, most of them were only dimly aware of what was to come, but they all looked eager enough. He put that to Ranthar's enthusiastic training.

"When we flush them," Verkan said, "we rush. I want Fish's group to get past the station if possible. You just keep going hell for leather while we cover you. Attack quickly before they get organized and see if you can pin them down. There's more of them than there are of us, but they may not be so well-disciplined. I'm counting on that to carry us through.

"You men without firearms, you've been trained to use what you have. Be ready, too. Corporal Fish has some experience at this kind of fighting; he'll try to tell you where to hit them. Drop your supplies when we are committed to combat, but not before—and give them Hell!

"Any questions?"

"You think they'll be waiting for us, sir?" somebody asked.

"No. Fish and Gonzalez both agree, they wouldn't be able to keep a large group hiding in ambush for this long. They'll have guards out, but patience isn't their strong point. That's why I want a rush when the fighting starts. We'll be ready; I hope they won't be. It's our best chance. Other questions?"

"How fast will we be moving, sir?"

"As fast as we can without noise until we get close. I don't have to tell you to keep quiet. Your lives depend on it." He looked them over again. "Okay, fall out and go to the latrine. Last chance before combat, so force it if you have to. All of you. Be ready in five minutes. Dismissed."

"A Sunday walk, Captain," Ranthar said. "Nothing to it."

"Let's hope so, Sergeant. Got the grenades ready?"

"Yeah. Hope they go off right. How'd you happen to get a can of gunpowder from that store? Made a couple of nifty pipe bombs with that water pipe."

"Just did, that's all," Verkan replied. "Don't use them unless you have to, we aren't likely to get more."

Ranthar gave him a pained look. "Yes, sir."

"Captain." Verkan turned around, saw Susan Majors standing behind him. "Captain, I—be careful, will you. You don't know how much everyone here depends upon you. If you get yourself killed, it would be like taking the last hope away from these people."

"Thanks. I'll try not to."

II

It was pitch dark in the subway tunnel. The attack party moved slowly, careful to avoid the tracks. As the Company went along, they began to gather more agility at moving in the dark and picked up speed. All lights that might show in the tunnel had been extinguished, so that the combat force would not have light behind it to frame them for an observer. Each man clung to the cord attached to the man in front of him, his hand lightly brushing the wall to his left. Each of them lost in his own thoughts as he made his way carefully down the black tunnel.

Verkan was considerably more worried than he had let on, and tried to focus on the objective up ahead. For all his years in combat situations, starting as a drummer boy, he had never quite lost his before-battle jitters, and used his First Level mental discipline to keep himself from concentrating unduly on what might go wrong. His plan was simple and concise; and, given the situation, there was no other possible one. It was so little a plan as to be almost none at all.

As he slid his feet lightly over the concrete walkway between the tracks and the wall, he thought about the fallout shelter system which had been constructed at such great cost. There were cities, he knew, in which the citizens took pride in knowing and caring about the Civil Defense system; this had not been one of them. Federal law required that each suitable construction be modified to provide shelter spaces and be stocked—the modifications to be paid for by Federal subsidy.

He wondered why there were so few people in the tunnels. It had been a hot day when the missile had struck and many of those who had lived in the area might well have used the efficient rapid transit to go to the beach or cooler resort areas. He was trying to estimate how many people he might expect to find on the outside, between where they were and the tunnel exit, when he saw a faint glow in the tunnel ahead. They were approaching the bend.

The light was blocked out momentarily, and he felt Ranthar beside him. "We can just see, Captain," the Sergeant whispered. "Baker and I were about a hundred feet out further. They've got some kind of barrier up across the tunnel with one guard standing watch. While we were watching, a girl came out and gave him a cigarette and something to drink. I don't think anybody else is on duty—at least, at this end of the tunnel. Baker says the radiation level wasn't too bad in the tunnel, and it starts to drop off completely up from where we were. I think it's clear from there on to the next station."

"Okay," Verkan said. The whisper sounded like a shot, but he knew it couldn't be heard from more than a few feet. "How close do you think you can get?"

"Beats me, Captain. Maybe, I can take the guard out. It's a cinch we won't find out what's in the station until we move past him. The barrier must be thirty, forty feet from the platform."

Verkan continued to give whispered orders and the group silently formed into attack formation. As he moved forward, he became aware of the stench of death—an unmistakable odor familiar to him from other campaigns. When he reached the head of the column, Ranthar and his scout Diablos crawled forward, Verkan right behind them.

His hand brushed against something soft in the dark, then closed around a hard pole. He suddenly realized that it must be the spear they had given Avery Matheson, and that the body must be his. Somehow the man had made it this far. Verkan wondered if he had been seen by the leather jackets, or collapsed and died only a few yards short of his enemy.

The sentry was wearing a black leather jacket with some kind of emblem on the back. A scuffling sound from somewhere behind him was as loud as the roll of a drum, but the sentry did not turn. The leather-jacketed sentry held a rifle in the crook of his arm and was looking back toward the subway station. Every now and then he would turn and peer into the darkness of the tunnel, but then would quickly turn back toward the light.

A tin cup rested on the barricade across the tunnel. The barricade itself was formed from the remains of the ticket booths and telephone stands. The central portion was no more than waist high. Ranthar and his Diablos crept closer.

The attacking force froze as the sentry turned again to squint down the tunnel. He seemed to relax for a moment, then reached behind the barrier and lifted a large flashlight. As he turned it on, Ranthar rose in front of him.

Sergeant Ranthar carried a piece of telephone wire three feet long with wooden handles at each end. As the sentry straightened in horror, the wire looped around his throat. Ranthar jerked hard and the boy's cry was strangled before it could reach his lips. The rifle and flashlight dropped to the tunnel floor. As the party started forward again, there was another clatter. A pile of debris and tin cans fell from against one wall. One of the scouts had struck a tripwire.

Ranthar and his scouts, followed closely by Fish's group, vaulted the barricade and ran toward the station area. Verkan's group swarmed behind them, ignoring the body of the sentry, the wire still looped around his purple neck.

The subway station platform was on their right, with a smaller platform on the left side. Three armed men were just rising from benches on the left platform, as Ranthar and Verkan cut them down.

"Sergeant, cover Fish and his squad," Verkan shouted. "Get moving, Fish! Run you bastards!"

On the platform to the right a swarm of men were just beginning to fan out, many of them half-dressed or rubbing sleep out of their eyes.

"The rest of you take cover here at the platform edge," Verkan ordered.

There was rifle fire from the main station and one of the Diablos shouted and fell. Baker dragged him to the shelter of the station platform, while Verkan, Ranthar and the other riflemen laid down a steady fire.

Drawing his pistol, Verkan shot out the two lights behind his group so that the only lights came from the main station to their right. The Company was now in relative darkness firing into the light. He saw four or five of the Imperial Lords drop, or writhe as bullets struck.

From the opposite tunnel, Joey Fish called out, "All clear over here, Captain."

Two Diablos were firing wildly at the door of the station where some of the enemy gang had taken cover. Other members of the gang dashed into the station restrooms. Two attempted to hide behind benches in the waiting area, and Ranthar methodically splintered their cover with his big rifle, then dropped each of them as they attempted to run for it.

"Hold your fire," Verkan ordered. It was very still in the tunnel. His ears echoed with rifle shots. On the main subway platform against the right hand wall of the station, about fifteen people of various ages were spread about on the floor. One man was lying across a small child, while another was cradling his wife in his arms, sobbing loudly. Several did not move; the others were staring about wildly. Lying with them was one of the Imperials, seemingly unarmed.

Verkan counted almost twenty men with leather jackets sprawled on the platform in front of him, two of them still moving. There were also four unarmed men and a woman, whom he took to be civilian casualties. One of the men moved feebly, but he could see that the woman and at least one of the other civilians were dead.

Directly in front of him were the main doors to the shelter. At least four armed men had taken cover behind them and must still be there. There were other hostiles in the men's and ladies' rooms of the station.

Verkan sent a Diablo to the left platform to gather the weapons of the three gang members who had been shot and were lying on the floor.

"What'll I do about them Imperials if they're still alive, Captain?" one asked.

"Slit their throats, so they won't bother us again. Bring those guns back here, as well as anything else they might have. You'll have to work in the dark. Oh, and bring their jackets and belts. We can use leather goods."

The boy gulped, then said, "Yes, sir." He crawled across the tracks, careful not to raise his head above the level of the platform until he was in the dark area beyond.

There was a small barricade in front of the ladies' room. Verkan was unable to see what it was made from, but estimated it was tough enough to stop light-caliber rounds. What Ranthar's rifle might do to it was another matter. As he watched, there was a shot from that direction, and the bullet whanged from the concrete of the station floor, a yard away from him.

"You men in there," Verkan called out. "You want to talk, or do you want us to clean this place out?"

"Who are you bastards?" a voice from the men's room asked.

"That's not important, is it? What is important is that you're caught like rats in a trap. We can keep you there until you starve to death. Or I can throw grenades in with you and really mess you up. Which is it? Talk or shoot?"

"What's to talk about? What you want, man?"

Joey Fish crouched along the edge of the platform until he reached Verkan. "Let me parlay with them, sir. I know how to deal with them."

Verkan nodded.

"I want one of you out where I can see you," Fish yelled. "Send Crazy Eddie out here."

"That your gang, Joey the Fish?" the voice from the men's room asked. "Where's El Toro? Who's that Do Right out there with you?"

"Send Eddie out and find out for yourself," Fish shouted back. "That's the way it's done, sir," he told Verkan. "I've made treaties with the Imperial Lords before. You tell me what you want and I'll get it. Really, Cap'n, this is the best way if you want to talk with those guys. Me and Eddie will meet out there in no man's land, between both gangs, and chew the fat."

"What are they doing now?" Verkan asked.

"Tryin' to make up their minds as to if they ought to talk. You got 'em in a crack, Cap'n, they don't know whether to shit or go blind. They sure don't want to surrender, but you got 'em bad and you can squeeze hard."

The enemy spokesman shouted, "We'll send Crazy Eddie when you show somebody. First you got to let Jacks come in with us."

"Is that Jacks over against the wall," Verkan asked.

"Yes, sir. Jacks is the sharpest mechanic they have."

"Tell him he can go in," Verkan ordered. "Hold your fire, troops."

"Go on, Jacks," Fish cried out. "We got you in our sights anyways. You be dead anytime we want."

The jacketed boy with the civilians rose and dashed for the men's room. The others, on the platform where Jacks had been laying still, were crying and or groaning. They did not call out to Verkan or say anything loud enough for him to hear.

"All right, Joey. Here are my terms. Safe passage for everybody, and that includes all my people below here, past this station. I want all of the food out of the Civil Defense lockers. Tell them anything you think will work. We keep all the weapons we've already got, as well as those off the bodies on the platform. They're ours by right of arms. If they give you any trouble, tell them we'll shoot up all their food and water, then grenade their rooms."

"I don't believe we can trust these guys, Cap'n."

"I don't, either. I just want to see how desperate they are, and if they're ready to make terms."

"Okay."

"I also want to learn whether or not they have any hostages inside the restrooms. If they do, find out if they'll let them go. But don't act too interested in them. I don't see how we could protect them if it came to a real battle—"

Verkan was interrupted by firing from the far side of the tunnel. He could make out Ranthar lying on the tunnel floor, firing down the tunnel into the dark and flashes of small weapon fire. There was a scream as someone took a hit.

"What's there, Sergeant?"

"Were four, now five, Captain. I saw them coming just now, and they aren't friendly. Started shooting as soon as they got close."

Corporal Fish shouted into the dark tunnel. "If you guys are the Imperials, we've got a truce. Hold it."

"Who says?" a voice demanded. "I ain't heard no truce."

Fish turned back to the men's room. "Get Crazy Eddie out here and tell 'em, or we start lobbin' grenades." He paused. "Better haul ass."

After a moment, one of the Imperials came out of the men's room. "This is Eddie," he shouted. "We got a truce. Stop shooting!"

Fish climbed up on the platform, leaving his weapons with one of the Diablos. He and Eddie sat on the floor of the station and began speaking in low tones.

David Mills crawled over to Verkan. "Can we trust that kid, sir? How do we know he won't sell us out to the Imperials? They're birds of a feather."

"We don't know, but if we can't trust him we haven't got a Company. Now, back to your post."

"Yes, sir. But—but, sir, this is dangerous. You can't trust those hoods."

"Back to your post. Now!" Verkan put some bite on the last word.

"Yes, sir." Mills scuttled back to his squad.

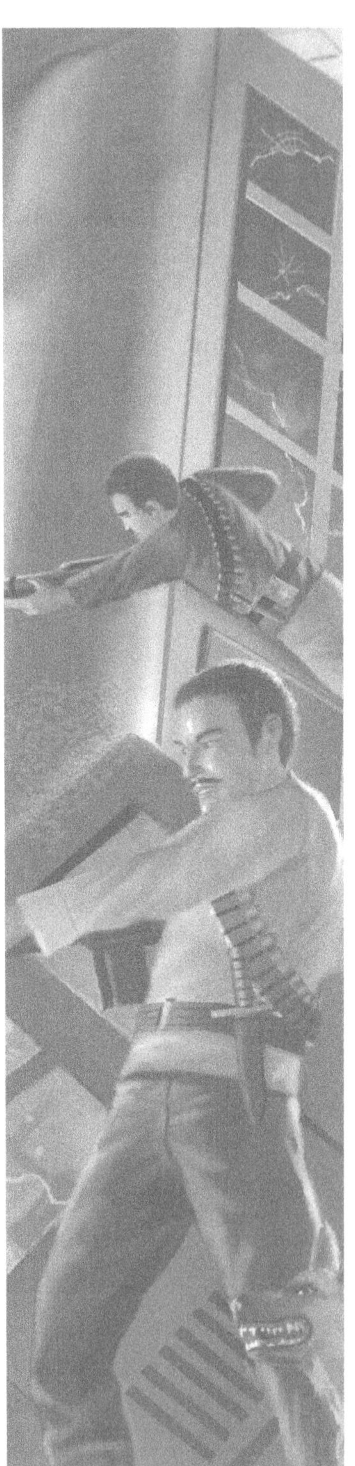

TWENTY-TWO

On the platform Crazy Eddie, a tall well-built boy between eighteen and twenty, suddenly stood with a gesture of dismissal. "Like hell, man!" he said loudly. "Whatch ya mothers think ya got goin' on, a goddamn army? Ya'll ain't getting' notin' from us but a ticket off our turf."

Fish also stood. His voice rose as he said proudly, "Yeah, we got an army, man. Not a bunch of punks like you. We got a real army with a real captain. We got grenades, too. You want some, we give 'em to you. Now go tell your boss-man what I said, and tell him my captain ain't goin' to wait all night, either. Go tell him!"

Joey Fish walked contemptuously away from Eddie and jumped down beside Verkan. "They're scared, Cap'n. Those civilians over there are all that's left of the people that was in the station. El Toro said there was almost two hundred of 'em in the station, with women and kids, when he was there. They must have killed all the others… Freddy says the food over there is mush, it's nothing. They got a lot more, but he says they don't wanna give it up. But he had smokes in his pocket, maybe they sent some fool out for food, too."

"What terms will he agree to? Verkan asked.

"He won't let nothin' go. Not people, not weapons, not water, not food—nothin'. They will agree to stay in their holes and order the people up the tunnel not to bother us, and we can bring the others up, too. They won't bother 'em."

"What will his boss say?"

"I don't know, sir. We only see a few Imperials, but there's some of the South Brooklyn Boys there, too. I saw a couple of Gowanus Boys and some South Brooklyn Devils. Probably as many of them as Imperials since we killed a bunch. I don't know the Devils much, but they're supposed to be tough. Hopheads, greasers, some of 'em. Motorcycle gang. They won't want to give up nothing'."

"Baker," Verkan called.

"Yes, sir."

"Take the Diablos and go up and relieve Sergeant Ranthar. Send him to me now."

Barker crouched and led his men down the tunnel.

"Mills, take that spear and put out the light over there. The one that's behind Ranthar." Mills smashed the light, making the tunnel even darker. In the station, the Civil Defense lighting system illuminated the platform poorly, leaving pools of shadow near the walls and in the corners.

"What will you have, Captain?" Ranthar asked.

"How much trouble is that gang ahead going to be?"

"Well, you see the situation, Captain. All they've got to do is fire down the tunnel at us. What little light there is, it's behind my troops. I think there are four, and they went back around the bend. We'll probably lose two, three men getting them."

"What are our casualties now?" Verkan asked.

"One of the Diablos got gut-shot. Doc'll have to work on him, if he lives that long. I don't think we can save him. Recruit Fuller's dead. Baker took something in the arm, but he says he's all right."

"Fuller?" Verkan asked.

"Family man," Ranthar replied. "Wife, kid about eight. Wife helps with the cooking."

Verkan nodded; he remembered the wife, a tall, lanky redhead. "And two more if we take out that group, now that they're warned. So I make the best deal I can with this outfit. Okay."

At Fish's summons, the leather-jacketed negotiator appeared on the platform. "Boss says ya'll are full a shit. Don't have any damn grenades. You did, you woulda used 'em."

"I have plenty," Verkan announced. "I don't particularly want to waste them on you, but if you don't come to terms fast—I will."

There was no reply.

"First squad! Prepare to advance! Sergeant, prepare to throw!"

Verkan shook his head slightly as Ranthar prepared to throw one of his pipe bombs.

"Wait up!" a loud voice echoed out of the restroom. "Say you got grenades. Ya'll can't get us all. Watcha want?"

"I told your man what we want."

"Not all that mush. Man, we'll run short of eats."

"All right. Half the food. And two of those ten gallon water cans. Free passage for my entire outfit. And your prisoners."

"Not our prisoners. Give ya'll the rest, jus' not those suckas."

"If you run short of food, what will you do about them?" Verkan cursed himself as he asked. The little group on the platform stirred, started to rise, then fell flat again as a shot sounded from the ladies' room.

"Tha's my lookout," the unseen spokesman said.

"No. They come with us, either peacefully—or over your dead bodies."

"You muthafucka's fight, they die!"

Suddenly from the platform a girl cried out: "I don't care if they kill us, I'm going to talk. Those black-hearted bastards murdered innocent children, raped women and little girls—played with us. Torture, too! Kill them all. Kill them!"

A young girl, not yet twenty, rose up and ran toward the edge of the platform. "Kill them! The bastards, kill the—"

A shot from the ladies' room felled her. She lay on the concrete screaming for a moment, then tried to rise. She cried out, "O God! Damn them, kill them, kill them all."

Ranthar hefted his bomb, but waited for orders.

David Mills fired his 30-06 rifle at the barrier in front of the ladies' room, worked the bolt, fired again. From up the tunnel, firing broke out again.

"No, damn-it!" Verkan shouted. He was too late. Baker led his squad up the tunnel, charging the group around the bend. As the men ran, they fired, just as Ranthar had drilled them, although they had never had the ammunition to practice the maneuver.

Verkan turned to the station itself, fired through the barricades. Screams of pain, shots fired back and curses answered him. He ordered the men with weapons to fire at the center doors and into the restrooms.

Then he called to Mills. "Get up there and herd these people across the platform. Anybody who can't walk, leave them. Move it, man! We don't have enough ammo to keep them pinned in long."

From the ladies' room a girl's voice screamed, "Please, please don't throw the bombs. They won't let us out! Please stop shooting. Oh, whoever you are, please, please!"

"Continue to fire!" Verkan ordered. "Cover Mills. Sergeant, if anyone fires on him, heave that bomb!"

Ranthar laid down his rifle and lit a piece of fuse, laid it and the pipe-bomb on the platform before he took up the rifle again.

Up the tunnel Verkan could see flashes from gunfire, then a light around the tunnel bend. He saw Diablo Hernandez take aim, fire, then the light swing in a crazy arc and suddenly go out. Before it died, Verkan saw one of his men go down, the others rushing madly around the bend of the tunnel. There were more shots, then quiet. Another light came on around the bend, stayed on briefly, then went out.

There were no more shots.

Mills herded the last of the prisoners to the edge of the platform, dropped over the side himself, carrying a small child. Three figures remained in the prisoners' corner, one of them not moving. The not very pretty girl who had started the battle lay halfway between them and the edge of the platform, moaning softly.

There was a babble of voices, then a cry from an older man as he saw several jacketed Diablos. "Oh no, God. Oh, God no—not more of them!"

"Shut up!" Verkan ordered. Then more gently, he added, "Please. You are safe now, but please be quiet. I have things to do."

He turned. "Sergeant, get Baker's report on the double. Corporal Fish, have them send Crazy Eddie out here again."

"Don't think they will, Captain. It was us broke the truce, they ain't likely to trust us no more."

"Us!" Mills shouted. "They shot that girl. Captain, let me go get her."

"No."

"They shot her," Fish said, "But you shot at them first."

"What did you expect me to do?" Mills asked.

"Obey orders, like the rest of us," Fish growled.

"Hold it," Verkan ordered. "Mills, we'll deal with you later. Corporal Fish is right. Our truce did not cover prisoners. Your gesture of sentiment cost me at least one man, and may have endangered my getting our party past this station, not to mention the food stores we negotiated for. That's a high price to pay when we don't know if you saved anyone. If we are killed, those people are a lot worse off than before."

"Yes sir…sir, can't I go get that girl? I don't know where she's hit, but it looks bad. Can't I go get her?"

"No. You'd never make it, and I don't have the ammunition to cover you. Go up the tunnel and report to Baker."

He motioned one of the men prisoners, who appeared the least shell-shocked, over. "How many of them are left?"

The man frowned. "There's a dozen or more in the restrooms. The filthy cowards…."

He turned to Joey Fish. "Tell them if they trust us or not, they have five minutes to agree to our terms, or we will clean them out. Same terms as before, except there is no longer a prisoner problem."

"But there is! My daughter's in there with those savages…that was her screaming in there. They forced her in there!" one of the former prisoners shouted. A middle-aged man, his suit torn and dirty, stood up and ran to Verkan, grabbing his shirt and crying, "You've got to get her out. My Beth, she's still in there with those animals! She didn't want to go in. One of them made her his girl, because his didn't make it to the station. Please help me."

"STOP IT!" Verkan shouted. "Sit down, sir. Now!" His tone of command was momentarily effective. "Corporal Fish, you have your orders."

The Corporal shouted the ultimatum to the Imperials still in the station. A voice, Verkan thought a different one from the previous spokesperson, answered, "We'll think it over, big shot."

Sergeant Ranthar crawled up to Verkan. "The bend is secured, sir. Lost one man, Cranston, he's dying. Baker has another hole in his shoulder, as far as I can tell from an old US Army thirty caliber slug. Clean entry and exit on that one. The one he took before was a .22; it's still in there. There were four of them, like I thought. The boys didn't take any prisoners. We got two rifles, a pistol, couple of knives, looks like a lot of ammo. They were kids, denim and jackets like out there."

"What's the radiation around the bend?"

"Don't know yet, Captain. Baker's coming back for his Geiger counter; he set it down here when he took over that post up there."

Verkan nodded. "Think he'll be able to operate it all right?"

"Yeah, I tied up his shoulder. Need to get the Doc to look at him, but I think he's fit for light duty."

"Can you see anything up ahead?"

"Yes, a subway train. Lights shining on it. And a light shining kind of diagonally out of the next station where the train is. Best damn security system you could get in this tunnel. Whoever's there knows what he's doing. Looks like a pro, Captain."

Ranthar ran his fingers through his hair and took a deep breath. There was the faint smell of death in the air. "Also, up around that bend is the damndest stack of bodies you ever saw, sir. All kinds. Looks like some of those tribal wars we ran into on Fourth Level— There's a break in the overhead, or something, cause it doesn't smell much down here, but Captain, there must be a hundred and fifty or more bodies stacked there like cordwood."

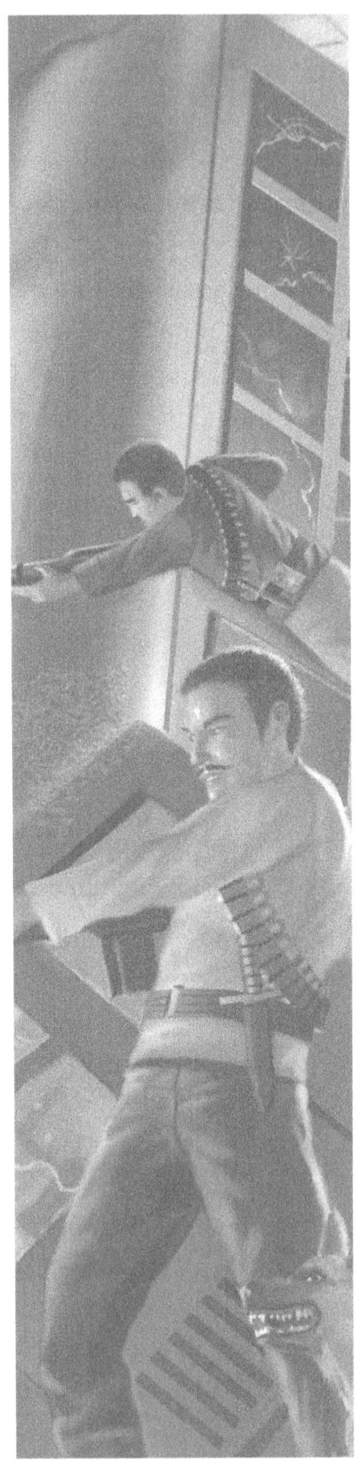

TWENTY-THREE

I

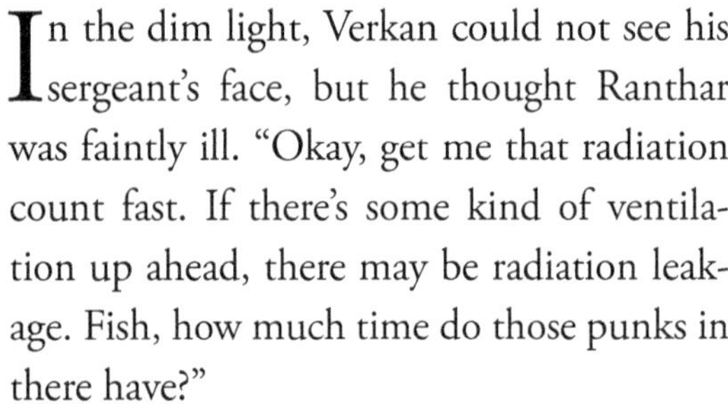

In the dim light, Verkan could not see his sergeant's face, but he thought Ranthar was faintly ill. "Okay, get me that radiation count fast. If there's some kind of ventilation up ahead, there may be radiation leakage. Fish, how much time do those punks in there have?"

"Just about used up, Captain."

"Sergeant, how good is your fuse? Can you trust it?

"I think so, Captain," Ranthar answered. "I timed some of it back at the last post."

"All right." Verkan led Ranthar to one corner of the platform, where they could see the men's room door plainly. The barricade in front of it was splintered, and the glass had been shot from the half open door.

"Can you get through that opening?" he asked.

Ranthar studied the distance. "Not from here, Captain—not sure. But look, it's dark along the wall here. You go back over and shout at them some more, sir, they haven't seen us here yet. I think I can get up there and do the job."

"Don't get killed, Jard."

Ranthar grinned, then left.

Verkan went back to the group near the center of the platform and began to shout orders. "Stand by to make assault. First squad will make the assault, second squad will fire to cover. Grenadiers, prepare your grenades!"

"Open fire!" Verkan ordered.

The four riflemen he had motioned to began to fire at the restroom and the main station doors. Verkan watched as Ranthar lit the fuse match below the level of the platform so that it could not be seen, and now had it wrapped in a leather jacket taken from one of the enemies, as he slithered up to the station itself. Verkan started firing his own rifle.

From the corner of his eyes, he saw the sparks of the grenade fuse twirl through the air toward the washroom door. Ranthar bounded up, dashed across the station and dove head first over the edge, hitting the track level in a tumbling roll. Bullets were whizzing over his head.

"Get the girl," he ordered Mills quietly, slapping him across the shoulders. As Mills scrambled up the edge of the platform, there was an explosion from the men's room. In the confined space, it sounded like a much larger explosion than it was. Inside the room they heard several sharp screams.

"What the hell!" the enemy spokesman yelled. "Hey, man. No more of them goddamn things!"

The girl in the room with him also screamed again, then another girl's voice was heard, "Oh please, don't, oh please...."

It was quiet for a moment. Mills grasped the wounded civilian girl by the shoulders and backed toward the platform edge, dragging her to safety. There was a shot from the main station doorway, the bullet striking the concrete inches from Mills. Verkan returned fire, and David dropped over the platform. Willing hands lifted the girl, putting her on the track ballast. She lay very still, and Verkan recalled that he had not heard her cry out for some time.

"Dead?" he asked.

Mills bent over her. "No, sir. There's a pulse."

"Take care of her, then." He fired again at the station doors.

II

The unseen spokesman shouted, "Okay, big man, you got your deal. Take the stuff, get off my turf. We won't hassle you."

"Cease fire!" Verkan ordered. "Corporal Fish, your squad will cover those doors. If anyone puts a head out—blow it off!" Then more quietly, he asked, "Corporal, can we trust them not to fire if somebody goes in after the food in the cabinet?"

"I don't know, sir. I wouldn't volunteer for the job."

"Well, we'll worry about it after we get everyone else past the station. Baker, what's the radiation count?"

"It starts falling right around the bend, sir. There's a hot spot just outside that workroom door where they stacked the bodies, but we closed the door on it. That didn't help the radiation much, but it's a deep room. Just a band of hot air coming out from there, probably won't hurt you if you get past it quick. Closed the door because of the flies, sir. God, that's an awful sight."

"All right," Verkan said. "Sergeant Ranthar, take charge here. Signal the women to start coming up the tunnel. Don't start anything with this group. I don't want anyone else hurt. You men understand my orders? Don't start another fight here. But, if they start one—finish it."

There was a murmur of agreement. Verkan took two Diablos and moved up the tunnel and around the bend, watching for the tool room door so they could run past it to escape the radiation Baker had reported. His flashlight picked it up ahead. The door had come open again, and as they neared the room, Verkan saw the corpses. There were men, women, children, thrown randomly in the room. The stench quickly became overpowering despite the faint breeze they felt blowing from the tunnel into the death chamber. The stench followed them after they dashed past the door, and one of the Diablos was sick.

Verkan swallowed hard and continued to march up the tunnel. As they approached the next station, he extinguished his light.

He estimated the distance between stations as perhaps a quarter mile, or five city blocks. It was difficult to judge distances underground, but he remembered from the station map that the two seemed unusually close together—maybe this one was an express station. When they got closer, he could see the train pulled into the station. The train was lighted, and, with the lights from the station, fifty to a hundred yards of the tunnel were illuminated. The lights themselves were well-placed, and could not be extinguished from the tunnel. It would be necessary to step well into the lighted area to shoot them out. Although, he could not see them, he guessed that there were guards in the train, looking out through its transom windows.

"Sergeant Ranthar was right," he told his men. "This is professional. If those people up there want to fight, we've got a hell of a job."

They moved on toward the train, staying carefully out of the lighted area. As they drew close, they heard voices. First a single voice, then a chorus of others in unison. At first, Verkan could not make out the words, but then he suddenly recognized them.

"O Lord, save the State,"

"And mercifully hear us when we call upon thee."

"Imbue thy Ministers with righteousness."

"And make thy chosen people joyful."

"O Lord, save thy people."

"And bless thine inheritance."

"Give peace in our time, O Lord." The voice wavered as it spoke the words.

The chorus answered: "For it is thou, Lord, that makes us dwell in safety."

"Glory be to the Father, and the Son, and the Holy Ghost."

"As it was in the beginning, is now, and ever shall be, world without end, amen."

One of Verkan's Diablos whispered the words again, "World without end." Then he laughed, a short strained laugh.

Verkan gathered his men against the wall. "It looks like we won't have much trouble," he whispered. "But don't count on it. Be ready to hit the dirt and get away fast if anything starts. Remember, we're badly outnumbered."

He stepped out to the center of the tunnel and shouted. "Hello, train people."

A light mounted on top of the train came on, shining down the tunnel. Verkan dropped to the floor and squeezed behind a rail, taking aim at the light. He did not fire.

"Who's up there?" Verkan shouted. "This is Captain Verkan, here. Who are you?"

"Verkan? Never heard of you," was the answer. "This is Lieutenant Hart, NYPD. Come out where I can see you."

"Not just yet, thanks." Verkan replied. "I had enough trouble at the last station. Are there many of you in there?"

"Enough. How big is your outfit? And what are you captain of?"

"I have seventy troops and about the same number of civilians, but haven't sorted them out from the last station, yet. Another platoon coming up later. We also have heavy weapons. If you are a police lieutenant, I'm glad to see you. If you aren't, you're in trouble."

"Army, huh?" the voice queried. "How are we going to work this, captain? You don't trust me, and I don't trust you. I heard the fight down the line there. You clean out those punks?"

"Yes." Verkan thought for a moment. "Look. How about I send in one man to look you over—that okay?"

"I don't like it, but I don't know what else to do. I'll send you one of mine to get a look at your outfit, all right?"

"Wait one minute." Verkan turned back to his men. One of the Diablos was shuffling slowly back down the tunnel. "Hernandez! Where are you going?"

"Hell, Cap'n, that cop knows me. Hates my guts."

"Stand fast, soldier. That's one thing you don't have to worry about. So, that means it really is a police lieutenant up there?"

"Si, Cap'n," Hernandez told him. "*Es verdad.* He's the toughest cop in the precinct. He—look, sir."

A short, balding man in clerical clothing was coming down the tunnel from the train, walking in the lighted area toward them. Lieutenant Hart shouted, "Father, get back here. You don't know who those people are!"

"No, I don't," the priest answered, as he walked faster. "But none of us are going to get anywhere like this. I'm Father Dutton," he said to Verkan, peering into the dark at the edge of the lighted area. He came up to Verkan. "Of Christ Church. Those are some of my people back there. Why, hello, Francisco," he added to the Diablo.

Verkan studied the priest carefully. He wore the usual cassock of the Catholic Church, his gray clothing stained and smeared. A rosary hung halfway out of his breast pocket.

"Father, I am Captain Verkan. I have a group of survivors back at the last station. Hernandez, do you know this man?"

"Yes, sir. I lived in this neighborhood before my old man split, and we had to move. He was the priest here when I was a kid. Yes, sir, that's Father Dutton." Hernandez shuffled for a moment, then said, "*Hola, Padre.*"

The priest nodded in return.

"Excellent," Verkan said. "Father, this stretch of the tunnel is pretty well clear of radiation, so it won't hurt to go through it twice. Can you come with us?" Remembering the bodies in the tool room, he added, "You won't have to come far. Hernandez, double-time back and report to Sergeant Ranthar. Tell him he's to bring everybody past the station and get the line to here. Stop them about halfway between the bend and this station. Have them wait for me to send word. When he's got the civilians past the last station, he can do what he likes about the extra food we negotiated, and assume command of the rearguard. Got that?"

"Yes, sir."

"Okay, take off. I want to look over this place before you get back." The Diablo ran down the tunnel.

"Father Dutton," Verkan continued, "tell your man to turn off the light on top of the train. I want to hear what you say when he can't see you."

"Lieutenant," the priest called out, "turn off the light for a moment, please. Not your security lights, just that big one. It's all right."

After a pause, the subway tunnel was dark again except for the area near the train.

"Now, Father," Verkan said, "is it all right up there? Are they holding anyone hostage? If there's anything wrong, for God's sake tell me. We're in a bad way down below and I have to know if it's safe to bring my people up."

"If by all right, you mean can you trust Lieutenant Hart—yes. But, it's not all right. We are low on food and water. The tunnel up ahead is both radioactive and blocked by criminals. The building above the station collapsed and filled the stairs with rubble and part of the station itself fell on us. I have fifteen injured people to care for."

"Yeah," Verkan signed. *This just keeps getting better*, he thought. What's next? "Well, let's go meet your Lieutenant Hart. Stay here, Private Espinoza."

TWENTY-FOUR

I

Lieutenant Hart had been on the subway train when the klaxons sounded. The train had pulled into the station, and many of its passengers ran off it up the stairs. Others from above were trying to get down into the shelter. While Hart was trying to restore order, the bombs fell, destroying the portion of the station near the entrance. The debris that fell when part of the ceiling collapsed had narrowly missed the Lieutenant. As a result, he was left with sixteen men, nine women and four children who were uninjured, and another fifteen people who still lived, and an even larger number of dead. His armament consisted of his police revolver, half a dozen pistols—carried by various men and conductors—and by sheer good luck, a full box of ammunition.

He had found Father Dutton among the litter, stunned but able to function. With the Father's help and some of the others, he had attempted to care for those who had been injured.

The shelter was rated for two hundred people. Its equipment locker was intact, but the food locker had been broken into by

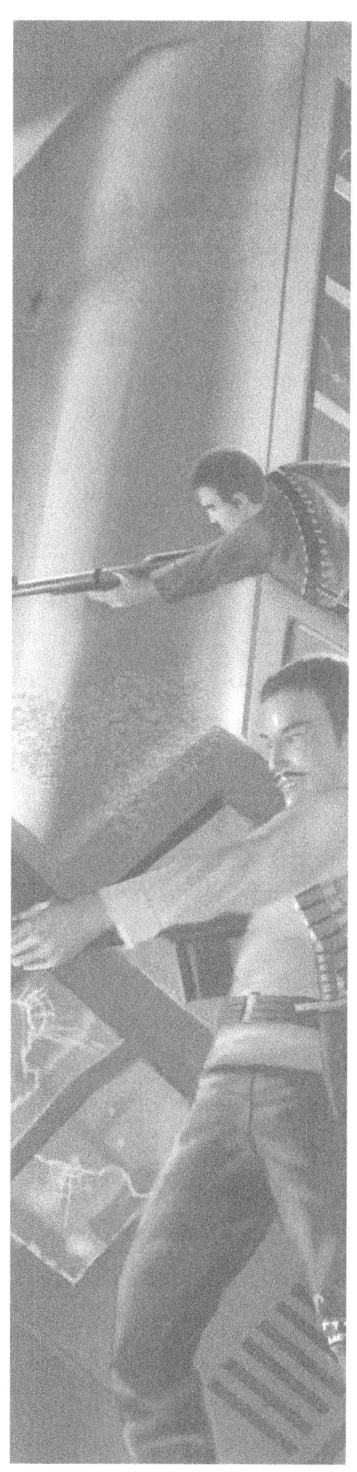

rats, its contents never replaced. Consequently he had batteries for the lighting system. In addition, the train crew were able to rig up lights to operate from the storage batteries on the train, but they had been on short rations from the beginning.

With the transit cop from the train and half a dozen armed men, Hart had held off attacks by the Imperial Lords and the South Brooklyn Boys on the third and fifth days, and had set up the defense system Verkan had noted. The lieutenant allowed Verkan to inspect his inadequate defenses with a resigned air.

He turned to the clergyman, then rubbed his gray eyes. "Father, if this guy's not on the level, we're all dead. Hell, he's not even in uniform. Where are his men?" he asked. The policeman was close to collapse from exhaustion.

"No, Rudolph. If Captain Verkan and his men are not on the level, as you put it, we're dead anyway," the priest answered. "With his force, we may be able to move up the tunnel. He may even have food and water to spare. Without him, what can we do? You asked me to pray for deliverance, are you sure this is not God's answer?"

"Yeah, but…" Hart shook his head sadly. "Did you know any of his men?"

"One of the boys. I remembered him when he was a lad. It's too late to do anything but to trust him, Rudolph. He sent for the rest of his army."

"All right, all right, I'm weary to death of this game, anyway."

He walked over to the big military man. "Captain, since you're here, look around. You'll be able to see everything without me. Please don't disturb my guards in the train." Hart went to a bench and sat, his face buried in his hands.

"The lieutenant has not slept a full night since the bombs fell," Father Dutton told Verkan. "The street gang you just passed have kept four or five men prowling around, just out of pistol range, almost all of the time. Every once in a while they fire on the train. The gang in the station above us sends a scout down to look us over two or three times a day, as well. We don't even know who they are, they won't answer when we call out to them. But, once when we tried to approach them, they fired a shot over our heads. If I had told the lieutenant that you had street gangsters in your army, he would have tried to shoot it out with you right here."

"Aren't you taking a chance, Father? On me?"

"Not really."

"Not you, too," Verkan said. "Are you going to say that Francisco Hernandez, deep underneath, is a nice boy so you can trust him?"

"No, Captain. I was going to say that Francisco has always been an insolent little brat, and any man who had him saying sir and walking with his head up is worthy of respect, if not trust. But you miss my point. Without you, there is no hope at all for any of us."

Verkan was guided by the priest around the station. The men were on guard in the subway train itself. The conductor-engineer of the train nodded when Verkan was introduced, then went back to his post, staring up the tunnel. The Transit Authority policeman, a tall man in his early thirties, smiled pleasantly and shook Verkan's hand.

"I'm George Wykowski," he said pleasantly. He was still wearing his special police uniform, his belt laden with handcuffs, nightstick and other implements of his trade. "Do you think you can get us out of here?"

"I hope so, Mr. Wykowski. Can you tell me anything more about what's up ahead of us?"

"No, I can't. I got a look at one of them in the flashlight once, and he didn't look like the street gang type. That station's near the University; there are some pretty tough people who hang around it, you know. Excuse me, Captain, I need to sit down. I'm bushed."

Wykowski sat down on the bench, stretched and said, "Won't you join me? You must be tired, too."

"Thanks. I'll do that, but not for long. If I stay down too long, I may not be able to get back up. If you can hold out, Mr. Wykowski, my sergeant will have the gear to make hot coffee up here in an hour."

A smile broke out on Wykowski's face. "Man, that's the nicest thing I've heard since we've been down here. We haven't had coffee or much of anything else since the bombing. Now, about what's up ahead. You know some of those political parties at the University have what's pretty close to a private army. It might be some of them up the tunnel. Then there's the pushers and dealers who hang around the place. I don't think it's the students; they'd talk to us."

Verkan heard a shout from down the tunnel. "That'll be my sergeant," he told the Transit cop. "Let's go and make sure your guard at the other end of the train doesn't take a shot at him."

II

It seemed to take forever, but finally the lead elements of the Company came into sight. Susan Majors was leading, with the Diablos marching beside her, carrying litters or towing shopping carts. One of them had made up a song to the tune of *When the Saints Come Marching In*, and the Diablos sang it proudly. Half the verses were obscene, and the boys slurred the words only slightly. Behind them, the other women and children carried the other stores. It was a ragged group, but their pride was in sharp contrast to the listless expressions on the faces of Hart's survivors.

Verkan couldn't help but feel proud of his wretched gang of would-be soldiers.

When they reached the station, the Diablos set down their burdens then double-timed back down the tunnel. Sergeant Ranthar came up a few minutes later.

"No incidents, Captain. I didn't want to send anybody up on that platform after the food and stuff, but this guy here volunteered." He indicated one of the prisoners the Company had liberated from the Imperials. The man was dressed in expensive sports clothes, now grimy and ruined. A little blonde girl, perhaps three years old, clutched his hand. "He said they sent him out on the streets two days ago, and he doesn't feel so well. He wants us to take care of her. He removed the supplies from the locker. On his last trip, for good measure, he grabbed up all the rifles he could carry from the dead kids on the platform."

"Has Doc Pearson looked at him yet?" Verkan asked.

"He says there's nothing to see, but if it's as hot on the street above that station, as it was above ours, he's not going to last a week."

"He said that about Eduardo Gonzalez, too."

"Sure, but will this guy have all the volunteers for blood donations El Toro got? He's a lot older, too. Although, he's in decent shape."

"Doc's generally right."

Ranthar waved the man over.

Verkan turned and looked straight into the man's eyes. "You're damn right we'll take care of your little girl."

Doctor Pearson set up his dispensary in one of the cars in the subway train. The girl Mills rescued was his most critical patient, with a bullet lodged just below her lungs. Palua, the wounded Diablo, had been hit in the abdomen, but with a full-jacketed bullet. Pearson thought that if he could keep him quiet for a time he could save him. Baker's shoulder was more easily managed. Verkan saw that his Company was settled comfortably, and went to sleep.

The next morning, Verkan examined the new report on quartermaster stores. They had sixty pounds of rice, forty-five pounds of oats, thirty pounds of soy bean flour and fifty of wheat flour from the Imperials, in addition to a sizable quantity of chocolate and six ten gallon jerry-cans of water. They had also added thirteen new mouths to be fed. Hart's able-bodied and wounded added another thirty-four. Subtracting their casualties, he found that the Company was only slightly better off than it had been with regard to food, and much worse with regard to water. They had to find new sources of food and water within a few days, or the situation would quickly reach critical.

He also had an incipient mutiny situation. Ranthar reported it quietly. "It's Russell, Verkan. Even back at the last station, he was itching to start something, but he saw me watching him and the Diablos stood fast to orders. He's unhappy as hell about leaving those girls as prisoners to that street gang. The father of one of those girls is going around the Company right now talking up how we ought to go back and wipe out those kids. Couple of mothers want their girls saved, as well."

"Just what we needed," Verkan said flatly. "A mutiny. And now we have these new civilians, Hart's people and my Company all mixed up together, and it won't be possible to keep the Company away from the others. Let's go see Lieutenant Hart."

The lieutenant was in much better shape after his first night's sleep in a week. Verkan, Ranthar, Pearson and Hart used an hour inspecting resources, human and material, available to them. Verkan took this opportunity to explain the actual nature of the Company to Hart. After the inspection tour, they returned to a section of one of the train cars, which the Diablos had screened off as Verkan's orderly room. A Diablo stood guard outside the entrance, saluting as Verkan and Hart entered. Coffee was brought by another Diablo within moments of their arrival.

"How many of those kids do you have?" Hart asked. "They look pretty handy to have around."

"I have thirty-two of them. Diablo Espinoza is missing one hand, Corporal Gonzalez is on the disabled list and Diablo Palua will be out of action for a while. They're my shock troops." Verkan lit his pipe. Looking in the pouch, he estimated two more bowls to go. "Go on, have your coffee, Lieutenant."

"It's not fair to the others," Hart said. "I had my water ration for the morning."

"The amount of water consumed by having a cup of coffee is insignificant. Having or not having it won't affect when we run out by minutes, much less hours. Suit yourself, but if you don't want it, I'll drink it myself.

Verkan leaned back and sipped the hot coffee. "These train seats are much more comfortable than what I had back at the last station."

Hart attempted to copy Verkan, stretching his leg in from of him and tasting the coffee, but he was unable to do so. He sat very straight and turned gray eyes at him. "Look, Captain. You're right about this being a different world from what it was a week ago, and maybe you've got the best way for facing it. But I'm a cop. I've been a cop all my life. If there's anything left of city government, I work for it. I'm too old to change outfits. Can my people be allies with yours? We can decide what to do on a permanent basis when we get out of this tunnel."

"What kind of alliance do you have in mind?" Verkan asked. "I can't have you pulling one way, while we go another. I can't have you interfering with my internal administration, either. I may have to shoot someone for disciplinary reasons. What does your cop instinct say about that?"

"I'll worry about that when the time comes. Look, Captain, we can agree that if your people don't bother mine, mine won't bother yours. Mine get in your way, I'll handle them. And if I don't like where you're taking us, we quit on the spot."

"You understand that our regulations must be reasonably uniform," Verkan said. "I cannot afford a great contrast. We can see how this alliance works out. I don't see what else we could do anyway. I can't and won't conscript people into the Company. One thing, though: don't quit and then do something hostile."

"Yeah, I've got better sense than that. Is it a deal?"

"For now," Verkan replied. *This organization of mine is getting completely out of hand,* he thought. *But, Ranthar and I can't make it alone, so we need their help. Until we don't.*

Verkan raised his voice. "Sentry!"

The response was immediate. The Diablo entered, his rifle ready, saw the two men seated relaxed with coffee, and came to attention.

"Sir."

"Send Marie with more coffee, please."

"Yes, sir." The Diablo saluted, received a response and marched out the door.

"What was all that about?" Hart asked.

"I merely wanted you to witness something. As stated before, don't quit me and do something hostile." Verkan smiled at him. "I may have an overly developed sense of the dramatic, Lieutenant, but I do like my allies to know where they stand."

"It's impressive as hell, Captain, I agree to that. The Diablos were outside my precinct, but I've heard of them. I sure as hell would like to know how you can turn them into fine upstanding citizens."

"They're hardly that. They are soldiers. The military has been making good soldiers out of thugs and barbarians like them for five thousand years. They can't be made into citizens; they aren't civilized, and won't be. Your

Mister Wykowski is a citizen. So are you. For all your copying of military procedure in police regulations, you still deal with a different kind of person than a soldier."

Marie brought in the coffee. "Anything else, Captain?" she asked. When Verkan said there was not, she saluted and marched out as crisply as had the sentry.

Hart noted that she wore a small pistol on her belt.

The lieutenant regarded his second cup of coffee for some time before he drank it. "Things are pretty desperate, Captain. How long do you figure we can feed this motley group?"

"Three days on short rations. We are also down to about that on water. If we don't get out of here pretty soon, we're in trouble."

Hart nodded. "Well, with your army I think we can make it. Up ahead we've got troubles. Maybe it's a street gang, maybe they're crooks—but it's trouble. They heard that gunfight last night and are going to be on guard. We have to get through the station they hold, and we have to do it fast. I think I have a way."

Verkan's eyes filled with interest. "How?" he asked.

"You got any cigarettes? Thanks, I haven't had one in a week." Hart sat back, enjoying the cigarette and coffee. Verkan watched him intently, but said nothing. "Okay, Captain, it's like this. About fifty yards ahead here that tunnel starts downhill, and it runs downhill past the next eight or nine stations. That's roughly three, maybe four, miles. The stations are spread farther apart the further away from downtown we go. Then the tunnel flattens out for another two miles, and there's one more station. Just past that, the tunnel breaks out. The track goes on for another mile and a half over a bridge before there's more tunnel. If your people can help push this car off this train for fifty yards, I think it will roll all the way to the outside. It'll sure as hell get us to a mile from the end."

"How steep is this grade?"

"Enough to keep a car moving, I'm pretty sure. I had to chase a guy up it on foot one time, and you notice it. Leads down to the river where the bridge is."

"Think the crew up ahead have blocked the track?" Verkan asked.

"I don't know. If they haven't, we can roll right past them before they know what's happening. If they have blocked it, well, you got a pretty damn big army and a lot of guns."

Verkan leaned back and closed his eyes. *In seven or eight miles*, he thought, *the radiation ought to have abated quite a lot. Perhaps enough that we can survive outside*. It was upwind from the downtown areas that were hardest hit. Since he had no way of knowing whether the bombs were ground or air burst, he could not estimate what damage the area at the end of the tunnel might have suffered. It was possible that some food supplies could be had there. Certainly, more than they had here.

"Yes, Lieutenant Hart, I think you've got a plan. All right, let's get the crew together and get this stuff packed up to roll. We can move on out in four hours."

"Cutting it close, aren't you?" Hart asked.

"No point in staying here. I'd rather be where there are some knobs to twist while we still have food left. There's nothing to be accomplished here." He raised his voice again. "Sentry, pass the word for Sergeant Ranthar."

Hart left to explain the new relationship to his group as Ranthar entered.

"Sergeant," Verkan ordered. "Assemble the Company."

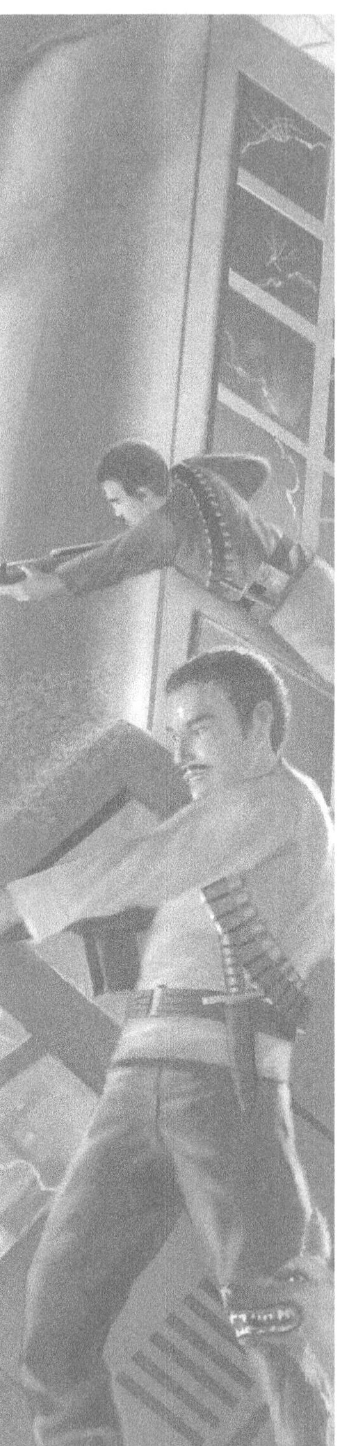

TWENTY-FIVE

I

Ranthar assembled the civilians and armed men as best he could. The Diablos stood rigidly at attention, rifles grounded, along one side of the group. Baker, Mills, Guliksen and the other troops standing somewhat less formally in the center. Susan Majors and the noncombatants of the Company were grouped together, while the newly freed civilians from the last station milled about despite Ranthar's attempts to keep them still.

Eduardo Gonzalez sat on his litter with the women. The other disabled and injured were installed in the railway car Pearson had converted into his sick bay. Verkan noted that Ranthar stood facing the assembled group, his rifle cradled in his arms.

Some of the other civilians were speaking rapidly to each other.

"At ease," he told the group. "I have news for you. It's that we may see daylight at the end of the tunnel system by tomorrow noon. Perhaps much earlier than that, if all goes well." He paused to let that sink in. "However, before we get out of here, we'll have to fight our way past the next station up the line.

"There are seven or eight more stations after that one about which we know nothing. But we won't be fighting on foot, we'll roll past them in a car from the subway train. Lieutenant Hart says it's downhill all the way."

Excited whispers broke out among the civilians. David Mills looked around at his wife and grinned wildly.

Then a woman shouted, "What about my Miriam? She's back there with those criminals. Are you going to leave without her? Do you know what they're making her do?"

Bob Russell shouted, "She's right. We can't abandon those girls. Who's with me to go get them out?"

"Ten-shun!" Ranthar shouted. "I trained you lot, now show it!"

Verkan spoke quietly. "Madam, I'm afraid that we have to leave her with them. Her captors are now alerted, and I do not have the force to fight them now that they are on guard. I could lose half my Company. At best, we would have to use bombs to flush them out of their strong rooms, and that would be as likely to kill the girls they hold prisoner, as it would the enemy. I can't even starve them out; they have more food than we do."

His speech failed to quiet the woman. The man who had seized Verkan's shirt the night before was also shouting. Lieutenant Hart came up and stood with the civilians. Russell began to speak loudly. "We can't just abandon those girls. We *have* to do something. You're the military expert, Captain Verkan, it's up to you. You've got to do something!"

"Diablos, right face!" Sergeant Ranthar commanded. "Left oblique, march." He halted them in the space between Verkan and the assembled Company. "Right face. Port, arms." The Diablos now stood facing the milling group, their rifles held across their chests.

"BY DAMN, SHUT UP!" Ranthar ordered.

The grim faces of the Diablos quieted the group as much as Ranthar's command. "Next man that talks out of turn is under arrest," Ranthar said. "Captain, the Company is formed."

"There is nothing I can do," Verkan said. "They may not outnumber us as a combat force, but we'd have to dig them out of their strongholds. I doubt if the bomb in the washroom killed many of them, since it was not made with shrapnel. They are alerted, they have a strong defensive position and more supplies than we have. Our job is to get out of this tunnel, and that is what we will do. Sergeant, assign the Company to packing gear and get the train ready to roll. Private Russell, come with me."

II

Back in the orderly room inside the train, Russell stood at attention before Verkan's desk. A Diablo stood outside as sentry.

"Private Russell," Verkan began coldly, "I only partly regret that we did not shoot you out of hand as an example to the others. Then I would not have the problem of what to do with you. By the way, if you put your hand on that pistol at your belt, you're a dead man."

"You have no right!" Russell protested.

"I have every right. You freely joined this Company. Now you are attempting sedition. I haven't charged you with anything more than talking in the ranks, yet, but you could easily manage something more serious."

"But you're wrong, Captain," Russell said. "You don't just leave those girls to those savages while their mothers cry. It's not human! You just can't do it."

"Damn it, man. Can't you get it through your skull that I have no choice whatsoever. Look, would you like to go up there alone and try to get them out?"

"It would do no good. Besides, I wouldn't be alone."

"Exactly. It would do no good, and you would drag some of my Company with you into a completely futile death. Private Russell, get this. I have a limited number of combat troops. I have an unknown number of hostiles ahead of me. My mission is clear, I have to get the Company and its dependents out of here. If I let part of my force get killed on this stupid errand, I may not be able to complete the primary mission. Do I have to shoot you to make it clear?"

"No, sir."

"Turn in your weapon. Right here, lay it on the bench. Now, Private Russell, you are on latrine duty until I take you off. You will go tell Ranthar that any miserable job he has that needs to be done, you are to do. If I catch you whispering to either the civilians or my troops, I will shoot you down on the spot. Is that clear?"

There was no answer.

"Is that understood, Private?"

"YES, SIR."

"Then get out of here." Verkan followed the man out of the train.

Outside, the Company was repacking its gear. Verkan went to find the train crewmen to discuss the use of the car for their exodus. In the station, Ranthar was shouting orders.

III

Susan Majors found him back in the orderly room. "I have the sick room report, Captain," she told him. "That girl you rescued last night has never been conscious. Someone told us her name was Lynn, but that's all anybody knew about her. She wasn't pretty enough for one of the gang members to adopt her as his regular girl, but apparently several of them used her."

Susan was as matter of fact in her report of this as she had been about the food and water supplies.

"Diablo Palua will recover, we think, but he won't be fit for duty for weeks. Corporal Baker has been returned to light duty, but Dr. Pearson says to take it easy on him."

Verkan nodded. "Thank you, Miss Majors. How are Lieutenant Hart's people?"

"Bad. Oh, I could tell you about Mrs. Gocka, and little Johnny Rafferty, and all the others, but mostly it's just bad. They had two weeks to get as many of them well as they could, Captain. The ones who were disabled are not likely to recover without special facilities. Broken backs, legs not set properly, some need traction but we don't have it. Oh, Verkan, it is bad."

She sat for a moment, struggling with herself. "What will it be like ahead?" she asked more calmly.

"From what Hart told me, I'd say our chances are fair. The first problem is whether or not those yahoos down the line are stronger than we think, or have the track blocked off. If they don't, we blow right past them without their knowing what happened."

She nodded. "And you're going to just go and leave those girls in the last station."

"You, too?" Verkan stood, hoping to terminate the conversation.

"Oh, sit down, Captain Verkan; not me, too. If you say there's nothing to be done, then there's nothing to be done. I've learned a lot about myself and about women in the last few weeks. We aren't like men. We can adjust to anything. Those girls have men. If they're any use as women, they'll be taken care of. I don't want any of our men killed on their account. Isn't that horrible? My sociology professor would disown me if he heard me talk like that."

Verkan returned to his seat. "It doesn't sound much like what you've said to me before," he admitted.

"The world has shrunk a lot down here," she said. "I find myself concerned with basic things, and not much else. I guess most women are more oriented to pure survival when it comes right down to it."

Susan smiled at him. "It's a lot nicer to be friends with you, anyway. I said some pretty horrid things, didn't I?"

"Nothing I didn't expect. You come from a different world than mine, Miss Majors. Probably a lot nicer world to live in than mine."

"But it's all your kind of world, now," she replied. "I guess the rest of us had better start getting used to it." She looked at him again, more intently, making Verkan nervously shift his weight. "Your Sergeant tells me that you are here to rescue your wife."

Back on safe territory, Verkan relaxed. "Yes, Dalla. She's in a small town upstate. I was on my way to meet her when all hell broke loose."

"Well, I hope she's safe, but if she isn't...."

Verkan squirmed on his seat. "Dalla's a survivor, believe me. She's been in worse jams than this one and has come out smelling like a rose, to use an old cliché."

Susan nodded her head. "We'll see. I told you women look at things differently. We're adaptive and can get pretty *real* when we have to. Now I'd better get back to the packing, I want to know where they stow everything. I'm having my people make lists of where everything is so one of us can find it when we need it. We have quite a lot of equipment that was in this station, and I don't think Lieutenant Hart will need all of it."

She stood. When Verkan said nothing, she laughed. "I do believe I've frightened the great warrior. See you later." She left, still laughing.

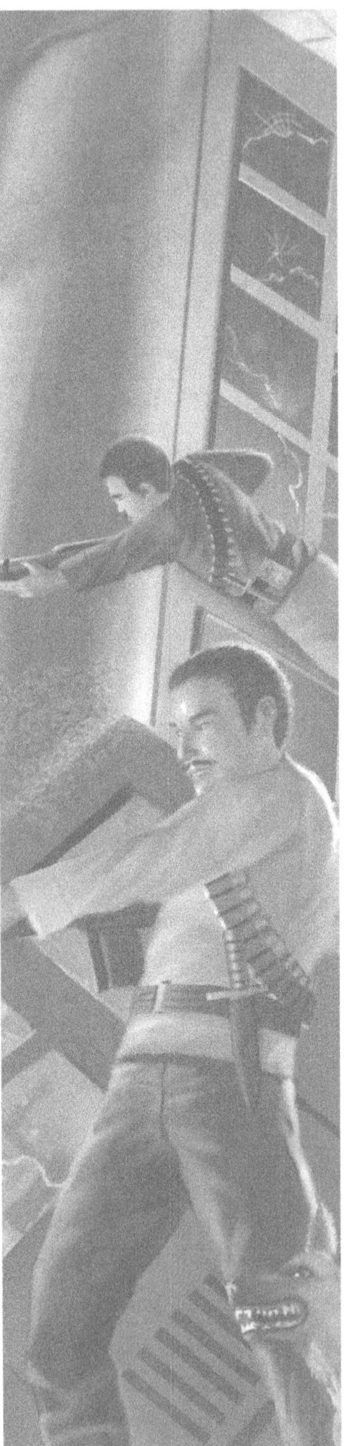

TWENTY-SIX

I

"We're about to roll, sir," Ranthar reported. "I've got the women assigned to places under the seats. I've got the doors and most of the sides of the rear car near the back so we can get in and out if we have to, leaving four thicknesses of junk and seats as a rail along the back to duck behind, and I've got benches out of the station piled in front of the car. It isn't a tank, but it'll do."

"Water and stores all protected?" Verkan asked.

"Yes, sir. I'm having trouble getting that priest to take a station under a seat, though. Says he'll help us push."

"I'll see Hart about that. We may need a priest before the day is over. Okay, get all the walking wounded that can carry arms up in front of the car to watch out ahead. Load them up, Jard. Let's get this thing, whatever it is, on the road."

"Yes, sir."

"By the way, how are you planning to stop it?"

"There's a hand wheel on the rear deck, sir. A little exposed, but I've got junk piled around it best I can."

"Right. Let's go."

When the train was loaded, the men and younger women pushed. It moved slowly at first, then began to creep along, everyone straining to move it to the sloping part of the track. There was no sign of the enemy as they strained and cursed to push the car. Someone began to sing. Others took up the refrain as the car began to pick up speed. They reached the downhill stretch, and the women and children were shoved aboard, the men pushing, walking along, pacing faster, faster.

Ranthar called cadence: "Hup, two, three, four, hup, two, three, four, hup, two, three, four, hup two-three-four, hup two three four, hup-two three four, double-time hoah, hit, hut, hit, haw…"

"All but the afterguard get aboard!" Verkan shouted. "Women take your places. Get down. You, too, Father. Battle stations…sounds like a navy. Anybody know a sea chantey?"

One of the men sang *What Will We Do With a Drunken Sailor* in time with the pace of those still running. Verkan heard a girl's voice join in, lilting, exuberant. It was Susan Majors, he realized.

The afterguard clambered aboard the rear deck. Verkan and Ranthar followed them, and he made his way through the packed aisle to the forward end of the car. After a few minutes, he thought he could just see lights ahead. Behind him the sea chantey continued, and he thought momentarily of calling for silence, but decided against it. All the troops were aboard now.

"Baker, that you on the spot?" Verkan asked.

"Yes, sir."

"Get ready to throw in one. Hold it, hold it….OKAY, NOW!"

The light lit up the tunnel ahead. A hundred yards away they could see the station, its lighted platform in contrast to the gray light in the tunnel itself. Outside it would be midafternoon. Some kind of barricade was set up on the tracks, but it did not appear substantial.

A shot was fired from ahead, then another, then a third. Verkan heard bullets strike the bench armor Ranthar had placed in front of the car. The forward wheels of the car struck the barricade. The air was rent with the sound of wood being crashed and splintered. Then a screeching noise that hurt his ears. The car began to move slower, perceptibly slowing....

"We're dragging something, Captain," Ranthar called. "Afterguard, over the side." Ranthar and his crew jumped off the platform. As they did, the bow gunners fired into the darkness. Verkan couldn't see any targets, but he heard sharp screams and shots from the station. Baker swiveled his light about wildly, searching for something for the gunners to shoot. As he did, the lights on the platform went out.

A spotlight appeared from one corner of the station and swept over the railcar. It outlined Ranthar and his sweating crew reaching under the wheels of the car to pull something away before half a dozen riflemen shot it out. More flashes came from the platform, and the bow gunners fired back.

They were three-quarters through the station, but the car had slowed to a walking pace. Verkan heard Ranthar curse, then heard a scream.

Ranthar shouted, "Goddamn thing's caught on the other side, too."

Firing continued, and Verkan took aim at the flash from his right, firing his pistol at it.

"Got it!" he heard from behind. It was Mill's voice, tinged with pain, but a note of triumph sounding through.

"Ranthar!" Verkan called. There was no answer. Verkan clambered over the benches, stepping on the huddled forms of women and children in his haste to get to the after end of the car. As he did, he heard El Toro shout, "Get the Sergeant, Diablos!"

More men jumped from the train. It seemed pitch-dark now, everyone's eyes were dazzled by the spotlights which had played about the station.

Pearson shouted, "You can't go out there!"

"Like hell, I can't, Doc," El Toro said. The car was no longer slowing noticeably, but it was not moving very fast.

"Over the side! Push you bastards!" Verkan ordered. He shook his head momentarily to clear it. No time to worry about Ranthar. He found his way blocked by someone, roughly heaved her aside to get to the rear of the car. People were everywhere.

Shots rang out.

Then he heard El Toro shout, "That's it, heave him aboard. Now push like hell, come on you sonsabitches, push. Hup, do, tree, four, hup-tow-three-four hup" the voice stopped in mid-count.

"We're moving," a girl's voice cried out. "We're past 'em!"

Verkan reached the end of the car. It had picked up more speed, moved faster all the time. He cursed as he realized that the track would have been level in the station proper, cursed himself for not thinking of it earlier. "Okay, everyone aboard," he ordered. "Who got left behind? Ranthar, report!"

There was no answer. Verkan felt someone standing beside him, realized it was Joey. Their eyes were again adjusting to the low light.

"El Toro got left, Captain," Fish stood stiffly. "He got hit smack in the head. He was tryin' to get the sergeant on the car."

"Is Sergeant Ranthar dead, too?"

"Don't know, sir. El Toro got Ricardo and me to throw the sergeant aboard. He was hit, and Toro stood in the back of the car and pulled him in. Then he started to count, and they shot him off the train."

"Afterguard!" Verkan called crisply. "Mills?"

"On board, sir. I lost two fingers under the train."

"Hernandez?"

"On board, sir."

"Kelsey?"

"On board, sir."

"Reardon"

"On board, sir."

Verkan continued to call the roll. Everyone was aboard. Finally he said, "Ranthar?"

"I have him, Captain," Dr. Pearson said. "He's out cold. I can't see what's wrong with him in this light. Pulse is strong, anyway."

"How many wounded, Doc?"

"Don't know, sir," Pearson answered. "Not many."

They had gone through the station—Verkan found out later from Susan Majors—in less than forty seconds total. It had seemed like hours.

"Rig a light for Doc," Verkan ordered. "Screen it with blankets so that it won't blind the rest of us. Corporal Fish, take over the afterguard. I'm going forward again."

II

The next station was deserted. The light revealed a score of bodies draped around it; none of them moving. As they approached it, Baker looked at his radiation meter, hit it lightly—and looked again. "Hot as hell," he announced. "We're lucky we're moving through it so fast. About as bad as the ventilators were a week ago."

"Read out," Verkan ordered.

"High, high, falling a little, steady, steady, falling again...now, back to tunnel normal, steady, steady—"

"That's enough," Verkan interrupted.

"Yes, sir." Baker replied. "It could be just this station. Maybe a bomb went off overhead? A leak in the waterproofing? Runoff from drains pooled there and soaked in?"

"I don't know," Verkan admitted. "But if it's still that high, what's it like outside?" The end of the tunnel is only three, no, three and a half miles from here. Baker, you better hope that was just a pocket, something freakish, or we're not going outside for a damn long while."

TWENTY-SEVEN

I

The car rolled on, making approximately nine to ten miles an hour down the tunnel. There were more lights ahead, as they approached the next station. Verkan stared ahead intently. There were no obstructions on the track.

"Radiation level?" he asked Baker.

"High but lower. It's been falling a tad all the way since the last station, not enough to report, but it's down a little." Baker put down the counter and turned to his spotlight.

"Just hang on to the spot for a minute," Verkan said. "They can see us coming but there's no point to giving them a target."

He raised his voice, "All troops, stand by. Battle stations. Here we come."

They rolled into the lighted area of the station. Thirty or more people were on the platform, lined up for food which was being served from a kettle on the cook stove. Someone shouted and everyone turned toward the train. There were children in the line, and one of them waved at the car. Verkan saw no hostile movements.

The car streaked thought the station, slowed for a moment, then began picking up speed as it got back to the incline. Just beyond the station, a group of men stood in the tunnel itself. They carried rifles. As the train passed by, one shouted, "Who the hell?"

They rolled on, gaining speed. Baker returned to the Geiger counter, saying, "Falling, maybe just a tad more. It's under the yearly safe dosage they got marked on here—yeah, I'm sure it's falling…"

Verkan wanted to discuss their situation with someone, but Ranthar was still unconscious and Dr. Pearson was busy with David Mills' hand. He found himself standing next to Susan Majors.

"I think your friend is all right," she said. "He seems to have been struck in the head with a piece of wood when they pulled it from under the train wheels. He has a definite concussion, but Dr. Pearson doesn't think the skull was broken. He may have headaches for a couple of weeks, but I believe he's going to be all right."

"Thanks," Verkan said. "That helps."

"There's something else, isn't there?" she asked.

"That last station. They had guards posted on the downhill side. There wouldn't be much point in guarding the uphill side since the station above them was contaminated, but I'm wondering what they were guarding against. For that matter, why haven't they tried to leave the tunnel? It's not very far to the next station."

Verkan peered ahead, down the station, but couldn't see far in the dim light. It seemed to be getting darker, he noticed.

The subway car rolled on, the grade getting less and less steep until it finally leveled out. The train continued to coast along, slowing more and more.

"Get that light on, Baker, and watch your meter. Afterguard, over the side. Keep this car moving as long as you can."

He started to make his way forward. "Take care of Jard for me," he told the girl.

The afterguard, then other able-bodied men, finally the women as well, piled out and pushed the railcar along. The sea chantey rose again, and after it was finished, the Diablo's song, the words modified now and less suggestive. The Company was in good spirits despite the loss of Corporal Gonzalez. Only Marie cried softly as she trotted alongside, pushing the train.

The bow lights blazed through the darkened tunnel, showing nothing ahead. When they were close to the next station, at the end of the tunnel, the train ground to a halt.

"Radiation still low?" Verkan asked.

"Yes, sir, fallen maybe a little more. Definitely under the yearly tolerable dose."

"Okay, Baker. Bring your box. Corporal Fish, assemble the Diablos. Lieutenant Hart, can you come with me, please?"

Verkan climbed down from the car. With the bow lights off, he peered down the tunnel, but could see nothing. There were few ventilators in this region, or those there had lightproof baffles, for there was no light except from the car. It was very still and a little damp in the tunnel.

"Where the hell are we, Hart?" Verkan asked. "I think we came a long way for only three miles."

"I'd agree, Captain. I'm trying to think of where we might be. It only makes sense that we'd see the light at the tunnel's end."

Verkan went back to the train, asking, "Does anyone here know anything about the track layout in this area?"

George Wykowski came forth. "I've been down this line a number of times."

"Good. Come with us, George."

The three men with two Diablos started their march toward the outside. Pearson was left in charge of the car, with those not in the search party standing guard behind the train. They walked in silence, the illumination coming from a dim flashlight held by Verkan.

He counted his steps as they moved through the dark. He estimated eight hundred yards, when the tunnel took a sharp bend to the left and started downhill again.

"What the hell?" he asked.

"I know," George said from behind him. "There's a switch in the track, Captain. It's back there just after the last station we passed. The line runs off along the river and then starts down into the tunnel under it. I don't know how we got on it, but we're on the interurban track."

"And where does that come out?"

"In a shopping center just the other side of the river. It's, oh—two miles from here. You have to go under the river to get there."

"And our car's eight hundred yards back," Verkan said. "We'll never push it this far. Or could we?"

"Hard enough pushing it fifty yards, Captain," Hart reminded him. "Think what it would be to do it sixteen times that far."

"Oh, no sir," George Wykowski interjected. "You can't feel it, but that track must be going downhill all the way. It wasn't so hard pushing it when it stopped, was it? It didn't seem so to me."

Verkan shined his light down the tunnel. "Do you suppose the structure is intact? I'd hate to push this thing and then find water blocking our way. Still, no point in standing here. Wykowski, take a light and run down that tunnel. Count two thousand paces before you start back, and see if the tunnel looks all right to you."

"Yes, sir." Wykowski trotted off down the tunnel, his light swinging rhythmically as Verkan and the others walked back to the car. As they drew closer, they could see its lights.

"Now, see, Captain," Hart said. "Doesn't the car look to be above us? I'm sure it's downhill from here."

"Could be," Verkan admitted. "Not a lot of grade, but I guess you're right. I don't want to go back if I can help it. Coming out in Bakerville makes a lot of sense. It's not so far to less populated areas. The sooner we're away from New York City, the better I'll feel. What about you, Hart?"

"I've been thinking about that while we were talking. If you don't mind, I think I'll take those who want to go with me and go back up the tunnel to where we intended to come out. That crowd in the last station we passed didn't look wild, either. So, if we can't get out, maybe we could share with them."

They had reached the railcar, and everyone crowded around them to ask what happened. A trio of Diablos were singing a popular song—*Wee-ooh wim-o-weh. Wee-ooh wim-o-weh. Wim-o-weh o-wim-o-weh o-wim-o-weh o-wim-o-weh. O-wim-o-weh o-wim-o-weh o-wim-weh. Wim-o-weh o-wim-o-weh o-wim-o-weh o-wim-o-weh O-wim-o-weh o-wim-o-weh o-wim-weh*—while others were beating time on the sides of the train.

"Did you see the sunlight?" one of the women asked.

The air of excitement faded as Verkan told them the situation, but did not die completely away. While the others were milling around, Verkan called Father Dutton, Lieutenant Hart and Dr. Pearson away from the car.

"How many of the group from the lieutenant's station can walk?" he asked.

"Of the injured? Not many," Pearson replied. "He has at least twelve that will have to be carried."

"Yeah. Now, how many are going with you that can carry them on makeshift litters? And what are we going to do with the rest? I think trying to tote them a mile of steep grade from under the river, not knowing what we'll find at the other end, is more than I bargained for. You may have to stick with us to carry your injured. Sure you want to stay behind?"

"Let's see what the others say, Captain Verkan. Now that there's a chance of safety, some of your company may want to split off."

"True enough. What about you, Doc?"

"I'm with your Company. The only thing that matters with me now is Jimmy, and you'll take better care of him than anyone else."

"Father Dutton?"

"I have no choice. My parish is back there. If there is anyone left alive, they'll need me. I can't leave without finding out."

They assembled the others. "Decision time, again," Verkan told them. "Lieutenant Hart intends to take a group back up the tunnel. He believes that the people back at the last station will be friendly, if he can't get out at the other end of the tunnel. I'm inclined to agree with him, but we don't know how they are set with rations. My plan has always been to leave the city, and directly ahead is the shortest route. Those of you who want to go with Hart, Verkan's Company wishes you the best of luck. Now, who's with me?"

"Do we know anything at all about what's ahead at the end of the tunnel, Captain?" David Mills asked.

"Not a thing," Verkan replied. "All I know is that it is further from the detonation zones, so there will be less fallout. Or I hope there will be less. It may even be in another fallout pattern entirely, but I doubt it."

There was more excited murmuring from the group.

"You people decide for yourselves. I'll be over here. Those that want to stay with the Company can come see me." He walked a ways down the tunnel, followed by Corporal Joey Fish.

"How many you think will be with us, Cap'n?" he asked.

II

It took nearly an hour to sort them out. All of Hart's original group, except George Wykowski, elected to go back. In addition, the liberated prisoners from the Imperial Lords station, as well as a few of the original Company, drifted off. Bob Russell went from family to family, persuading many to return with Lieutenant Hart.

There was never any question about the Diablos or David Mills and his family. Baker was surprised he was even asked, and Guliksen took only a few moments to make up his mind. Verkan was even more surprised when George Farris, Russell's companion in the aborted attempt to try the Diablos, elected to stay with the Company.

Betty Fuller and her eight year-old daughter asked Verkan, "Can we stay with you? I've never had to decide anything important without Ronald, and now that he's dead...." She was close to tears, clutching the child's hand and looking up at Verkan.

"Mrs. Fuller, you've earned the right to stay with the Company, as long as there is one. But are you sure you'd rather be with us? It might be safer with Lieutenant Hart."

"I don't know. I can't decide things like that. What do you want me to do?"

Verkan thought for a moment. His original plan had been to leave the city so that he could rescue Dalla. Not knowing how much of the city still stood, nor what conditions were like in the rural area he was headed for, made it impossible for him to predict what conditions might be like outside the tunnels. Regardless, he didn't think they would be good for a young widow who couldn't make up her mind. "Go with the Lieutenant, Mrs. Fuller," he told her. "Go help her pack," he told one of the others.

Some elected to remain with the Company. When they had sorted themselves out, he found that he had twenty-two able-bodied Diablos, counting Espinoza as able-bodied, in addition to Palua in sick bay and Marie. He had six other men, five with families, Dr. Pearson and Jimmy, Mrs. Fuller and several children. Ranthar had not yet regained consciousness. The rest were set to go with Hart.

There would be more than enough to carry Hart's wounded and injured. The Company would have little trouble taking care of its own.

It was also agreed that Hart's group would help get the car moving down the track until they reached a definite grade. Those unable to help would remain behind until Hart's men could come back for them.

It took another hour to unload everyone from the car, frame litters for the injured and pack the food and equipment Hart's group would take with them. Verkan fashioned carrying litters for his own wounded and loaded his gear into packs and the shopping carts to save time when the car came to a halt, somewhere under the Hudson River. Hernandez reported that the tunnel was still intact, although there was perhaps six inches of water in its lowest point. Verkan and Wykowski decided this was normal seepage which would stand now that the tunnel was no longer being pumped daily. Eventually, it would fill up with water.

With everyone pushing, and the much lighter load inside, the car was set moving more easily than before. They strode alongside it, but there was no singing. The party had taken on a somber air. Verkan saw Susan at the rear of the car, pushing with both hands, a Diablo to each side. She had not asked to stay with the Company.

Within two hundred yards, the grade was noticeable. The car rolled along with little effort from those pushing, and Verkan climbed aboard. From the rear deck he waved to Hart. "Good luck!" he called out.

Father Dutton raised his hand in blessing, and Verkan turned and made his way forward into the car. There would be no goodbyes. Hart's party dropped behind, and the Company women, then men and finally the afterguard swung aboard. They were on their way.

PART THREE

TWENTY-EIGHT

I

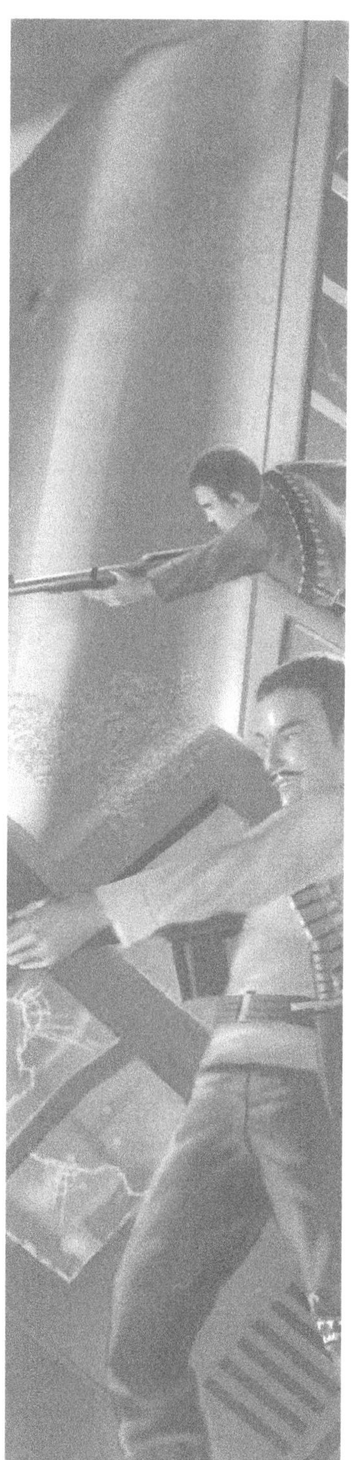

The tunnel slanted down sharply after they rounded the bend. The train picked up speed, moving faster than anyone could run for long. The air became damper and the last dim traces of daylight vanished. Baker's searchlight stabbed before them, tracing rough stone walls, then glinting off a pool of water ahead. The walls were wet on either side now. The radiation monitor showed no perceptible count as the car moved under the river itself.

"When we hit the water, she'll slow down," Verkan shouted. "I want everybody able to push off this thing as soon as it slows down enough to keep up with. Keep it moving as far up the other side as you can."

"Aye, aye, sir," Corporal Fish shouted from the other end of the car, producing the first laughter since the group split up.

"What's the gloom?" Mills asked. "Verkan's Company is on the move. Who'll join me for a cheer. Hip hip hurrah, hip hip!"

Others joined in. Just after the last HURRAH echoed through the tunnel, they struck water. “Over the side, you sonsabitches,” Fish ordered. “Push!”

Verkan stayed with Baker and Diablo Espinoza in the bow of the train, searching ahead. Behind them, the Company splashed in the water, shouting now, some laughing.

“Hey, Hernandez, did you say six inches?” somebody yelled. “I’m up to my knees.”

“You always did have short legs, Farris,” Fish shouted. “Push harder!”

The car moved through the last of the water, starting up the other side, slowing now. The grade was quite steep.

“Man the handbrake!” Verkan ordered.

The car moved slower, slower, despite Fish’s shouted oaths. Finally it halted and two Diablos turned the handwheel frantically. It was very still and humid in the tunnel.

“Well, that’s it,” Verkan told them. “From here on it is Shank’s Mare. No use standing around discussing it.”

II

Corporal Fish and his Diablos led off, their rifles held ready. Baker walked behind them, the Geiger counter clutched to his chest and a pistol in his good hand. Verkan was next to him, listening to the whispered reports. “Going up a little, Captain. Still within lifetime tolerable.”

The rest of the combat force marched behind Verkan and Baker, some of them burdened with the Company’s wounded. Ranthar was still deathly still on his litter. When Verkan asked Dr. Pearson what he could do, he was told that there was nothing to be done. No operation seemed required and without full facilities nothing would be possible. For Verkan it was the worst of all possible situations for a Paratimer: he was stranded on a primitive world without adequate medical aid to help his friend and valued cohort.

“The Sergeant is a strong, healthy man,” Pearson said. “He’ll heal or he won’t, but there’s nothing more I can do for him.”

They moved in silence. With part of the combat party burdened with wounded, there was no question of moving without lights, although he would have preferred to do so. Up and up they went, the air drying a little now and not so clammy. The stone walls of the tunnel replaced with plasti-tile, Moorish-looking mosaics catching the light of flashlights and the lantern.

Then, far ahead, they could see a small point of light. Everyone sped up and the chatter grew louder. As they moved ahead, the light grew brighter, becoming a definite disc, a circle. The black of the tunnel interior became gray, brighter, until they could see color.

Whispering instructions, the combat force turned their burdens over to Doctor Pearson and the women, then moved ahead faster, soon outdistancing them.

"Count's up a little, sir," Baker noted. "But still not up to year tolerable. That's daylight up there. Real sunlight. God, I'm white as a slug."

Verkan waved the column behind him to a halt, moved cautiously with the combat force. Fish's Diablos fanned out to either side of the tunnel. There was no sound from up ahead.

They reached the tunnel mouth. Ahead were platforms on either side, lined with shops and stores, an underground concourse. Above them light streamed through a jagged hole in the girder roof.

A bird flew up from the station floor, its wings beating thunder in the empty concourse. There was a muffled cheer from those in the Company close enough to witness it.

Broken glass was liberally strewn on the station floor. Still searching the barren chamber, Verkan motioned Baker to the tunnel entrance.

The counter clicked rapidly, subsiding as Baker changed the scale. "Not too bad, Captain," he announced. "You wouldn't want to live in it, but it's safe out there for a few hours. We could go look around if you want to, but I'd better come along to watch out for hot spots."

Verkan nodded in accord. "Bring up the company," he said quietly. The word passed down the column until Espinoza, the last man in the combat force, sprinted back to tell the women where they crouched in the dark.

Sunlight splashed into the concourse, a little pool of it lying just outside the tunnel exit, lighting the tracks as they ran through the station. Verkan stepped into the light, felt the warm sun on his face and arms, and turned to watch the Company assemble in daylight behind him. The first party of women carried Sergeant Ranthar, and Susan Majors carried the left front pole of the litter.

"You went with Hart!" Verkan said.

She looked at him, a puzzled expression on her face, then laughed. "I did not."

"But you didn't tell me you were coming with us."

"Why should I? I'm part of the Company. You mean you never noticed I was with you?"

"No. It was dark."

III

Verkan led Corporal Fish and three Diablos across the concourse to the stairs, Baker following closely with his counter. The windows in the shops on the lower level were smashed, their pieces lying in intricate patterns on the mosaic floor. A bookshop was next to the stairs, its stock scattered on the floor, books lying open like bedraggled butterflies on the floor. Others were still on the shelves, their bright jackets in contrast to their brothers and cousins scattered nakedly about. Verkan made a mental note to visit the shop before the Company left the concourse.

The radiation count mounted as they climbed the stairs, but Baker pronounced it safe for a brief time. The concourse was only one flight down, and they soon reached the surface.

The ruins of a shopping center lay about them. Fires had burned through some of the stores. Others stood vacant, their windows broken and doors smashed open.

He stood, glorying in the afternoon sun, and looked at the ruins of a city. Much of it had burned, either in the first moments of the attack, or later, when fire raged on unchecked by man. Around the ruined shopping center were the husks of suburbia, houses burned, houses crushed and the ruins of places for which men had worked all their lives. There were no living people.

In the center of the mall where he stood there was a statue, bronze on a granite pedestal, a man, bent with care, his head lifted defiantly—a strong man, bronze muscles rippling in the sunlight. Verkan walked over to it and stood looking up at it until Baker called him. Before he turned away, he read the inscription: "This replica of ADAM by Rodin is contributed to the people of Bakerville by the Bakerville Chamber of Commerce; American Legion Roy L. Capek Post; Rotary Club...."

"Captain, come look," Baker was calling. "Corporal Fish has found something!"

He reluctantly turned from the lonely bronze figure and followed Baker past a hardware store and a clothing store to the back of a looted furniture outlet store. It had not burned, but every drawer had been ripped open and there were patterns in the dust that settled after the windows broke in the bombardment. Patterns indicating that rugs and various pieces of merchandise had been removed.

"Look! Back here, sir," Fish shouted. "There's a van. Not much gas in it, but we can get it running all right."

A large delivery van stood inside a loading bay of the furniture store. The metal doors behind it were twisted and crumpled, and would require several hours of work to get them open, but that end of the building stood intact.

"We can load most everybody in here, Captain," Fish said. "Some junk in here, we can throw out." He turned and said, "Reardon and Hernandez get busy on them doors."

Verkan inspected their new transport. It was a medium van, a standard size for the delivery of furniture on this time-line, with wood lining inside. A large pile of furniture pads lay in the center of the truck.

"Cut me some gunports in the side of this thing," he ordered. "You'll have to go back down to the hardware store for the hatchet and saw. They don't have to be neat, but I want to be able to fight mounted, if we have to. Baker, let's go see if we can find something to run this thing with."

A few automobiles stood in the parking lot, but only one appeared to be intact. Verkan found a stick and used it to measure the contents of the gas tank. "There's a good bit in here, maybe ten gallons," he told Baker.

"Now we have to find a way to get it out of the car. Look around the lawn over there and see if you can find a hose. I'll look for a can."

The hardware store was burned out, as was a Western Auto parts store. A few crumpled cans were in the debris, but Verkan did not trust them to be leak proof. He searched for another store.

A cleaning establishment yielded several plastic garment bags, which he used to line the best of the cans. Using a length of hose Baker found behind a ruined hamburger joint, they siphoned off gasoline and carried it to the truck.

The Diablos were busy pounding the garage doors with chair legs and pieces of metal ripped from bed frames, attempting to straighten the bent frame of the door in order to open it. Another crew chopped holes in the sides of the van.

"It isn't all that hot," Baker told him, "but I wouldn't want to stay here any longer than we have to. We could even sleep here, but it's safer in the tunnel. There's no problem with a day or two in this level of radiation exposure, but I sure wouldn't want to live here."

Verkan nodded. Leaving the crew to their work, he went back into the tunnel to speak with the rest of the Company.

"It's bleak up there," he told them, "but not as bad as it could be. New York City took a hit about four to six miles from here, as near as I can tell. At the apex of an isosceles triangle from there and the station we started at. Fallout must have drifted downwind pretty quickly, because it's not strong here. We'll drive out of here."

Someone cheered.

"May we look outside, sir?" Jimmy Pearson asked. "Can we go look at the sun?"

Verkan said, "Yes, but only for a minute. Then get back here quick; I don't want you kids out in that any more than you have to be."

The children trooped out, dashing across the concourse and up the stairs, Jimmy leading them.

"Ranthar's waking up," Doctor Pearson told him. "Don't let him get out of the litter for a while. He took a nasty crack on the head and I don't want him raising his blood pressure."

"Thank goodness," Verkan muttered. He made his way back down to the tunnel where Susan sat beside the stretcher.

"Here he is," she told the pale form on the litter. "You remember what the doctor told you. Keep your mouth shut."

She looked up at Verkan. "You let him alone so he won't get excited. I didn't help carry him all this way just to have you give him a relapse."

"Hi, Captain," Ranthar said in a low voice. "They tell me I can't get up. Everything's a little fuzzy yet."

"Damn right you can't get up. You stay there until the Doc tells you otherwise. That's an order. How are you, Jard?"

"Little woozy, Captain. We at the end of the line? We get out here now?"

"Sure. You'll get to ride in a furniture van on top of some furniture pads."

"Thanks. Wow, I got a doozy of a headache, sir."

"Close your eyes and get some sleep. We won't move out until tomorrow morning." Verkan stood, looked down at Ranthar, then turned to walk back to the exit.

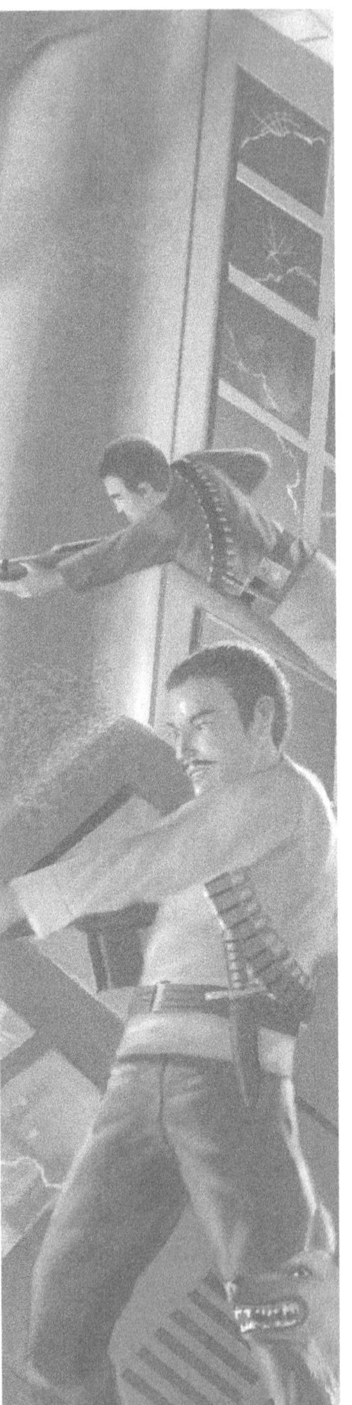

TWENTY-NINE

I

Dalla was in the kitchen making lemon tea on the old wood stove someone had discovered in one of the storage sheds, when she heard an insistent knock at the front door. Jeane was doing better, but was still confined to bed. James Dixon was out making himself useful as one of Maldar's scouts. She turned and made her way to the front door. It was Valthan, one of Maldar's field agents playing national guardsman; he was almost out of breath and there were sweat stains on the pits of his arms. When Maldar had realized how defenseless the small town was, he had sent his men to the Danbury armory to pick up whatever they could find in the way of uniforms and firearms and ammunition.

The way Maldar told it, the armory had already been partially looted, but that a small squad had remained behind protecting what was left. Rather than start a firefight, they'd tossed in a couple of sleep-gas grenades. Then they had loaded an old lorry and three vans with all the ammunition and firearms that were left in the armory. They'd been fortunate to find an old .50 calibre machine gun and brought it with them.

Since that time they had raised a local militia and were busy training some two-hundred volunteers. About a third of them were WWII vets, and they helped a lot. Maldar was most worried about large-scale raiding parties coming from the big cities. That would happen sooner or later, no question about that. Even the locals with their heads buried in the sand realized that.

"Hi, Dalla," Valthan said. "We've spotted a big band of bandits coming down the main road; there's well-over a hundred and fifty cars, jeeps and trucks. We estimate about six hundred and fifty effectives. So we're badly outnumbered." Maldar had hand-picked the best of locals for his temporary militia, most of whom were more than willing to fight for what was theirs, but still had less than three hundred men.

"Then you're going to need my gun, too," she said.

Valthan nodded, but she could tell he didn't like it. Everyone, as far as she was concerned, was too worried about what Verkan might think, rather than about doing the right thing. She was no shrinking violet, like Jeanne Dixon, to say the least.

Dalla followed Valthan, noting that he was walking briskly as though he expected her to keep up, which she did without difficulty. The local villagers had been working for weeks with tractors, two old skip loaders and trucks—at Maldar's direction, to build an eight-foot high stone wall around the village proper except to the south where the settlement bordered the river. The wall was solid, but with convenient murder holes for defense. She could see a dust cloud rising from the west fields as part of the attackers' convoy broke off to hit them from the back. Maldar was busy sending a hand-picked crew to oversee the rear defense, but it left him shorthanded at the front gate.

When she saw that Maldar was free, she came over. "Sergeant, what can I do to help?"

From the look on his face, the words "get the hell out of here" were probably what he was thinking.

Instead, he shrugged, then pointed to a small tower where several men were huddled over a .50 calibre machine gun that Maldar had brought back from the armory. "Give her your rifle," he told one of the younger men standing around. Then he turned to Dalla, "You've used a 30-30 before, right?"

She nodded.

"Okay, I know you're an expert shot."

She smiled to herself, careful to keep it from showing. *So hubby does brag about me.* She looked the rifle over; it was a Winchester 30-30 in good shape. *Somebody gave this one some TLC.* She quickly fired a couple of ranging shots, noting that the 30-30 pulled just a bit to the left.

"Dalla, I want you to take out anyone who's a threat to our machine gun nest. And any commanders you see. Can you do that?"

"With pleasure, sir."

"Good. We're going to hold off on the machine gun until they get up-close, then create maximum casualties before they know what's hit them. We've also got some grenades and a few other surprises."

Oh, goody, she thought gleefully. *This is going to be fun.*

One of the new militiamen, an older man with a Gabby Hayes beard and a thick Yankee accent, cried out. "Hey, they wanna play cowboys an' Indians."

He was probably referring to the way the raiders were encircling the village, looking for weak spots. Meanwhile, some of the more anxious attackers were shooting at the wall with the occasional ricochets. Their only casualty was one of the younger militia men who got a splatter of rock splinters in one eye; meanwhile, the enemy was wasting ammunition. She noted that Maldar had established fire discipline, as none of the militia returned fire.

A group of pickups and jeeps drove closer to the wall. A tall man with a black cap and beard, wearing a blue jacket, stood up in the lead jeep with a megaphone and began to shout: "THIS IS GENERAL SHAWLEY OF SHAWLEY'S RAIDERS. SURRENDER NOW AND WE'LL JUST TAKE WHAT WE NEED. SOME OF YOUR FOOD AND WEAPONS, BUT WE'LL LEAVE YOU AND YOUR WOMEN UNHARMED. YOU HAVE MY WORD. NOW, YOU HAVE TWO MINUTES TO MAKE UP YOUR MINDS!"

Dalla turned to Sergeant Maldar. "Does he actually think we'll take his word as gospel?"

Maldar chuckled. "Look around you. Most of these saps would buy it if we weren't here."

She could read the hope in the faces turned toward Sergeant Maldar. *Outtimers are so pathetic in their delusions. This country hasn't had a war within its borders since the Civil War—and it shows! The minute these barbarians get through the gates, there won't be anything worth having by the time they leave. The healthy young men they'll enslave, the old, infirm and weak—they'll kill. The younger women will be raped, and any who resist will die. The survivors will become concubines or sex slaves. The elders will be killed along with the younger children of both sexes, except for a few pretty young girls close to puberty.*

"YOU'VE GOT ONE MINUTE LEFT!"

She looked at Maldar.

He gave her an evil grin. "I want you to put a shot right down the gut of that loud-hailer. Can you do that?"

"In my sleep," she replied, bringing her rifle up and aiming, compensating for a slight pull to the left. She figured the leader was well within the two-hundred yard range where these 30-30 Winchesters were most effective. Stupid or over-confident, she wasn't sure what he was. But it wasn't a mistake he was going to make again.

Dalla fired and her slug hit dead center; the white megaphone exploded, sending out shrapnel along with bloody pieces of the leader's head. About half of the raiders fired their guns in a reflex of anger, a few shots struck their own men and cars.

No fire discipline, Dalla noted. She surmised they were not used to getting bit back by these small villages.

A big red tractor with a front mounted blade—in normal times used for clearing snow off roadways—led the charge with about ten cars flanking each side and another dozen following. From what she could determine, their goal was to bulldoze the gate and open the village up. Not a bad plan....

"See if you can take out the tractor driver," Maldar ordered.

The raiders had mounted a welded plate of steel in front of the driver's seat, providing him with a thin eye-slit. She needed more of an angle to hit him directly and there was no time to move to the left. Her first shot spannged off the plate, inches away from the eye-slit, as did her next shot. Still, they had been close enough to make the driver pull to the right, where he slammed into an old beetle-shaped Ford sedan, which swung around in front of the tractor, bringing them both close to a halt as the tractor blade tried to drive the Ford into the ground and got the rear bumper caught in one of the tractor's wheels.

"Good work!" Maldar shouted. There was a ragged cheer from the rest of the militia, with the women shouting loudest.

The tractor and its cohorts were now close enough that Sergeant Maldar ordered the old M-2 Browning machine gun to fire. His first shots took out the tractor's front tires, then he made cheese parings out of the little jeeps and pickup trucks. Several of the cars exploded when rounds hit their gas tanks, spewing burning shrapnel, dense black smoke and body parts around. Firecracker bursts from rounds cooking off and cries from wounded bandits rent the air. The snipers took care of those who survived the initial rounds, leaving another twenty or so dead and dying in front of the gate before they could escape.

"They won't try a frontal assault like that again," Maldar observed with satisfaction. "If their leaders have any brains at all, they'll pack up their leavings and get the hell out of here. But I wouldn't count on it. We'll have to blood them another time or two before they wise up."

"What about the rearguard?" Dalla asked.

Sergeant Maldar pointed to one of the squads. "There won't be any further action here for a while. Go support the rear."

They saluted smartly and took off at a trot.

Maldar smiled proudly. "Not bad for a pack of farmers and tradesmen. Fortunately, a lot of them are veterans of the last World War."

II

"Can I go up and see the sun again, too?" Susan Majors asked Verkan. "Betty Fuller can handle our wounded."

"How's Palua?"

"No change. Dr. Pearson thinks he'll be all right if we can keep from bouncing him around too much. You'll have to take it slowly in that van."

"Right. Come on up here, there's something I want to show you." He led her up the stairs and across the shopping center to the statue. "Did you ever see anything so magnificent in all your life? If the human race can produce that, we'll survive."

She looked at the great figure in silence. The statue seemed alive in its strength and determination, concerned about challenges ahead, but confident, indomitable. Then she turned to the ruins all about her.

"I'm glad you showed me this, Verkan. It makes the rest of it a little easier to live with. Where are all the people?"

"This town was far enough from the blast area that it wouldn't have killed too many people directly," Verkan told her. "The fallout would have killed quite a few, so there should be bodies scattered around—yet there aren't any. Somewhere around here there's enough people holed up to bury the dead. Schoolhouse shelters, basements, I don't know. There's no shortage of safe places, or they'd be using the tunnel. That concourse wasn't rated as a shelter, or at least I didn't see any signs designating it as one. People have been through this place to get the more obviously useful stuff. If they come back, I just hope they're friendly."

"You didn't happen upon a woman's clothing store, did you?" she asked. "We all look a fright, and we're filthy. I'd give anything for clean clothes and a bath."

"The clothes store I saw was burnt out, but there's a dry cleaning place over here that has some stuff hanging up in it. Let's see what they left us."

Inside they gathered up all the clothes they could find. "I don't care if it fits or not," she told him. "It's clean. Funny, how excited I can get just thinking about clothes that aren't dirty and covered with blood. And the prospect of a bath and hot coffee. You never notice things like that when you have them, but they're the most important things in the world when you don't."

They returned to the tunnel, herding the children in front of them. After the sunlight, the tunnel seemed even darker. Outside, the sun was almost set. The German Shepherd Verkan still called Dog joined him, sniffing at his pants legs.

Their evening meal was nothing much. The food supplies they had would not last more than two more days, even on short rations, with a few emergency items beyond that. After supper, water was brought from the pool standing at the bottom of the tunnel and everyone was able to wash behind a screen of blankets rigged up in the tunnel. The women selected items from the clothing found at the dry cleaners.

Verkan moved over to the wall where Ranthar's mattress was lying.

The troops sat around the cook stove and talked, then fell to making up new verses of the song the Diablos had sung earlier in the day. The words were not brilliant, but it didn't seem to matter.

"Pretty bad, huh?" George Wykowski, who had just joined them, asked Verkan. "I wish we could think of something clever, but we're all too tired. At that it's better than what the Diablos used to sing."

"Depends on your point of view. There was a certain wild improbability to some of their verses."

Ranthar sniggered.

"It sounds like they're having a good time," Verkan observed.

"Most of us didn't think we'd ever be happy again," George said. "Yet, here we are singing like school kids."

"Good for morale," Verkan said.

"Join them, Captain," Ranthar said. "Sounds like a good party. Wish I could get in on it myself."

"Thanks, but I'd better see to the guards." Verkan hoisted himself to his feet. "And I want to make sure that truck's secure. We probably should have left the moment we found it."

As he walked through the concourse with George Wykowski, he was shadowed by Corporal Fish and three other Diablos. Outside, there was a crescent moon, casting an eerie light over the shopping center. A large shape darted across in front of them, and Verkan unslung his rifle hurriedly before he realized that it was a dog, lost or abandoned.

"There'll be a lot of them," Verkan said. "Some of the breeds will survive, and I suppose there will be some who simply can't stand it. They'll keep looking for their gods until they die of loneliness."

George nodded. "I had a dog, but...."

He left unsaid that it was probably gone for good by now.

Verkan looked over at Wykowski and asked, "I was wondering why you didn't leave with Lieutenant Hart. Why did you join up with the Company?"

Sergeant Wykowski grimaced. "Hart's a good man and a tough cop, but he lacks imagination. And that's something we're going to need to survive in this new world of ours, Captain. I believe you have both experience and imagination."

Verkan nodded.

"Look, Captain!" cried Private Hernandez. He pointed across the shopping center, beyond the first street of ruined houses. "A light. I saw a light, a bright one, sir. There it is again!"

"Yeah," Verkan said. "It looks like a searchlight of some kind. Well, that tells us where the people are. We can go look for them in the morning. I wonder if they're friendly."

"Why, why wouldn't they be, sir?" George asked.

"Short rations, for one. Fear of strangers and the unknown. Or just mean. George, just because we're out in the suburbs, don't get the idea that everybody we meet is going to welcome us."

"Good point."

They reached the furniture store, and Verkan called out. "It's me. What's the situation?"

"All quiet," Mills reported. "There are rats here, sir. Scared me half to death at first. But nothing else."

"Keep a sharp watch, Mills," Verkan ordered. "I'm going to put another guard out in the shopping center. We saw lights not half a mile from here, and I'd hate to lose that truck. Stay out of sight and keep your eyes open."

"Yes, sir."

"They're so happy back there," George mentioned. "But out here it's still guards and guns. What's going to happen to us, Captain?"

"We're going to survive. I wish I knew why we haven't heard anything on the radio. Somewhere there must be generators still going and transmission towers still standing. The government shouldn't have collapsed this completely." Verkan had been on a number of time-lines after a nuclear war, but this was the first time he'd been caught up in one.

"Well, let's get inside," he continued, "and make everyone get some rest. There will be plenty to do in the morning."

They went down the stairs and across the concourse. The Company was singing again, "The Bonnets of Bonnie Dundee" and Dr. Pearson was leading them. They paused to listen to the last verse, Pearson's voice wavering but clear, triumphant:

He waved his proud hand and the trumpets were blown,
The kettle drums clashed and the horsemen rode on,
Till on Ravelston's cliffs and on Clermiston's lee,
Died away the wild war notes of Bonnie Dundee.

THIRTY

I

It had taken Kostran Galth more time than he had expected to get a temporary conveyer-head set up in Westchester near the New York/Connecticut border. They had spent the last ten-day trying to locate Chief's Assistant Verkan. He had eight hundred Paratime field agents at his disposal; so far, not a single lead. Half of them were combing the northern exits from New York City, while another two hundred were checking out western Connecticut and the balance were scattered through Massachusetts.

One of his field agents came into the temporary headquarters set up in a deserted school administration building. Most of the locals had bugged out shortly (and wisely) after the strikes on New York City. Radiation levels were still slightly higher than normal, but for the most part they had fallen to within an acceptable level.

"What is it?" he snapped. There was no way he was going to return to Home Time Line without Verkan and his wife.

"I think we've got a lead on Dalla's location. We picked up someone who knew of a seeress who predicted the bomb attack on New York City; it's gotta be Jeane Dixon."

"You're right. No one else saw it coming, not even the experts. Did he have any information on where she's staying?"

"Yes, a small village named Silchester."

"Okay, get the map coordinates and let's get going. I'll contact our teams in New York and Massachusetts."

"What about the teams searching for Verkan?"

"The trail's too cold. Either he's holed up with Dalla, or…?" That was one place he didn't want to go.

II

In the morning it rained, a hard, driving rain at first which settled to a light drizzle. Baker tested the radiation level and pronounced it somewhat reduced except for a few places where the runoff had collected. When the rain abated the women of the Company collected water in ground cloths to replenish their water supply.

Verkan decided against carrying the injured in the drizzle and used the time to explore the shopping center for useful items. He collected books on basic mechanics, agriculture and farming in the concourse book shop before going up the stairs. Now that Ranthar was awake, Dog was persuaded to leave his side where he had stayed the entire time the sergeant could not move. Now he padded after Verkan and his escort.

The first intact store they found, when they left the center of the shopping center, was a woman's wear shop, one of many which the shopping center had originally contained. Verkan sent Espinoza, who was not the Company runner, back for Susan and some of the other women, with instructions that they could take one item for dress wear, but should concentrate on shoes and practical clothing. He went on in search of other establishments which had not burned.

The sporting goods store was still standing untouched, but contained very little of use. Verkan collected some men's clothing adapted for hunting, but all the knives, guns, ammunition and tools had been stripped from the racks. He left a Diablo to patiently sort through the piles of junk on the floor which looters had thrown on the floor in their haste. "Be sure and look in all the drawers and cabinets for tools, gunpowder, and, of course, ammunition."

From the looks of the store, Verkan didn't think he would be successful.

Most of the rest of the shopping plaza had burned. In those stores that remained they found little of interest. Verkan did find a telescope in a gift shop and a box of wineskins which would be useful as canteens. The others also found lighter fluid and flints, sewing kits and other gear, but nothing which excited them.

The ladies had discovered plastic raincoats in the women's wear shop and passed them out to the others when Verkan returned. The back of the shop had also had a fabric section, and several bolts of cloth were added to the Company's stories for immediate use as blankets and bandages, as well as eventual use as clothing.

The Diablos had located half a dozen abandoned cars with gasoline. One had its gasoline siphoned out and put into the truck. The others were to carry passengers and three were to act as scouts for the truck. By noon, all their gear was loaded and the van was driven around to the head of the stairs. Their injured were covered with ground cloths and the plastic raincoats and carried up to be loaded aboard. The Diablos had fashioned a hammock for Palua from a bolt of sailcloth, and the air mattress, covered with bunting, was placed over him so that the jouncing of the van would not aggravate his wounds.

Verkan inspected the van with the Company loaded aboard. He was pleased to notice that Fish had cut forward firing gunports as well as those along the sides, and that he had stacked their bolts of cloth and other heavy goods around the edges to serve as protection in case they were fired upon. After he was carried, under protest, to his place in the forward end of the van, Ranthar nodded to Joey Fish, saying, "Well done."

Diablo Reardon proved to be the best driver in the Company by common consensus, first by the Diablos, and—after he had related his experiences fleeing from the police in stolen cars—the rest of the company. With Verkan seated beside him in the driver's compartment, they drove toward the place where they had seen the lights the night before. Verkan ordered Corporal Fish to keep a sharp watch on all sides through the gunports and to have the Company ready to fight if attacked. They had knocked out the glass partition between the truck body and the driver's compartment for ease of communication. The scout cars took the lead and the others followed behind in their wake.

After a few blocks, they saw the Civil Defense signs pointing to shelter. Reardon followed them through the streets of empty houses, some in ruins, others still standing but abandoned. Here and there an older house with a basement showed signs of being occupied, windows boarded up, dirt shoveled around the foundations to aid in attenuating fallout, but the streets were deserted. Fire had claimed some blocks, left others untouched.

They rounded a corner of a street of standing houses and saw a shelter ahead. It was a school, surrounded by its playgrounds and parking lot. Out in front the United States flag hung limply from a pole, soaked by drizzle.

"Back around the corner again, Private Reardon," Verkan ordered. "That's far enough. Now you get out and stay over there where you can watch. Be prepared to get the women the hell out of here."

Verkan walked to the back of the truck. "Corporal Fish, bring me four men and stay behind me. Put two more in with Reardon in case we need covering fire. Let's go."

As they started around the corner toward the school, Verkan's dog leaped from the truck and ran to heel behind him. He looked at the animal for a moment, decided that he was already wet and thus further exposure to the rain would not disturb the occupants of the truck with his shaking any more than they were already threatened, and walked on. Fish, Mills and three Diablos followed him, rifles held loosely across their bodies.

They reached the edge of the playgrounds, when Verkan heard the whine of a bullet before the crack of the gun that fired it.

"Hit the dirt and spread out!" he ordered, diving onto the sodden grass of the playground, his rifle butt taking the shock of his fall. He looked across the sights at the two-story clapboard school building, looking for an open window or a telltale movement.

"YOU OUT THERE. STAY WHERE YOU ARE." The voice spoke through a public address system.

"Who are you?" Verkan called. "I am Captain Verkan Vall and these are survivors from New York City enlisted in my Company. We saw your lights last night and came to find you."

"WE ARE SURVIVORS OF THIS NEIGHBORHOOD. STAY WHERE YOU ARE."

"It's a little hard to talk from this distance," Verkan shouted.

"LEAVE YOUR MEN BEHIND AND YOU CAN COME CLOSER. STAY FIFTY FEET FROM THE BUILDING, AND WE WILL SEND OUT A MEMBER OF THE COMMITTEE."

Verkan shrugged. "Corporal Fish, you're on your own. I'm going up to talk to them."

"Yes, sir."

Verkan rose and walked swiftly toward the building. Dog paddled behind, his nose at Verkan's knee.

"LEAVE THAT DAMN DOG BACK THERE!" The speaker blared. "YOU BRING HIM ANY CLOSER AND WE'LL SHOOT HIM!"

Puzzled, Verkan ordered Dog back to Joey and told him to stay. The Shepherd whined, but stayed put. Fifty feet from the building, Verkan halted, waiting. A door opened, and he saw a man, perhaps forty years-old and dressed in a worn brown suit, come out and stand near it. He did not approach any closer.

"What did you say your name was?" the man asked.

"Captain Vall Verkan? Who are you?"

"Sounds foreign, where are you from?"

"South Africa."

The man nodded. "My name is Richard Walker. I'm a member of the committee which governs this shelter. Did you say you came from the City?"

"Yes, through the subway tunnels. We haven't heard a single word from anyone since the bombs fell. What's the situation up here?"

"Ah. The subways. That explains it. Have you seen the rats?"

"There were some in the shopping center over by the tunnel last night. We didn't find any in the subways. Not much to eat in the parts we were in."

"Because there's a plague, Captain Verkan. If you haven't heard any of the radio broadcasts, you wouldn't know, but some cities have been utterly destroyed by it. We don't know where it came from. Something the enemy dropped on us, or possibly endemic to the areas but always controlled before—we don't know. But we're taking no chances. That's why you have to stay where you are and we don't want your dog around us."

"Have you heard of any cases locally?" Verkan asked.

"No. Closest was about a hundred miles west from here."

"What is it like in the rest of the country? Have you heard anything on the radio?"

"Yes. They broadcast at one-thousand kilocycles every evening at six. President Kennedy is dead, his cabinet is dead, there's a General Lemnitzer, from the Joint Chiefs of Staff, who claims to be acting as head of state until we have some other method of replacing him."

Lemnitzer, the name rang a bell in Verkan's mind. On one of the Europo-American Subsector time-lines he was an important figure in the war against Cuba.

"If you are a military officer, you're supposed to report to the nearest District Commander, if you can find him. Otherwise, the radio says you can act at your own discretion to restore order."

Verkan was nonplussed. "My God, man, it sounds as if the whole country is destroyed!"

"It's pretty bad. This area is one of the least damaged. They expended most of their bombs on the big cities, Washington, D.C., Boston, Philadelphia, Atlanta, Baltimore and, of course, New York City, set firestorms going across a third of the nation, as well as their missile strikes against our bases. General Lemnitzer says that the enemy has also ceased to exist as a civilized society."

"Have there been any other attacks since the first day?"

"Not here," Walker replied. "There were some in other areas. There was a second and third wave of missiles, not many—from Soviet nuclear subs, I heard. They went mostly after our bases in the South and Midwest. I don't know much about it, I'm only telling you what we get from the radio."

"Any idea of what it's like north of here, upstate or New England? My wife's up there and I was taking my people there."

"You mean up Route 84? It'll take you through Connecticut, but I'd stay clear of Boston. A couple here in the shelter tried to get out that way two days ago. But you can't get through. Some of the locals have roadblocks set up; they're not letting anyone in. They're scared of plague, just like we are. They say they're short of food, not enough for even their own people. I wouldn't try going there if I were you; they're armed and mean business."

III

Dalla was making a late breakfast when she heard a sharp cry from the back bedroom where Jeane Dixon was staying. She'd been out of bed for the past few days and her color was much better; Dalla hoped this wasn't a relapse.

She took the eggs off the burner since there wasn't much give or take with a wood-burning stove. Then left to see what was disturbing her famous psychic.

Jeanne was sitting up in bed, her hair sticking straight-out, as though she'd just plugged her finger into a light socket. When Dalla drew close, she grabbed her upper arms as though they were all she had left to hang onto in this world.

"What is it?" Dalla asked.

"THE ARMY OF THE BEAST! THEY'RE COMING!" she cried, tears streaming down her face.

"Slow down, Jeanne. What's the Army of the Beast?"

"Thousands upon thousands of men dressed in black sowing death and destruction towards all. They call themselves the Beasts of God. They're coming this way. They'll be here any day!"

Dalla wasn't sure how seriously she should take this prophecy; however, if Jeanne was right, there might be real trouble on the way. "Okay, calm down, Jeanne. This little village is not a big target. They'll probably strike first at New Haven, then at Waterbury. We probably have a few days. I'll tell Sergeant Maldar and have him send out some scouts so we'll know when they're coming."

"Thank you, Dalla. Thank you so much!"

"What do you think?" she asked Sergeant Maldar.

He shook his head. "I'm not up on this psychic business, like you are. But it does sound worrisome. Most of her recent predictions have been on the money, right?"

"Yes, I've made recordings of most of them. I'd like to take her back to the Rhogom Institute, but I'm afraid she won't do well on Home Time Line. Her sense of reality is already shaken, and now she's in the habit of blaming herself—as if anyone in power would ever listen to her—for the horrors that are going on in this time-line. Another major shift in time and place, and she'd probably have a complete mental breakdown. As it is, it's only her husband and the familiar surroundings that are keeping her tethered to this world."

"Yes, but should I take her warnings about the Beasts of God seriously?"

"I would," Dalla said. "You know how seriously they take their religions on Europo-American. Cults and sects, even without cause, spring up out of the woodwork here all the time. A devastating and unforeseen attack like this one could spawn all kinds of deviltry and mass psychoses."

"Okay, I'll send out some scouts and see if they can pick up any intelligence. If these Beasts of God are half as bad as she claims, we'll start hearing all about them real soon."

THIRTY-ONE

I

Back at the truck, Verkan explained the situation to the Company. "They're scared," he told them. "They're afraid we might have some plague-ridden fleas aboard, so they aren't about to let us in their shelter. And, they don't have any food to spare, so we've little choice. There's no question but that we could manage to make a living here for a while from what we could loot from the surviving houses. People leaving them wouldn't have taken everything, and some of them are dead anyway. But we'd end up having to fight the locals for food that's left; the smartest thing to do is to continue to head north.

"We always intended to go there, or I did—that's where my wife is. So it might as well be now. There's only one problem—the plague. Doc, is there any way of dealing with that?"

"The radiation should have taken care of most of the rats and fleas, but DDT should take care of the survivors—for the short run. Lots of it. Nothing's better at killing fleas. If no one's got it yet we can keep them from

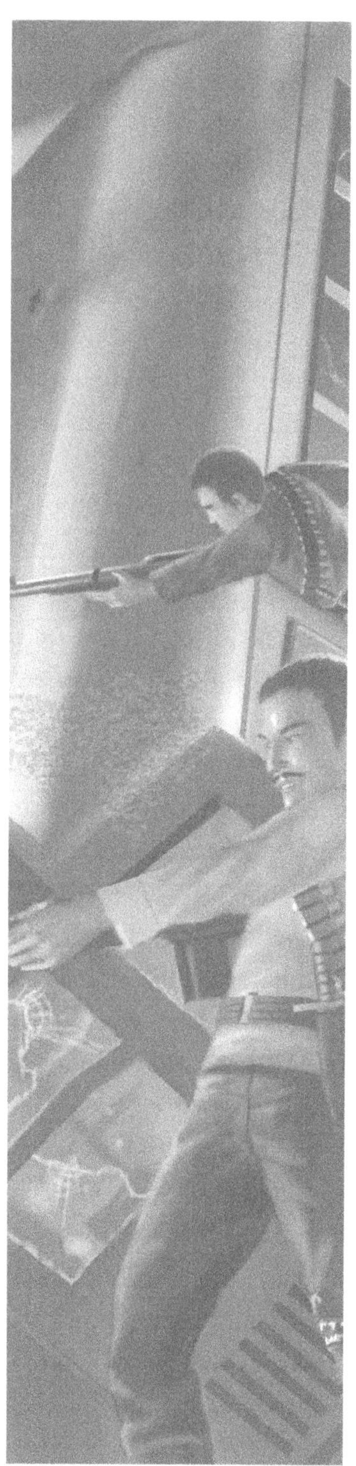

getting it by avoiding being bitten by fleas. For the long run, well, I studied how to generate immunization serums in medical school. Get me where I have some horses to work with and I'll try it. Of course, you'll have to find me a plague victim, but from what you were told that will be easier than we'd like it to be."

"Yeah," Verkan said. "All right, all aboard. Walker said the road block is thirty miles from here. I know where it's got to be, somewhere around Waterbury. The road runs through a valley there, and there's just damn little bypassing it. Dynamite a bridge or two, and nothing does. Let's see how good they are with their dynamite; I'd rather go around those farmers than kill them. Let's roll."

They drove through the deserted suburbs in silence. Two more shelters were seen along the route, but no one stopped to investigate them. A few minutes later, they came to the edge of the suburbs and turned down the highway. It led over low hills to the central valley.

When they had crossed the hills and left the city behind, the countryside appeared on the outside to be perfectly normal, if deserted. Baker pronounced the radiation levels sufficiently high enough to prevent anyone sensible from living in the area without protection, but not dangerous for a few days. Farmhouses stood undamaged in places, but here and there doors stood open.

Verkan decided that some of the farmers might well be living in their own homes, in basements, probably with earth shoveled on the floor above, if they'd read any survival manuals, or even stubbornly refused to admit that there was slow death in the air. The city drizzle had turned into a steady rain which would keep people indoors if there were any, and they saw no one.

Eleven miles short of Waterbury, Verkan directed Reardon to turn the van off on a side road, a single-lane asphalt strip overgrown on the side, trees hanging across the road and scraping against the sides of the van, their rasping noise startling the people inside. The scout cars followed. The road twisted and turned across the hills on the side of the valley so that Reardon couldn't drive more than ten miles per hour for fear of slinging the passengers from side to side on the sharp turns.

"What is this thing, Cap'n?" Reardon asked. "Worst road I ever drove."

"It's called a 'farm to market road.' A political device to get the votes of every farmer who lives along here. Now that farm votes aren't so important, they don't keep them up very well, but it's still here. It was designed to go past every ranch house in the area."

"I believe that," Reardon said, as he cranked the wheel to bring the van around another ninety-degree turn. "This thing ain't no sports car, you know, Cap'n. It's going to wear me out." He shifted down to get the truck going again.

It was late in the afternoon when they topped a small ridge to look down on the stream below. A single lane girder bridge spanned it, and across the far side a heavy makeshift gate, constructed of iron rails, closed it off completely. A hastily built concrete block hut stood next to the gate. A large hand-lettered sign on Verkan's side of the stream said simply, KEEP OFF OR GET KILLED.

II

Dalla was the first one to get to the door. She was shocked to see Kostran Galth in full National Guard uniform. "Hi Colonel," she said, as she wrapped him in her arms and bussed him on the cheek. "You're a welcome sight for these sore eyes."

They hugged tightly for a few moments.

"You too, Dalla. We were getting worried until one of our scouts got information on your precog's location."

"Yes, with her talent, it's tough for her to hide anywhere for long. People visit and ask for a reading, and she's almost under a compulsion to give it to them. It's hard to keep her under wraps."

"You can say that again," Jeanne said from behind. She was out of bed and either reading or wandering the house aimlessly. Lately she'd been seeing images of a Great Beast with sword in hand tearing its way through the local towns and villages. Her eyes were framed with what looked like black bruises, but at least she was staying out of bed and her hair was combed.

"I've come to get you to safety," Kostran said. "We've got a temporary conveyer-head set up in Westchester, New York. And, we've got air transport so that's not a problem. Plus, enough men to guarantee your safety."

"Phew," Dalla let out. "I'm glad to hear that! It's going to be really bad here shortly. Jeanne's had a vision about a huge band of murderers who call themselves the Beasts of God. Jeanne's been seeing them in visions rip out the local towns and cities, murdering, destroying everything in their path and raping women and children without pity. They're madmen set to kill anyone and everyone in their way; the bombs destroyed their hold on sanity, or they were like this all along, but didn't have *permission* to let go."

"How far away are they?"

"Jeanne's having trouble getting an exact fix, but from her latest vision it sounds like they've just destroyed what was left of New Haven and are on their way here, or to Waterbury, which is a bigger target."

"We'd better do something about them right away," Kostran said. "I'll have some bombers brought in from nearby Europo-American time-line bases outside the Beria Belt. I think there are some in Florida that will do perfectly."

"Florida?" she queried.

"Sure, the Bermuda Triangle is right there. We use that all the time for operations that can't be covered up any other way. Rosedale's another one, but it's in the southwest."

Dalla laughed. "You guys don't miss a trick, do you?"

"Nope. How do you think we've kept our operations on the Europo-American Subsector quiet for so long? It's gotten to the point where no one, except a few saucer nuts, will listen to reports of unidentified flying objects. We don't use saucers so I expect someone once ran across a conveyer dome and decided it was a downed flying saucer!"

"So, how are you going to stop the Beasts, Galth?"

"The final way. We'll bring in some DeathCon VI bombs and drop them on the Beasts of God; they'll die by the thousands, like cockroaches."

III

"Stop and back up!" Verkan ordered. "Quick. He's seen us, but I want to get back over that ridge fast."

As Reardon backed the van out of sight of the bridge, Verkan jumped out and ran to the rear doors. "Corporal Fish, take your ready group and go down the side of this ridge, back here where they can't see you. Get across that stream without their knowing you did it, and get behind them. I don't want any shooting unless it absolutely has to be done. Some of you are going to have to be living with these people for a long time; the place my wife is staying isn't more than fifteen miles from here. Besides, we'll be glad of guards at that bridge once we're across it. I'm going to try to talk my way across, watch for a chance and do what you think is best, Corporal. But remember, no shooting unless you must. Now, move out."

"Yes, sir. See you on the other side."

Verkan pointed to the scout cars. "You guys stay here for now."

"Okay, Reardon, move," Verkan ordered as he sprang back in the cab. "Take her down to about twenty feet from the bridge and stop. We'll have a talk with whoever's there."

The truck lumbered down the steep grade to the level ground a hundred yards below. As Reardon brought the van to a halt, Verkan climbed down from the cab and shouted across the stream: "Hello, the other side. Who's there?"

"YOU CAN'T CROSS," an amplified voice from the blockhouse answered. "I'VE GOT THE BRIDGE SET WITH DYNAMITE. YOU TRY TO GET ACROSS, I'LL BLOW HER TO KINGDOM COME. GO BACK TO WHERE YOU CAME FROM."

"I came from over there," Verkan said, raising his voice. "I'm Captain Verkan, my wife's staying in Silchester, at Mrs. Crosthwaite's place. You know the place?"

"Sure, but never heard of you," the man with the loud hailer said. "Some strange city lady and her friend are staying there with Mrs. Crosthwaite. The batty dame claims she sees into the future!"

"That friend you're talking about is my wife."

"I don't care where you and your wife are staying, mister. It's where you came from. We're not letting anybody from the city get over here. There ain't enough for us, and we—sure as Job's troubles—don't need the plague over here. Go back, mister."

"It's not mister, it's Captain," Verkan shouted back. "For all I know, I may be the senior officer in this district. Haven't you heard on the radio that military officers are supposed to report to the District Command?"

"Can't help you, Captain. If you are a captain. We decided nobody comes across here. Only reason we didn't blow the bridge and be done with it is we want the pasture land on the other side. You want to talk to somebody, go to Waterbury. They'll let you through there if you're who you say you are, but I can't do it."

"Mister, I belong over there," he shouted. "I have my wife in that house, and I don't even know if she's alive. Now are you going to let me by, or should I unload my troops. There's a lot of us, we could take you."

"Sure you could. But the first shot you fire, I blow the bridge, and my brother and neighbors come across that ridge like nothing you ever seen. If you think you can fight all of us in our own county, you're not much of an army man. Now get the hell out of here!"

"This is ridiculous," Verkan shouted. "You can't keep me from getting to my wife."

"Hell, mister, I got a wife—and children, too, at home. Look, you go to Greenfield. They got the authority to let you by, if you really are army. Maybe they'll even let you go if you ain't, if you can prove you got family out here. But I can't do anything for you. I was told to let nobody over this bridge, and I'm letting nobody over it. Now, go."

"All right. In Greenfield, you say?"

"Yeah, at the big bridge. There'll be people there who can let you through."

"You can at least tell me about my wife. Was anything hit out here? Any fires?"

"No. We got fallout drifting north, but nothing else. I hear the city's gone, that right?"

"Yes. There are people in shelters in Bakerville, and there are some people left in the city, but most of it burned up."

"The hell you say. There must have been fifty thousand of them came out here the first week. We stopped letting them through after the second day, they all wanted to stay here, there's just not that much out here for all those people."

"Yes." Verkan stalled for time, asking questions, volunteering information about New York City, anything to buy time.

Finally, the voice became stern. "Enough chitchat. Get out of here, mister, or I'll call my brothers. I don't know what you want, but you've been here long enough."

"All right," Verkan called out. "Back this thing up the trail, Reardon. Slowly. Take all the time you need."

As the truck lurched backward up the road, he saw Fish dart from the brush beyond the concrete sentry watch post. Two men followed him, then they disappeared behind the structure. He heard a crash, then a shout.

"Get moving back toward the bridge, but stay off it!" he ordered Reardon.

As the van started back down the grade, Verkan jumped out of the cab and ran down the side of the steep hill, across the bridge. Corporal Fish was coming out of the hut when he arrived.

"Got him, Captain," Fish said. "Ran up, busted down the door and grabbed him before he knew what was going on. There was a detonator thing, like you see in the movies for blasting, right next to him. We got to him just as he was reaching for it. What was it for, the bridge?"

"Yes. Is he all right?"

"Well, he's out cold; but yeah, he's okay. Old geezer, sixty, seventy years old, but a tough old bastard. I had to clout him twice."

"Search through his pockets and see if you can find the keys to that gate. That gate would take a day to get off without a proper sledge hammer, and we couldn't saw through the chain much faster."

"Yes, sir." Fish went back to the guardhouse, as Verkan waved the van on across the bridge. They located the keys and opened the gate, then locked it behind them.

"Should we tie the old coot up, sir," Fish asked.

"No. Leave him be. By the time they catch us, we'll be home. And they damn well won't get me out of there. Load up, Corporal, we're on our way. Well done."

As they drove off, someone began to sing. "And don't get in our way when the Company marches on." The fifteen miles went swiftly. At Verkan's direction, Reardon took side roads keeping them well out of the town of Silchester. Part of the country was fields and ranches, but then they entered a more heavily wooded area.

"It's just over the next ridge," Verkan said quietly. Turning to the opening in the van, he shouted, "five minutes."

Susan came to the opening. "Are we really there? I—I know there will be other problems, but I've begun to feel that once we reach your fortress we'll be safe. Like going to the castle in Medieval times."

Verkan said, "There were good reasons they built those stones fortresses."

Susan nodded, saying, "The old feudal barons were hard to bear when times were good, but I'm beginning to understand why they were around for so long. When the barbarians came down the road, it must have been wonderful to know that up in the castle was a man who could deal with all of them and have time left over for other things."

"What other things?"

"*Droit de seigneur*, for one. Oh, Verkan, is that it?"

They topped a small rise and could see across to the village. It was surrounded by a larger stone wall running eight to ten feet in height. Not a bad defensive move against smaller forces. *I wonder what they'll do when the hordes from Boston arrive?*

Rising above the wall from the courtyard inside it was a flagpole, the American flag standing out proudly in the afternoon breeze, the late afternoon sun shining through it.

"That's it. Reardon, blow the horn. Three longs, two shorts, three longs. Keep doing it."

"YES SIR," he shouted. Inside the van, someone struck up the song the Company had composed, others joined, until the entire Company was singing loudly.

"Pull up in front of the gate, and sound two longs, three shorts, one long. That ought to do it."

The horn had hardly died away when the gates were thrown open. Leading the charge, was his wife Dalla, with a big smile on her face.

Verkan ran up the path and threw his arms around Dalla, twirling her around, ending with a big kiss. It felt great to finally have her in his arms again.

When he released her, Dalla wiped tears from her eyes. "I was getting worried," she said.

"Our journey had its moments," he replied. "But we're all safe now."

"We heard about the bombs. No radiation poisoning?"

Verkan shook his head. "We were safe down in the subway tunnels. Besides, our rad tolerance is far above that of the locals."

Dalla let out a sigh of relief.

"How are things going with Jeanne Dixon?"

"She's the real thing, but I'm not sure she's got the temperament for it. I'll work up a report for the Rhogom Foundation, but I don't think she's going to be useful for them."

"Good," Verkan said. "I don't think she'd take to being a lab rat."

Dalla shook her head. "No, no, no...."

II

They returned to Sylvia's house and went into the parlor. Maldar Dard was sitting there patiently. Verkan gave him a thumbs-up. Galth spent the next half hour or so catching Verkan up with their big search and their final location of Dalla. He concluded with, "Maldar, with what little he had on hand, did a great job of fortifying this place. They held off one big attack from some raiders from New Haven."

"They saved the village," Jeanne Dixon piped in.

Dalla nodded. "I'd of been lost without Maldar. He and his squad even showed up in National Guard uniforms in an armored vehicle with a machine gun. They really saved the day."

"Your wife didn't do such a bad job with a 30-30. She took out the opposition leader with one shot!"

Verkan beamed. "So it looks like our job here is done."

"Not quite," Dalla interjected. "We can't just leave our new friends here in this village unprotected. I know you got rid of half a dozen armies from Portland down to Baltimore with DeathCon VI bombs, but what about the smaller ones to follow. This chaos and mob violence isn't over by a long shot."

Verkan nodded. "Yes, and I've got my Company to settle in. I don't want to leave them unprotected."

"Your Company?" Dalla asked.

He quickly explained the creation of Verkan's Company, leaving out most of the messy details. "Yes, I've got to see them settled in before we leave for home."

Dalla nodded. "I understand, I really do. This whole experience has been an eye-opener for me. Participating in the battle gave me a new look at just what it is you do and why you love doing it."

"I'm glad to hear you say that, because I know someone who isn't going to understand."

"Ahh," Dalla interjected. "Our friend Chief Tortha Karf."

"Oh yeah," Verkan said. "I can already hear the brow-beating, dressing down, and fault-finding in my ears. I do love these Europo-American idioms."

Dalla laughed. "That old bear. I'll just cuddle up to him and nuzzle his chin. Then he'll start turning soft."

Verkan nodded. "Yes, the old dear will start to slobber, just like an old bulldog!"

They both laughed, then hugged each other.

The End

www.ingramcontent.com/pod-product-compliance
Lightning Source LLC
Chambersburg PA
CBHW060557310726
48982CB00008B/1151/J

* 9 7 8 0 9 3 7 9 1 2 7 1 3 *